THE SAVAGE TRUTH

THE VAMPIRE WORLD SAGA BOOK 4

P.T. HYLTON

JONATHAN BENECKE

WHAT CAME BEFORE

ALEX GODDARD is the captain of the Ground Mission Team, an elite task force that supplies the ship New Haven with resources recovered from the vampire-infested Earth's surface.

The people of New Haven recently learned of the existence of another city, Agartha. Built into the side of a mountain, Agartha is protected by one hundred intelligent vampires, led by JADEN.

DANIEL FLEMING, New Haven's charismatic leader, believed in Resettlement, and he tasked former GMT member FIREFLY with leading the effort to bring humans back to the surface of Earth—an effort that ended in tragedy as Firefly and all the Resettlers were turned into vampires by MARK and AARON, disgruntled vampires Jaden had once tried to help.

With the help of Jaden and his vampire army, the GMT was able to defeat Mark and Aaron and free Firefly and the Resettlers. They then defeated Fleming and restored the City Council of New Haven. Alex, along with her commanding officer CB and her team of OWL, CHUCK,

PATRICK, and ED, then began the difficult task of locating the parts Fleming had stripped from the ship.

Jaden launched his own plan for Resettlement, one he'd been formulating since the fall of human civilization, and he recruited Firefly and the vampire Resettlers to help put his plan into action.

PROLOGUE

DR. MICHAEL STARLING stepped into the conference room, the fate of the world tucked into a folder under his arm. His two senior team leads stood as he entered. The air was thick with anticipation, and even from across the room, Starling could see the sweat standing on Jeff's brow. They all knew what was at stake.

Starling glanced up at the monitor mounted on the wall. Nothing had changed since the previous day, when he'd looked at it last. The screen displayed four simple lines of text: Project Black Horse, Project Pale Horse, Project Red Horse, and Project White Horse.

Project Black Horse and Project Pale Horse were both displayed in red text, indicating a halted status. The other two were yellow. Starling knew that by the end of the day, his project, Project White Horse, would be listed in green.

The room was silent for a moment, except for the sounds of the newscast playing on the television mounted in the corner. The female anchor's voice filled the room.

"—are calling last night's battle in Pittsburg astounding. What do you make of it, Tom?"

Another newscaster, apparently Tom, chimed in. "Well Paula, astounding really is the word. By all accounts, the city was considered lost. We're told the Pentagon was planning on pulling all military forces back to Philadelphia. They expected nightfall to bring the city's destruction. But that didn't happen. Instead, reinforcements arrived."

"Yes, they did," Paula interjected. "Video footage shows a small group of fighters, working their way through downtown Pittsburg methodically and efficiently. This lends more credence to the unsubstantiated rumors that some of the vampiric creatures are fighting on the side of humanity. Let's go to Pittsburg, where we have field correspondent Helen Groves standing by to—"

Rachel, the other team lead, clicked the remote, and the television turned off. She hesitated, her eyes wide as she looked at Dr. Starling. Finally, she nodded at the folder under his arm. "Is that...?"

"It is," he confirmed. "The ink's not even dry."

"And?" Jeff asked. His voice came out higher pitched than usual, and it held a twinge of annoyance. Starling couldn't blame him. None of them had slept more than three hours a night in weeks.

Starling looked at his two team leads, savoring the moment. "Eight days."

Rachel gasped and a hand went to her mouth, as if she were suddenly unable to speak.

Jeff, on the other hand, pumped a fist into the air. "Hell, yeah! Are you kidding me, right now? Hell, yeah!" He raised his hand, as if to give Dr. Starling a high five. Then he grinned and grabbed the doctor in a hug, instead. "We did it, man!"

Dr. Starling's face broke out in a wide smile. "Yes, we did."

Rachel threw her arms around both of them. Tears stood in her eyes. "That's even better than we'd hoped. It's hard to believe. This will all be over in eight days."

Starling felt his own eyes welling up. They'd worked so hard for this moment, and it was about to become a reality. The last few months had been so dark. So many had died. Humanity had been desperate for a way to fight the vampiric creatures tearing their way across the globe. But, now, finally, humanity had the means to stop them. And it would only take eight days.

Finally, Jeff let go of the other two and took a step back. "We have to tell the others." He paused. "Wait, did you tell General Carlsen yet?"

"I wanted you two on the call with me. You've more than earned it." Starling reached into his pocket and fished out his phone. "Listen, there will be plenty of kudos in the coming days and weeks, but I want to make sure you hear it from me first. Thank you. On behalf of the world, thank you."

Rachel grinned back at him. "You had a little something to do with it, yourself."

He didn't argue with that point. It was time to share the good news with General Carlsen.

Before he could unlock his phone, an alarm sounded.

"What the hell?" Jeff muttered.

They didn't have long to wonder what was happening. A moment later, the doors to the conference room burst open.

In less than five minutes, every member of Project White Horse was dead.

1

"YOU SURE ABOUT THIS, CAPTAIN?" Hector asked. "Almost sunrise. We could wait for tomorrow night."

Firefly drew a deep breath in through his nose. Though he no longer needed to breathe, he was finding it difficult to kick the habit. Besides, it was useful for smelling. Though the first hints of light had yet to peek over the eastern horizon, the sharp tang of sunlight stung his nostrils. Hector was right; it wouldn't be long before the sun rose.

Beneath that was another smell: the earthly, pungent rot of Ferals.

No, he wasn't about to give up on his plan now. Sunrise be damned.

He nodded toward the cave in front of them. "This is perfect. The ones we don't kill, we can drive out into the sunlight."

Mario grinned. "Then what? Spend the day huddled in this cave, like the animals we are?"

"You know it." Firefly raised his right hand and closed it into a fist, a signal to the twenty vampire soldiers behind him to prepare to breach the cave. Then he brought his fist down, and his team surged forward.

The first Feral was crouched on the ground, not thirty yards from the mouth of the cave. It hissed at Firefly as he charged it. When Firefly didn't stop, it leapt to its feet, its misshapen hands held in front of it like weapons, its hideous teeth bared.

It didn't stand a chance.

Firefly held his sword in a two-handed grip, just as Jaden had taught him. He struck hard, slicing the blade horizontally through the air. The blade barely slowed as it cut through the creature's neck.

As the Feral fell, Firefly was already turning toward the deeper part of the cave, looking for his next opponent.

He felt a rush of pride as he saw the battle taking place all around him. His team was moving quickly and efficiently. Their swords cut through the darkness, killing most of the Ferals before the creatures even understood that they were under attack.

It was so much different fighting the Ferals now than it had been in his human days. Even setting aside his vampiric speed and strength, the way the Ferals reacted was different. Every time he'd encountered them as a human, they'd been driven nearly mad by his very scent, and they'd attacked with a mindless hunger. They'd been forces of nature.

Now, it was different. Their instinct was to avoid rather than to attack. They'd fight to defend territory or to defend themselves, but not to feed. That made them less aggressive, but more cunning. While they didn't possess human intelligence, their powerful instincts made them dangerous enemies.

Out of the corner of his eye, he spotted a Feral crouched on an outcropping of rock, twenty feet up the wall of cave.

Hector saw it, too, and his hand went to the holster on his belt.

"Not an emergency," Firefly said.

He shot Firefly a displeased look, but he moved his hand away from his holster. Instead, he grabbed a small rock off of the ground and threw it at the Feral. The rock sped through the air and struck the creature hard in the head.

The Feral snarled and leapt at Hector. He removed its head with his sword before it even landed.

"See?" Firefly asked.

"Yeah, yeah. After we resupply—"

"We'll still need to be careful." Firefly cast his gaze around the wide-open area of the cave where his team was fighting. By his count, his squad of twenty had already taken out more than thirty Ferals. There were only a few left. Not bad, for less than three minutes' work.

Mario charged at a Feral in the deepest part of the cave. He brought his sword down in a perfect arc, but somehow the creature was ready. It leaned back and the blade sliced through its shoulder, rather than its neck.

The Feral threw back its head and let out an ear-splitting howl.

Mario struck again, and this time his blade hit the mark.

Though that had been the last of the thirty or so Ferals in the cave, Firefly felt something in his chest. It was like a wriggling mass of hunger and rage. He knew the feeling. He was sensing Ferals. A rousing horde of Ferals.

For a moment, all was silence.

Then Ferals began to pour out of side tunnels, filling the main chamber of the cave.

"Form up!" Firefly shouted.

His vampires immediately complied, collapsing into a

circle facing outward, making sure that they had every angle covered.

"This count as an emergency, Captain?" Hector asked.

"No. Stay focused. We've got this."

Hector didn't reply, but his face betrayed his annoyance at this order.

Firefly scanned the small horde racing toward them. There had to be fifty Ferals. Twenty against fifty wasn't great odds, but they'd faced longer.

The first wave of Ferals reached the team, hitting them from two sides at once. Steel flew, removing heads and piercing hearts. The Ferals were unarmed, but what they lacked in weapons, they made up for in aggression. Still, the vampires held their ground, taking down the Ferals as fast as they advanced.

Firefly glanced at the side tunnels. The Ferals were still pouring through. There had to be seventy of them, now. Still, as long as they held their formation, Firefly was confident that the vampires could—

"Ow!"

Firefly spun toward the scream. The shout had come from Caleb, a vampire with blazing red hair and a tall, gangly build. A Feral had sunk its fangs into his shoulder.

Caleb staggered forward, and Firefly cursed.

Mario was next to Caleb, and he quickly dispatched the Feral. But the damage had already been done. Caleb had broken formation.

Ferals raced to the gap created by Caleb's stepping out of line, breaking up the circle the team had formed. Now, the vampire soldiers had Ferals coming at them from all directions instead of just one.

Firefly cursed again. If they wanted to get out of this alive, they were going to have to resort to drastic measures.

He spoke loudly, so that all of his soldiers would be able to hear over the din of the battle. "I hereby declare an emergency."

As one, the vampires drew their guns.

"About time, Captain," Hector replied as he fired his first round, dropping a Feral who was lunging at Firefly.

Firefly returned the favor, shooting a Feral scurrying across the cave floor toward Hector.

He hated that he'd had to do this. Supplies were extremely limited on the island, and nothing was more precious to their survival than ammunition. Well, maybe blood. But both were limited resources, and had to be rationed extremely carefully. He and his team stuck to melee weapons on their nightly raids, saving ammunition in case of emergencies.

But now they had no choice. The Ferals just kept coming.

And slowly, Firefly had the terrible realization that even the bullets wouldn't be enough. They weren't going to win this fight. The Ferals were coming at them too quickly.

He looked around at his team. In the last few minutes, they'd scattered throughout the cave. They were all fighting their own battles. Any semblance of a military formation was lost.

He glanced toward the exit of the cave and saw the first light of morning seeping through the eastward-facing opening.

Damn, that meant that exit was lost to them. Their only options were to hold their ground or try their chances in one of the side tunnels. Assuming that they could even get to one.

A burst of static came through Firefly's radio, a faint, unintelligible voice underneath it. Firefly ignored it. Probably just a member of the recon team checking in before they turned in for the day. He didn't have time to deal with that now.

He fought hard, working his way toward the bulk of his team. It seemed like a futile effort. He'd lost count of the Ferals in this cave. As much as he didn't want to, there was a hard truth that he needed to face: he and his team were about to be overrun.

Suddenly, a bright light poured through the tunnel opening and the Ferals near it began to scream. The closest ones burst into flames.

It was as if the sun had suddenly turned its face on the opening of the cave. But the brightness, its abrupt appearance, and the electric smell it carried with it told Firefly it wasn't sunlight. At least not the natural kind.

Firefly smiled.

Four figures stepped into the cave. It was hard to make out their faces since they were backlit by the bright light, but Firefly didn't need to see them. Even if he hadn't been able to smell them, he would have known who they were.

The GMT.

As one, the Ferals turned toward the cave entrance, the vampire soldiers almost forgotten as the smell of living humans reached them.

The smallest of the humans leapt forward, stepping out of the illumination cast by the daylight mounted on top of their rover and into the shadows of the cave.

Three Ferals lunged at her, but Alex had her pistol ready. She dropped all of them before they reached her.

The GMT surged into the cave. The air filled with the sounds of gunfire as the humans joined the fight. Patrick's shotgun. Ed and Chuck's automatic rifles. Alex's pistol.

Firefly shouted to his team. "Form up, people. Press the Ferals toward the light."

The GMT worked at the edge of the daylight's reach, sometimes standing in its protection, sometimes, racing into the shadows after a target. They were efficient killers, dropping Ferals as fast as they could race forward.

Firefly's team was a moving wall. Most of the Ferals had their attention focused on the humans, leaving the vampire soldiers free to cut them down from behind and drive them toward the daylight. Some of the Ferals turned toward Firefly and his team and retaliated, their instinct to live apparently stronger than their instinct to feed, at least for the moment. The vampire soldiers easily handled the ones who took this route and pressed forward.

Firefly glanced up ahead toward the entrance. Alex had stepped out of the daylight and was about twenty feet into the cave. Somehow, three Ferals had wormed their way between her and the entrance.

"Shit," Firefly muttered. He dispatched the Feral in front of him and pressed his way forward, angling past the Ferals, toward Alex.

Sensing an opening, a few other Ferals had focused in on Alex, now. She was nearly surrounded.

She fired three times, and three Ferals fell. Two more quickly took the places of the fallen.

She spotted Firefly racing toward him. "You take those three. The other two are mine."

Firefly didn't argue. Not wanting to risk a shot toward Alex and the rest of the GMT, he went to work with his sword. The way the Ferals were focused on Alex, it was barely even a challenge.

Somehow, by the time he'd killed his three, she's already taken care of hers, as well.

"Thanks for dropping by," he said.

"We were in the neighborhood." She turned, standing shoulder to shoulder with him. "Can we kill the rest of these damn Ferals now?"

———

THE TWO TEAMS, human and vampire, made short work of the rest of the creatures.

Alex kept a watchful eye on her team as she worked. It wasn't so much that they needed her instructions; they'd drilled this scenario plenty of times. Every member of the GMT knew their role in the attack plan and was carrying it out. She watched to see if any of them got into trouble. Plans could fall apart quickly, and she wanted to be ready to support anyone who needed it.

She only had to step in once. Ed strayed a bit far out of the range of the daylight and a Feral snuck around behind him. Alex took care of the creature before it could attack Ed.

Within a few minutes, they were finished. The humans panted and wiped sweat from their brows. The vampires were oddly still. Chuck turned off the daylight mounted on the rover, allowing the vampires to mingle with the humans near the shadowed mouth of the cave.

They chatted for a few minutes, exchanging pleasantries and discussing what had transpired since the last time the GMT had visited the island two weeks ago. Though the vampires were friendly, Alex could hear the mild edge daysickness was putting into their voices. More than a few asked about the fresh blood supply that the GMT had brought them.

A large transport vehicle pulled up, it's tailgate flush with the mouth of the cave, and Owl hopped out of the driver's seat. While the rest of the GMT had been fighting, she'd been picking up the transport at the vampires' current base of operations, a hotel near the center of the closest ancient city.

"I hear some undead creatures need a ride," she called. The vampires piled in, staggering slightly as the effects of daysickness started to set in more strongly.

Just as Firefly was about to climb inside the truck, Alex grabbed his arm, pulling him aside.

She gave him a hard look. It was odd, seeing someone she'd known so well as a human, now living as a vampire. He was still the same old Firefly, in a lot of ways. His personality was largely unchanged and his silly grin remained the same. But his eyes... There was something unworldly in his gaze, something difficult to define, but unmistakably present. As much as he looked like her old teammate, Firefly had changed. He'd be walking the Earth long after Alex's bones had turned to dust. If he avoided being overrun by a cave full of Ferals.

He needed to step up his leadership game, especially considering the vital work that his team was doing.

He smiled, clearly happy to see his old friend. "You pulled our asses out of the fire. I appreciate it."

Her gaze contained less happiness. "That's what I wanted to talk to you about. What you did back there? Not okay."

Firefly blinked hard, confused.

"You left your team," she continued. "You broke formation to save me."

"They were fine. The Ferals were focused on you."

"You don't know that. Ferals are unpredictable." She paused a moment. "Listen, you're a leader. That means you have one priority. Keep your team safe. Me and the GMT can look after ourselves. We're outside your area of responsibility. I know what it's like to lose team members. After Hope died, I made myself a promise. I'm not going through that shit again. I'm not losing another team member."

She saw a twinge of annoyance in his eyes. Maybe it was the daysickness, or maybe it was the fact that she was trying to tell him, a man who'd lost every one of his Resettlers, what it was like to have someone for whom you were responsible die.

"Point taken." He stopped for a moment. "But after everything you've done for me, there's one point that's non-negotiable: I'm always going to have your back."

Alex cracked a smile for the first time since she'd arrived in the cave. "I appreciate it. It's good to see you, Firefly."

"Back attcha. Now, let's go home."

With that, Firefly walked to the entrance of the cave and climbed into the back of the transport vehicle protruding into the protective shade.

The vampire soldiers and the GMT rode together back to the base, Chuck following close behind in the rover.

Alex noted that, unlike after most battles, the warriors were quiet. For the vampires, it was probably the combined effects of daysickness and the anticipation of the fresh blood packets waiting for them back at the old hotel where Firefly and his troops were currently staying. For the humans, it was probably the strange feeling of being on the surface and feeling relatively safe.

It had been nearly two years since the battle in Denver. Since Fleming had been defeated. Jaden's plan for Resettlement had been underway for over a year now, and Firefly and his team were at the heart of it.

The site they'd selected for humanity's new home was the island formerly known as Puerto Rico. It was a biodiverse, mountainous island with a tropical climate, and it had been the location of humanity's last stand against the vampires. A surprising amount of infrastructure was still in place. Jaden had convinced the *New Haven* City Council that it would be the perfect location for humanity, once it was made safe.

But that safety would take time. Decades.

At over eight thousand square kilometers and a pre-vampire population of over three million, there were a lot of Ferals on the island. and plenty of places for them to hide. That was where Firefly's team came in.

Firefly and his army of one hundred eighty-four former Resettlers lived on the island full time now, slowly and methodically hunting down the Ferals in squads of twenty. They were accompanied by five of Jaden's vampires from Agartha. Four of these were scouts, assigned to roam the island and hunt out Feral nests like the cave Firefly's team had just raided. The fifth was a woman named Helen. She sat next to Firefly now, her arms crossed and a sour look on her face.

In Alex's experience, Helen seemed to consider it her job to tolerate lesser lifeforms like young vampires and the GMT. Though Firefly was in charge of the vampire army, Helen seemed to think she was in charge of Firefly. The way that she placed a casual hand on his arm suggested a deeper relationship between the two.

Patrick stifled a yawn. Alex couldn't blame him for being tired. The GMT was pulling double duty these days. Not only were they running supply missions to various parts of the world whenever they were needed, but they were also tasked with delivering Firefly and his team the items they needed to survive, namely, packets of blood and boxes of ammunition.

Still, despite how busy they were, Alex wasn't going to complain. She found the job invigorating. They were working toward a tangible goal, and the possibilities the future held were beyond exciting.

Alex and her team sat at the back of the transport, closest to the tailgate, where a bit of sunlight came through. She watched the countryside roll by and thought about what it would one day be like when humans made this their permanent home. She just hoped that she would live long enough to see that day.

2

_____

COLONEL BRICKMAN HURRIED through the streets of *New Haven*, headed for the Hub, his head down, careful not to make eye contact with any passersby.

If there was one thing CB would never get used to, it was being famous. These days, it seemed like he couldn't walk from his quarters to the canteen without some random stranger stopping him to ask about the time he'd taken on Fleming's faceless GMT in the underbelly of the ship, or to give him some great idea for how to speed up Resettlement.

It wasn't all bad. Spirits on *New Haven* were higher than he'd ever seen them. Part of that was the exchange program they'd set up with Agartha. A dozen citizens were selected each month and transported to Agartha, and an equal number of Agartha people were brought to *New Haven*. The program was one of General Craig's better ideas. The selections were made based on job and skill set, but even those who didn't have a realistic chance of being selected seemed to be cheered by the mere possibility.

And then there was Resettlement. Fleming's hurried plan had been shrouded in secrecy. The City Council was handling this one quite differently. They were nearly transparent with the citizens, providing weekly updates on the progress. More importantly, they set realistic expectations. Every person on *New Haven* knew Puerto Rico wouldn't be ready for human habitation for decades. Ironically, this actually seemed to get the people more excited about it. This wasn't just another batch of politicians making unrealistic promises. This was a methodical plan that would be carefully executed. It gave people hope of a better life, if not for themselves then at least for their kids.

And of course, it helped that it was Jaden's plan.

If CB was famous on *New Haven*, Jaden was a superstar. An ancient vampire who was actually on their side. He'd saved the GMT and fought to protect the humans. Jaden's legend had only grown when the exchange program started. People came back from Agartha with tales of Jaden's leadership and the way he and his true vampires ran things in the city below the mountains. In Agartha, there was no need for a GMT who risked their lives to obtain supplies. Everything the humans needed was provided by their vampire protectors.

CB found the whole thing exhausting.

He was nearly at the Hub when he heard a voice calling to him.

"Yo, CB!"

He glanced at the door twenty yards ahead and sighed. If it had been a bit closer, he might have been able to pretend he didn't hear the voice long enough to step inside. He stopped and turned, expecting to see another random citizen wanting a moment with their hero, CB.

Instead, he saw Brian McElroy.

Brian trotted toward him, a bright smile on his face. "CB! Glad I found you. How've you been?"

CB was momentarily confused by the question. He was Brian's boss and saw him nearly every day. Then he realized that it hadn't been every day, recently. Between overseeing the GMT, the badges, and various special projects, he supposed he'd let a few things slip. Now that he thought about it, it had been weeks since he'd exchanged more than a quick hello with Brian.

Still, that didn't mean he couldn't razz the man a little.

"I'm good. I'm surprised to see you. I didn't think you were able to fit any work into your busy social calendar these days."

Brian's face reddened.

Of all of them, Brian seemed to be making the most of his hero status. Between the key role he'd played in overthrowing Fleming and the fact that he'd gone on a few dates with Alex, he'd become one of the most eligible bachelors on *New Haven*.

Though the two years of female attention had given him a certain measure of confidence, the fact that he was blushing at the mere mention of his dating life proved that he was still the same old Brian.

"Listen, CB, I wanted to be the first to let you know. We did it. I got word twenty minutes ago. The final piece of the irrigation backup unit is up and running."

"That's...great." CB stared back at Brian, trying to understand why the man was beaming and why he was delivering this news at all. There were plenty of things under CB's area of responsibility, but the backup irrigation system wasn't one of them. "Anything else? The Council meeting is about to start."

Brian's smile faded. "You don't remember? The backup irrigation system is the last item on the list. We're done. We finally did it."

It took CB a moment, but then he understood.

"Holy hell. That's... Brian, that's great news."

During the last days of Fleming's rein, the man had focused all his efforts on Resettlement. To make even his hasty, ill-fated attempt, he'd drained *New Haven* of resources and stripped the ship of all but its most essential systems.

Sadly, what had taken Fleming only a few months to tear down had taken almost two years to rebuild. The GMT had spent much of that time searching the surface for the pieces of equipment needed to restore the ship.

And now, if CB was understanding correctly, Brian was telling him the work was finally done. The ship was back to its pre-Fleming form.

Brian's smile returned as he saw the light of understanding dawn in CB's eyes. "Pretty cool, huh?"

"Sure is." It would be nice to be able to share that news in the City Council meeting. Maybe General Craig would even give the GMT a few days off to celebrate, though CB doubted it. He wished he could do more for Alex and her team. They sure as hell deserved it.

CB realized he'd been staring off into space, lost in thought.

"You okay?" Brian asked, concern clear in his eyes. "You look tired."

CB almost laughed at that. Thinking back, he couldn't remember a time in the past two years that he hadn't been tired. But the last six months had been even worse. There were so many things constantly demanding his attention. Resettlement. Resupply missions. The badges. And Jaden and the vampires of Agartha.

He clapped a hand on Brian's back. "I'm fine. I appreciate the concern, though."

Brian wanted to say more, but instead, he just nodded.

"Hey," CB said, "now that the rebuild is done, you can focus on other things. What about that piece of tech you were working on last year? The little... What did you call it? The Silver Spray?"

Brian's face darkened. "It was a dead end. Too difficult to produce. All I have is the prototype."

CB nodded. "They can't all be winners."

"I do have a couple other ideas, though. There's this botanist named Gretta in the agricultural district. You know her?"

CB shook his head. "But if she's young and attractive, I'll bet you do."

Brian's face reddened again, confirming CB's suspicions. "We went on a couple dates. Point is, hearing her talk about her work got me thinking. Plants store and use the sun's energy, right? I'm thinking of ways we can synthesize the process and use it as a weapon. It's still in the preliminary stages, and it's going to take a lot of research."

CB grinned. "And maybe a few more late nights with Gretta?" The radio on CB's belt chirped. He held it to his ear, already knowing who it would be. "What is it, Linda?"

His assistant's voice came through the tiny speaker. "The General's asking for you, sir. You're late."

CB glanced at his watch. "Shit. Brian, I gotta go. We'll talk later."

He jogged the rest of the way to the Hub, going as quickly as the crowded corridors allowed.

By the time he made it to the conference room, General Craig, the rest of the Council, and the department heads were seated and waiting for him, as was Hayden McCready, the ambassador from Agartha. The Council had brought him aboard as an act of goodwill and so that Agartha would have a voice in the Resettlement-related decisions that were made on *New Haven*.

Jessica rolled her eyes, then shot CB a mischievous smile.

The look General Craig gave him was not nearly as pleasant. "Nice of you to join us. Now we can get started. Jessica, I want you to go over the communication shutdown that will occur next week when we bring the backup system online. CB, we will need to be sure there's extra security on hand when it does."

CB pulled his tablet out of his bag and added this task to his already overwhelming list of duties.

———

"THE CAVE WAS HERE?" Jaden asked, pointing to a spot on the large map spread across the table.

Alex shook her head. "A little north. More like here." She indicated another spot a bit deeper in the mountains. "When we got there, Ferals were rushing into the cave from a series of side tunnels."

Jaden thought a moment. "Hmm. I gotta wonder if our presence is driving them deeper underground."

"My thoughts, exactly," Alex confirmed. She took another look at the map. The area where they were sure they'd driven out the Ferals was so small in relation to the whole of the island. The task seemed daunting.

Jaden maintained a calm attitude about the project. Any time that she brought up the scope of the challenge, he reminded her that they'd known the difficulties going in, and that the project was on track.

They were sitting in a conference room in Agartha, reviewing the progress of the Resettlement project. Besides bringing blood and ammunition to Firefly's team, the GMT was also tasked with providing Jaden with regular updates. There was no way to directly communicate between Agartha and Puerto Rico, so the GMT brought the updates the old-fashioned way.

Today, Alex had brought Ed and Owl with her. The rest of the team was back in *New Haven*.

"When's your next mission?" Jaden asked.

"Four days."

"Yeah," Ed interjected. "And we've got nothing scheduled between then and now. It's almost like we're on vacation."

Jaden looked at the map for another moment. "Good. Anything else?"

Alex thought a moment. "Doesn't it bug you sometimes?"

"What?"

"The Resettlement project. You spent, what, a hundred and some odd years planning it? And now it's happening without you. I couldn't stand being cooped up in this mountain while all the action was happening thousands of miles away."

Jaden looked at her for a long moment before answering. "Yes, actually."

Alex tilted her head in surprise. Jaden always seemed so content. She hadn't expected that answer.

"Of course, I'd much rather be in the thick of it, fighting Ferals, carving out a place for humanity. But I'm needed here."

"So that's it? You're needed, so you miss out on the fight of a lifetime."

Jaden cracked a tiny smile. "The people here need me, Alex. I've helped guide the city for a century and a half."

"Yeah, well, while you're leading from under the mountain, somebody has to deliver your vampire friends blood and bullets. And save their asses from being torn to shreds in a cave."

"And it's much appreciated. Anything else?"

Alex shook her head. "I'm good, if you are."

Jaden stood at that, signaling the end of the meeting. "Oh, before you head out, Frank wanted to see you. He should be in the training room."

"Okay, I'll swing by."

Alex started to leave, but she stopped when Ed cleared his throat.

"Um, hey Jaden, I was wondering if I could ask you something."

Jaden looked surprised. Alex was a little surprised herself. As far as she could recall, Ed had never once exchanged words with Jaden. The big man's demeanor was also throwing her off. He was acting uncharacteristically meek.

"Sure," Jaden answering.

Ed didn't speak for a moment. He seemed to be trying to figure out the words to say. "I know you've been at this whole fighting thing for centuries. And you've seen me in the field. I was just wondering if you might have any, you know, tips you could pass along?"

"Tips?"

"To make me a better fighter. Ancient wisdom, or whatever."

Jaden raised a finger. "Ah, ancient wisdom, I can do. But you're going to have to put in a little effort."

Ed's eyes lit up. "Of course. I'm a hard worker. Ask Alex. I'm the first one in and the last one out of the gym every day."

"Good. Because it won't be easy. If you really want to be a better warrior, study Shakespeare."

Ed stared at him blankly.

"Report back once you have a good grasp on one of his tragedies and I'll tell you what to do next."

Ed nodded enthusiastically. "I'll get started right away. I really appreciate it, Jaden."

With that, Jaden marched out of the room.

Alex gave Ed a quizzical look. She considered razzing him about his question to Jaden, but she decided against it. Ed wasn't the type to ask for help from anyone, and she wasn't about to give him grief for swallowing his pride this once. "I'm going to see what Frank wants, and then I'll meet you at the hangar."

Ed and Owl nodded.

As Alex left the conference room, she heard Ed's voice.

"Hey, Owl, what's Shakespeare?"

Trying not to laugh, she headed for the vampire training facility. She found Frank squaring off again a large male vampire named Claude.

She watched them spar for a moment. Frank moved with the strength and speed of any other vampire, but without the grace and confidence she saw in Jaden and his team, and even in most of Firefly's crew.

It made sense. Frank hadn't been a warrior. He'd been a brave volunteer who'd agreed to be a canary in the coalmine, experiencing a hellish existence for the good of his people. But he wasn't a trained fighter, and it showed.

He lunged at Claude's leg, trying to grab it, but Claude deftly avoided the attack, spinning out of the way and tripping Frank, sending him sprawling to the mat. Lying flat on his back, he looked up and noticed Alex.

He grinned sheepishly. "Oh, hi, Alex." He turned to Claude. "Mind if we take a break?"

Claude held out a hand and helped the younger vampire to his feet. "Sure, but when I come back, you'd better bring it. I need you focused. Do Project Black Horse proud."

Frank glanced at Alex, then nodded.

Alex waited until Claude had left before speaking. "Good to see you, man."

Frank grinned. "Good to see you, too. Tell me, what's going on back on *New Haven*?"

Alex gave him the two-minute version of what had been happening on the ship since her last visit. As she spoke, he listened attentively, his eyes showing his hunger for every detail. He asked a few questions about the various systems on the ship, and Alex realized something: he was homesick.

It seemed odd. After all, he'd been locked in a cage and out of his mind for most of his stay on the ship. She would have thought he'd be glad to put the ship behind him, but that didn't seem to be the case.

"How about you?" Alex asked. "How are things down here? Enjoying life on the surface?"

He thought a moment before answering. "I don't know, Alex. Agartha... the city's great. But being a vampire... I just can't get used to it. After watching what they did to humanity back in my day, it's tough to get my mind around being one of them, you know?"

Alex crossed her arms. "It'll take time. Being a Feral for so long, I'm sure it can't have been easy."

"It was hell." His face was ashen. Then he forced a smile. "I'm sorry to complain. I'm sure it'll just take some time. I'll adjust."

She put a hand on his arm. "Hey, after what you did for *New Haven*, I think you've earned the right to complain. If you ever need someone human to complain to, I'm your girl."

He put his hand over hers. "Thanks, Alex. That means a lot. Truly."

She gave his hand a squeeze and then pulled away. There was something odd and intense about Frank. He was different from both Jaden's vampires and Firefly's. He seemed to feel everything so deeply, and he wore those emotions openly on his face. It was as if his enhanced vampire senses somehow extended to his feelings. Or maybe he'd always been like this.

Whatever the cause, the way he carried himself was so different from the warriors she spent most of her time around that it was both refreshing and unsettling for Alex. When he stared at her, it was like he could see to the heart of her.

She cleared her throat, feeling the sudden need to change the subject. "Hey, Claude said something about Project Black Horse? Is that a nickname, or something?"

Frank looked at the floor. "No, it's...something from the old days. It's not important."

The sudden change in his demeanor told her otherwise, but she wasn't going to push. He clearly didn't want to talk about it. Besides, sunrise was less than twenty minutes away. They needed to be ready to head back to *New Haven* at first light.

She said goodbye to Frank and headed to the cargo area where Owl and Ed were waiting with George, Agartha's head of engineering. As soon as the sun was up, he would open the heavy exterior doors and they would return to their ship, which was parked within the defensive perimeter protected by the automated fifty-caliber guns that had once shot down the away ship.

Moments before sunrise, Jaden hurried in.

"Ed, I heard you mention you weren't familiar with Shakespeare."

Ed's face reddened, and Owl grinned.

"Gotta love that vampire hearing," the pilot said.

Jaden handed Ed a small paperback book.

Ed looked at the cover. "*The Tempest*, by William Shakespeare."

"I know you don't have a lot of physical books on *New Haven*, so I thought I'd lend you this one. It's from our library."

Ed stared at the book in something close to awe.

Alex was just as surprised. While the digital library on *New Haven* was large, physical books were rare. They simply took up too much space. Alex had only touched a handful of them in her life. For someone from *New Haven*, this was a truly valuable gift.

Ed looked up at Jaden, his eyes fierce. "I'll protect it with my life. You have my word."

"Uh, okay," Jaden said, clearly struggling not to laugh at Ed's earnest response. "No rush. Just return it when you're done."

A few minutes later, they were aboard the away ship and headed back to *New Haven*. Though the flight was smooth, there was an uneasy feeling in Alex's stomach as they soared skyward. There was a nagging feeling that something was wrong, and it was driven by the strange look Frank had given her when she'd said the words Project Black Horse.

3

Shortly after the fall of Fleming, Tankards had instituted a new policy: the first round of drinks was free for any GMT member.

It was more than a publicity stunt or an act of civic pride; it was smart business. The GMT never had just one round of drinks.

That night, they were on their third round. Alex, Chuck and Patrick were taking turns playing a new game that had recently come to *New Haven* from Agartha and was currently all the rage, especially at the bars. It was called Tic Tac Toe. They played on erasable boards that Tankards had started giving out to the patrons, along with erasable markers.

So far tonight, Chuck was undefeated. It seemed he had figured out a way to ensure that the games either went his way or ended in a tie. Alex suspected that the existence of such a technique meant that the trend would be short-lived. The method would get out soon, and there would be little point in playing.

Ed sat in the corner while the other three played,

hunched over the book Jaden had lent him, squinting at the pages in the dim bar light. He read slowly, mouthing the words silently, his face screwed up in concentration.

Alex and Patrick were engaged in a game when Owl arrived and took a seat next to Chuck.Alex said hello without looking up. Then she noticed that Patrick's marker was hovering over the board. She looked up and saw his mouth hanging open as he stared dumbly at Owl.

She followed his gaze and saw the source of his surprise. Owl had always worn her hair relatively long, but now it was much shorter. The back was styled at an angle, so the left side touched her shoulder, and the right barely reached the bottom of her ear. And it was dyed bright pink.

Alex had seen the style a few times in the Hub, but only on the most fashion-obsessed women on the ship. And 'fashion-obsessed' had never been a term Alex would have used to describe Owl.

"Wow, Owl. You look great." She elbowed Patrick under the table.

"Uh, yeah," Patrick stammered. "You look super hot. Way better than usual."

Alex shot him a look.

"I mean, you always look hot. Sometimes I have a hard time not staring when you bend over, and—"

Alex's look hardened.

"You look very professional, is what I'm saying. The exact appropriate level of hotness for a co-worker."

She gave him one last look. Not perfect, but good enough, she supposed.

"It looks great, Owl," Chuck agreed.

Ed glanced up from his book. "Yep. Nice." Then he went back to reading.

Patrick frowned at Ed. He reached over and snatched the book out of his brother's hands.

"Hey, asshole!" Ed started to stand, ready for a fight.

Patrick raised a hand. "Relax. I just want to see what all the fuss is about." He cleared his throat and read aloud. "We are such stuff as dreams are made on, and our little life is rounded with a sleep." He tossed the paperback onto the table. "What the hell is this shit?"

Ed scooped the book back up, holding it protectively to his chest. "It's not for the unrefined mind."

"This, from the guy who farted into the PA system microphone last month," Alex said.

Owl nodded toward the book. "You'd better be careful with that. It's a loaner from Jaden."

The look on Patrick's face changed to one of understanding. He leaned back and crossed his arms. "Ah, it all makes sense now."

Ed grimaced. "You got something to say?"

Patrick shrugged. "If Jaden said chopping off fingers was cool, we'd have to start calling you the nine-fingered man."

"What the hell is that supposed to mean?" Ed stood up from chair. "We've got a centuries-old warrior on our side. Excuse me for trying to make use of him."

Both brothers were yelling now.

"Making use is one thing. Wearing a tee-shirt with his face on it is something else."

"They don't even make tee-shirts with Jaden's face on them!" Ed shouted. He turned to Alex, suddenly questioning himself. "Do they?"

Chuck stood up, putting himself between the Barton brothers. "Would you two chill? It's like drinking with idiot school children."

"He's right," Alex said. "Cool it. Both of you."

The brothers reluctantly sat down, Patrick going back to the Tic Tac Toe game and Ed going back to his book, each occasionally shooting the other an angry look.

Chuck shook his head. "It would be nice to have another level-headed guy around. Sometimes I miss Wesley. Maybe I should visit him."

"Don't you dare." Alex's voice was dead serious. "He's not part of this team anymore."

"Yeah, but he's always—"

"He made his choice. We have to let him live his life." She turned to Owl. "I really do like your hair. What inspired the change?"

Owl shifted in her seat uncomfortably. "I don't know. I guess I've been looking for something to set me apart."

"How do you mean?"

Owl thought a moment before answering. "Everybody knows us, right?"

"The GMT?" Alex asked. "Sure."

"And you're the tough, sexy leader. Ed and Patrick are the badass enforcers. Chuck's the smart one. You know what they call me?"

Alex knew, but she wasn't about to say it.

"'The other girl'," Owl said. "As in, 'Not Alex, but the other girl.'"

"That's not..." Alex started, then trailed off. "Not everyone thinks..."

"Yeah, they do. I wanted something of my own."

"So you went with, 'The one with pink hair'?" Patrick asked.

"Better than, 'the other girl.'"

Alex put a hand on her friend's arm. "Even if that's true, those people don't know you. They don't know the stuff you do for the team. Your insane pilot skills. The research you do for us. The dozens of times you've pulled our butts out of the fire." She smiled. "That said, if you want to be known as the one with pink hair, you have my support."

Owl's face reddened. "Not to change the topic as quickly as humanly possible, but how are the numbers looking?"

Alex's expression grew serious. "Not as good as I'd like. In the last month, Firefly's team averaged sixty-four kills a night."

Owl grimaced. "Not good."

Just a few months ago, they'd been averaging three hundred.

"The Ferals are learning to avoid them. They're in deeper hiding and are less willing to fight."

"If pre-infestation population records are to be believed, we're probably looking at three million Ferals on the island," Owl said. "Maybe more. A lot of people fled there as other parts of the world fell to the vampires."

"Yeah," Alex sullenly agreed.

If they managed to kill three hundred a night, that meant the island would be ready for Resettlement in thirty years. At sixty-four a night, they'd be looking at more like one-hundred thirty years.

Jaden didn't seem concerned. He said that when the population was depleted a bit, they could start using more aggressive hunting techniques. Using human blood to lure the Ferals would be suicide with millions of the creatures on the island, but once they'd thinned the herd, it would be a possibility.

The *New Haven* City Council was equally unconcerned. If Ed was a member of the Jaden fan club, then General Craig and the rest of the Council were the joint presidents. It seemed that they were consulting Jaden more and more on matters which they would have handled on their own in the past. Alex suspected that they were a bit jealous of Agartha and the fact that they'd had an immortal being guiding them through the past one-hundred and fifty years.

So, if Jaden said things were on track, the Council agreed.

Alex was conflicted on the issue. While she trusted Jaden, a little simple math made her question some of his claims. Still, he'd earned the benefit of the doubt, and she was doing her best to give it to him.

After she'd finished her fourth drink and lost another three games to Chuck, she reminded her team not to be late to the next morning's workout and left.

She'd fully intended to go straight to bed, but Frank's comment from the previous morning was still nagging at her. So she took a detour and headed for her office at GMT headquarters. When she arrived, she logged into her computer and opened a search window.

She typed the words "PROJECT BLACK HORSE" and hit enter.

There was only one result: a folder named "THE HORSEMEN." She clicked the folder, but instead of it opening, a system message appeared.

"NO ACCESS. THE FILE OR FILES YOU ARE ATTEMPTING TO ACCESS ARE RESTRICTED TO USERS WITH A HIGHER SECURITY CLEARANCE."

It wasn't the first time Alex had seen the message. She used to get it all the time when she was a recruit, and occasionally when she was a lieutenant. But she'd never gotten it since she'd been put in charge of the GMT.

As a captain, she had access to all military files. Or so she'd thought.

She sat staring at the system message for a long time, the

nagging feeling in her stomach quickly growing into something more.

JADEN LEANED against the metal railing, looking down over the makeshift hangar where the half-built plane sat.

For the past year, Agartha had been working on building their own ship. *New Haven* had been more than helpful, and Jessica and Owl had both visited a few times to lend their expertise.

Even with George's genius and lots of hard work, the process was taking longer than Jaden had hoped. Agartha had great records from before the infestation, so from a technological standpoint, they had everything they needed to get the job done. The problem was the complete lack of institutional knowledge. Every schematic and record they found in the computer system assumed at least a small level of experience in engineering aircraft. Agartha had none. All their efforts for the past one-hundred fifty years had been put into two areas: keeping their underground city safe and gathering supplies. Long-range travel simply hadn't been important.

Even the help *New Haven* could give was somewhat limited. They were very good at keeping their massive ship in the sky and at building short range away ships. What Jaden and Agartha were attempting was very different.

Jaden didn't want his people dependent on *New Haven* for trips back and forth to the Resettlement site. He was tired of counting on them for all the communication. So Agartha was building a transport plane that would have seemed old fashioned, even in the pre-infestation days. But in Jaden's opinion, the simpler they could make the aircraft, the better.

He was so lost in thought that he didn't sense the vampire approaching from behind until she was only twenty feet away. When he did, he cursed his absent mind-edness. If she were an enemy, he'd be dead right now. But as soon as he sensed her, he knew who it was. He greeted her without turning.

"Hello, Natalie."

She moved to the railing next to him, and the smile was clear in her voice when she spoke. "A little distracted?"

"Is it that obvious?"

"You've been quiet, lately."

He thought about that for a moment. He supposed he had been. Even after two years, he was still getting used to the absence of his most trusted confidant. "I've been thinking about Robert."

"I see." She paused for a moment. "I miss him, too."

Jaden glanced at her. She was staring off into the distance. Natalie and Robert had been in a relationship once, a long time ago. Still, time worked strangely for vampires. Memories from hundreds of years ago came back hard sometimes, catching you like a punch to the back of the head.

Natalie was younger than most of Jaden's team, having been turned shortly before the first wave, but she'd been through a hell of a lot. They all had.

"I think it's Resettlement," he said. "Saving the world... I'm used to having Robert by my side for that."

"Yeah?" she asked with a smile. "Sounds a little dramatic. You do that sort of thing a lot?"

"Only twice." He paused a moment, letting the memo-ries of those days wash over him. "The first time was a dictator who went a bit insane and was on the verge of unleashing his nuclear arsenal. Robert and I made sure that didn't happen. The public never knew, but the world leaders were grateful."

The smile was gone from Natalie's face now. "What about the other time?"

"A terrorist group developed a tailored super-virus and were preparing to release it in ten major cities. We almost failed that time, but Robert was very persistent. He drank from the terrorist leader himself." An image came to him: a darkened bunker filled with men holding automatic weapons. He and Robert had torn through the men like a righteous storm. "We kept that one to ourselves. The world never even knew it was in danger."

"Wow. Maybe you weren't being dramatic after all."

Jaden watched the workers below welding a piece onto the plane. "Honestly, though, I've never done anything as dangerous as Resettlement."

Natalie shifted uncomfortably. "Don't tell me you're having second thoughts."

"No. This is the only course of action. But it is a huge risk. Even exposing the two cities to each other…"

"That one wasn't your choice. They showed up on your doorstep."

"And I let them in."

Natalie shot him a look. "What else were you going to do? Let them die?"

"Five deaths against all of humanity? It has occurred to me that it might have been the wiser plan."

Natalie clapped him on the shoulder. "Look, I know I'm just a baby vampire compared with you and Robert, but I've learned a thing or two. And one thing I know is that you can spend an eternity second guessing your choices. A literal eternity, in our case. But you did the best you could. We all did. And you're Jaden. Your best is pretty damn great."

"I appreciate that." He didn't say what he was really thinking: that sometimes his best wasn't good enough. And if he didn't execute perfectly now, humanity would go extinct, and he and his friends would go feral.

The mistakes he'd made in the past had cost the world dearly. He'd saved the world a time or two, but he'd also damned it.

That was one mistake that he'd never stop trying to correct.

SOMETIMES, Firefly wondered what San Juan had looked like before the infestation. He imagined it had once been a peaceful place, probably not so different from the living quarters on *New Haven*.

Sadly, little evidence of that life remained today. San Juan had been the last known stronghold of humanity. After the Agartha closed their doors and *New Haven* was secretly launched into the sky, San Juan kept fighting. What remained of the world's military forces retreated there and made their last stand.

The brutality of those final battles was on display everywhere Firefly looked. Yet, it was also clear why Jaden had selected this location. Along with the destruction were weapons and military infrastructure. It wasn't perfect, but rebuilding what the greatest military minds of the pre-infestation world had created was a hell of a lot easier than starting from scratch.

It did present some unique challenges. Apparently by the end of the war, humanity was well aware of the effect that silver had on vampires. Many of the doors in what remained of the city were covered in silver mesh, and chains made of the stinging metal hung throughout the city.

Firefly and his team had learned to cope. They had an advantage that the Ferals did not – cognizant thought. They covered their skin when they went out at night, to avoid burns from dangling silver chains.

During the day, they slept in old office buildings, hotels, schools...wherever they'd ended the previous night's hunt. The places weren't really secure, but the vampires only used them during the day, when the Ferals were also sleeping. If they'd been human, their scent might have been enough to cause the Ferals to overcome their daysickness and attack, but there was no way the creatures were going to do that just to kill a fellow dead thing. Just another reason why the city's initial cleanout needed to be carried out by vampires.

Tonight, Firefly stood on the roof of what had once been called Coliseum Tower, a twenty-seven-story residential building. With his vampire eyes he could see as clearly in the darkness as he could in the daylight. The streets far below were still.

He sighed. Back when they'd started the cleanup, the night streets had been alive with Ferals continuing their centuries-long search for blood. Now there was nothing. The Ferals had learned to sense the danger his team presented them.

He spotted two of his squad members, Barbosa and Hargrave, in position next to an old pickup truck on the street below. He touched the radio on his chest. "We ready?"

After a moment, Hector's voice came through his earpiece. "Ready, Captain."

"Do it."

Though they were twenty-seven stories down, Firefly

could clearly make out their movements as Barbosa and Hargrave hoisted the pickup truck over their heads, carefully balanced it for a moment, then hurled it through the air.

The truck slammed into the building across the street hard enough to shake the concrete. The sound roared through the otherwise silent city as metal crunched and glass shattered, then there was another loud crash a moment later as the truck fell back to the pavement.

Firefly had vampires stationed atop buildings throughout this part of the city. All of them waited in silence for the response they hoped would come. Instead, they heard nothing.

He pressed his microphone. "Do it again."

"Roger that," Hector answered.

Barbosa and Hargrave hoisted another truck into the air and threw it against the building.

This time, they heard a howl come from the building.

"Hell, yeah," Firefly muttered.

"Stay frosty, people!" Hector yelled, and his voice echoed up to Firefly's ears.

A Feral leaped through one of the shattered windows and onto the street, confused and furious. Another followed. Three more leapt through another window and onto the street.

There were twenty vampires waiting. They attacked with their swords, striking efficiently and swiftly, just as Jaden had trained them to do. The fight was over in less than three seconds.

It was tough not to be disappointed. Firefly had hoped this technique might bring dozens of Ferals into the open. Instead, it had brought five. He sighed and touched his radio. "Hector, add five to the tally."

"Got it. That brings us to fifteen on the night, Captain."

It wasn't enough. Not nearly. They'd been killing the Ferals for a year and hadn't made a dent in the population. And it was only getting slower.

"All right," he answered. "Let's move on to the next building and see if we can draw more out."

As the team got set up, he thought about what Jaden would say about their situation. Time was on their side. Firefly needed to stop thinking in terms of human lifespan and start thinking like a vampire. One hundred years from now, he'd still be a young vampire.

They'd been at this for a year, but they were just getting started.

"We're set," Hector said through his earpiece.

Firefly moved to the other side of the roof for a better view. "Do it."

4

ALEX STOOD at the open door to Brian's office, watching him. He stared intently at his computer screen, alternating between bouts of frantic typing and scribbling on the pad of paper next to his keyboard.

Though it had been clear after a couple dates that they never would have worked out as a couple, she still thought his brain was fascinating. He gave himself over fully to his work in a way that she'd never seen in anyone else. The closest that she'd experienced was the way that the GMT acted during a battle, when total concentration was required to avoid certain death. Brian somehow brought that same level of focus to formulas and spreadsheets.

It was both baffling and incredible.

After about a minute, she started to feel like a bit of a creep watching him like that, and she knocked.

It took a few seconds before he even registered the sound. When he did, he turned and looked at her, and it took another moment before he realized who it was. His eyes lit up. One great thing about their failed, short-lived romance: Brian seemed to have finally gotten over his crush, and he and Alex were now closer friends than ever.

"Hey," he said, with a nod. "What's up, Captain?"

"Wanted to bend your ear about something."

"Sure thing." He kept his eyes on her, but the computer monitor was like a magnet trying to draw him back. He was winning the fight for now, but that wouldn't last. Alex knew him well enough to understand that he wouldn't be able to resist his work until he talked about it a little.

"How about you? What are you working on?"

He grinned at the question. Alex knew he didn't get to talk about his work nearly enough, and he always appreciated the opportunity, especially with someone he respected, like Alex. He turned back to the computer monitor. "Check it out."

Alex squinted at the charts displayed on the screen, but they meant nothing to her. "What am I looking at?"

"I'm studying cellular stability in vampires." He tapped the screen excitedly with his pen. "Look, we know vampire cells respond differently than human cells to certain stimuli, right?"

Alex nodded. "Like silver."

"Exactly!" he said excitedly. "I've been so focused on how to replicate those effects that I never dug into the whys behind it. Why are they different from human cells? If we can isolate those differences, we might be able to get to the root of what's different about vampires on a biological level."

"And that helps us, how?" Alex stared at a line graph on the screen. Something about cellular regeneration, but beyond that she had no clue what it meant.

"If we can isolate the biological differences, we may be able to find more effective ways to combat them."

Alex gave up looking at the screen and slumped down into the chair across from Brian's desk. "We already have that. The daylights."

Brian had made great strides in the daylight technology over the past two years. He'd developed smaller, handheld versions, which each member of the GMT now carried. Granted, there were some issues with powering the devices. Currently, each one only lasted about three minutes before it had to be recharged. They came in mighty handy in tough situations, though.

He shook his head, still grinning. "What I'm talking about would be much more powerful than a simple daylight." He paused a moment. "Honestly, I'm surprised the scientists working during the infestation didn't try something like this. It seems like a logical step."

"The way I understand it, the three waves happened pretty fast. Maybe they didn't have time."

"Maybe." Brian wasn't convinced.

"Well, if it helps us fight vampires, I'm all for it," Alex said. She sighed. "We need faster ways to kill Ferals. The way Resettlement is going, we'll be lucky if our grandkids set foot on the surface. I guess it's better to take our time with Resettlement while we're safely on the ship."

Brian gave her a strange look. "You think we're safe?"

She raised an eyebrow. "Of course. Do you know something I don't?"

"No, it's just..." He leaned forward and spoke more softly. "Last Thursday afternoon, did you feel that lurch?"

Alex tried to remember what she'd even been doing that day. A bit of turbulence wasn't uncommon on *New Haven*, so she didn't remember anything about a lurch. "No, I guess I didn't."

"Well, I was talking to Jessica, and she told me what

happened. There was an electrical malfunction. Small, but.. Basically, it tripped the emergency backup power system. Made it think the primary power was out. Thing is, it wasn't."

"I take it that's bad?"

"Yes, it's very bad indeed. Sending that much power to the engines could have been catastrophic. Thankfully, Jessica was standing right there. If she hadn't been, we might not be having this conversation."

Alex's eyes widened. "Jesus, Brian."

"My point is, this stuff happens. We try to prevent them, but mechanical failures occur all the time. *New Haven* has been flying for over one hundred fifty years. Engineering does their best to keep her fit, but she's getting older. All it takes is one malfunction—the wrong thing breaking at the wrong time—and we crash. We're all dead."

"Why are you telling me this?"

"I'm just saying, *New Haven* is safer than the surface, of course. And it seems safe, because we've lived here all our lives. But in reality, it's a risky way to live."

Alex felt a chill run through her. "Well, you really brightened my day."

He smiled. "My pleasure. Now, what was it you wanted to talk to me about?"

She hesitated a moment before answering. "Have you ever heard of Project Black Horse?"

He shook his head. "What is it?"

"That's what I'm trying to find out. Frank mentioned it when I was down on Agartha yesterday, just offhandedly. When I asked about it, he got...weird. Sounded like it was something old. Pre-*New Haven* maybe."

"Let's find out." Brian swiveled around in his chair, turning back to his computer. His fingers flew over the keyboard. "Huh. There's a record for something called the Four Horsemen, but I don't have access. Must be a classified military thing. Might need your credentials."

"You think I didn't try that before I bugged you with this? I got the same thing."

His brow furrowed. "That's odd. If it's military, you should have full access."

"That's what has me concerned."

He stared at the screen for another moment, then shrugged. "Well, if it's from the infestation days, that could make sense. They were pretty concerned about security back then. They might have had weird permission levels that aren't in use anymore. If you really want to know, I'm sure CB can get you access."

Alex nodded. "I'll ask him. In the meantime, keep your eyes peeled. Maybe there are other records."

"I will. But I need you to do something for me, too."

"Name it."

"Check on CB."

She raised an eyebrow. "Something wrong?"

"No, it's just... I talked to him the other day, and he seemed, I don't know, run down. He needs a break."

Alex chuckled at that. "This coming from the guy who once spent eleven days straight in this office. CB had to order you to go to your quarters and take a shower before the rest of the lab mutinied."

"Hey, you have to admit, I've gotten better."

Alex couldn't argue with that. He was taking actual days off and leaving the lab before midnight. She thought it might have something to do with the female attention that he'd been receiving recently, but if it helped him maintain a little work/life balance, she considered it a good thing. "That you have."

"As a workaholic, I know it sometimes takes someone slapping you in the face to snap you out of it. And you're a very good slapper."

"So, you do remember our second date," she said with a grin.

His face reddened. "Just talk to him, will ya?"

"On my way there now. Don't forget to look into my thing."

"Project Black Horse. Got it." He was already turning back to his computer, getting lost in the world of vampire cellular stability or whatever.

Unlike Brian, CB looked up immediately when Alex knocked on his office door. Also unlike Brian, he didn't seem entirely pleased to see her.

"Hey, boss," Alex said as she sat down in the seat in front of his desk.

She looked around, taking in the disorder. Paper wasn't exactly common on *New Haven*, but there were two stacks of it on CB's desk. Only the most crucial documents were physically printed, so every one of them had to be important. Then, there was CB himself. Alex wasn't sure she'd ever seen him look so tired.

"No offense, CB, but you look like shit."

He frowned. "I feel like it, too. Was there something you wanted? Other than to insult me, I mean."

"Yeah. Have you heard of Project Black Horse?"

CB's face hardened as she explained the situation and her lack of access.

"I was hoping you might be able to see the records," she concluded.

He frowned. "Honestly, I'm a little busy." He nodded toward the stacks of paper.

"Oh, of course. I just meant, when you have time."

"Sure." He turned back to the papers in front of him.

Alex started to get up, then hesitated. "Are you okay? I mean, is everything going well with Jessica?" CB and Jessica had been married for a little over a year. Leading up to the wedding, Alex had rarely seen such a happy couple. But now that she thought about it, she hadn't seen much of either of them in recent months. Together or separately.

"Jessica's fine," he answered without looking up. "She's... She's busy. Just like me. I haven't seen her as much as I'd like, lately."

She shifted in her seat a little. "Maybe it's not my place, but you need a break, CB. You're newlyweds. You need to take the time to enjoy it."

CB looked up at her and frowned. "Thanks for the input."

She knew she wasn't getting through to him. As Brian had said, sometimes people need a slap in the face. "I'm serious. You were lucky enough to find real love. That doesn't happen every day. Make sure you don't lose it."

Something in CB's eyes hardened at that, and he looked at her as if truly seeing her for the first time since she'd entered. "You know what we do here. You know what Jessica does. We keep this ship in the sky. It might not be popular to say, but that's more important than any relationship."

Alex frowned. "You better make sure your wife doesn't hear you say that."

"She feels the same way. And she's right. Maybe if we all do our jobs, there will come a day when we can relax and enjoy what we've earned. But today is not that day."

Alex shook her head. "We're not guaranteed tomorrow. You know that better than anybody. You've got a woman who loves you, CB. You've to got to—"

"Was there anything else?"

Alex stared at him for a long moment before answering. "No." She stood up. "Project Black Horse. Will you look into it?"

"Sure."

His voice wasn't exactly convincing.

———

FIVE HOURS LATER, CB left his office and headed back to his quarters. He felt bad for having snapped at Alex, but he also knew it was necessary.

Alex's tenacity was both her best and worst trait. Once she got her mind set on something, there was nothing that could stop her from digging to the bottom of it. CB had enough to worry about—too much, really. The last thing he needed was Alex investigating Project Black Horse.

When he reached his quarters, he opened the door gently, not wanting to wake Jessica. He saw that the light was still on in the living room, and he smiled.

"Hey. I'm glad you're still up. I missed you today. How about a late dinner and then—"

He stopped when he saw her. She was hunched over her desk, the computer still on, fast asleep.

"Maybe not," he said. While he was disappointed, he was also happy that she was getting some rest. Jessica pushed herself as hard as CB did. Maybe harder.

He gently lifted her from her chair and carried her to bed. She stirred as he set her down, but she didn't wake.

CB watched his wife sleep for a minute, then he laid down next to her, still dressed in his uniform, and fell asleep.

5

THREE DAYS LATER, Alex stepped off of the away ship and onto the ground just outside what had once been San Juan, Puerto Rico. Her conversation with CB was still in the back of her mind, gnawing at her like an annoying puppy. She had yet to get any answers on Project Black Horse, but she was still in a great mood.

Today was going to be a special day.

It had taken a month for Alex to convince both *New Haven* and Agartha of her plan to have the GMT make a few systematic strikes on the island to draw the out the Ferals. Jaden had spent so long planning Resettlement that he was reluctant to deviate from his vampire-centric approach. But even he had to admit that things were progressing more slowly than he'd projected. While he knew plenty about true vampires, there was still much about Ferals that he didn't understand. The Ferals were adapting to the presence of the vampire force more intelligently than he'd assumed they would.

Jaden's plan also hadn't predicted the existence of a fighting force like the GMT. While he'd known *New Haven* would need to occasionally send scavengers to the surface, he hadn't imagined that they'd engage the Ferals, let alone become so competent at dispatching them.

Those facts, along with Alex's persistent needling, had finally convinced Jaden to allow this test run. If it went well, it could be the first of many. Though Alex tried to protect her team from outside pressures not related to the mission, there would be plenty of eyes watching how they performed today. Firefly, CB, the *New Haven* City Council, and Jaden would all want detailed reports. And the results would determine whether they were assigned more of these missions.

Alex was convinced that the GMT could speed the Resettlement process along, so the success of the mission weighed heavily on her mind. She was ready and excited to prove once again what her team could do.

But first, they needed to check in with Firefly.

Firefly's team tended to move around a lot, sleeping in whatever building was convenient to their current hunting location. He carried a small tracking device, so that the GMT could find him on their resupply missions, and even a backup tracker, in case the first one broke. Owl insisted on the redundancy.

Today, he and his team were holed up in an old school building. When they got to the building, Alex led the way to the basement level.

"Glad the powers that be decided to finally bring in the big guns," Ed said as they walked.

Patrick grunted in agreement. "Well, you know what they say. When the amateurs aren't getting the job done, bring in the experts."

Chuck shot him a look. "I'd watch that shit. Vampires

have very good hearing, and the sun's up, which means they could be cranky. And hungry."

"You think I'm scared of them? If they were so tough, we wouldn't have to be here."

"It's not our toughness that's important today," Alex said. "It's our scents."

With that, she pushed open the door at the bottom of the stairs and they stepped into a windowless conference room. Firefly, Hector, and Helen were already seated at the table.

All three of the vampires looked groggy, but Firefly flashed his old team members a smile when he saw them. "Ah, breakfast has arrived."

Chuck glanced at Patrick. "Told you."

Patrick blinked hard and turned to Alex. "He's joking, right?"

Alex frowned. "Apparently Firefly's grown a sense of humor in the afterlife."

"Can we get started?" Helen asked, the annoyance clear in her voice.

Alex nodded and motioned for her team to take a seat.

When they had, Firefly spoke. "I still think this is a bad idea."

"I disagree," Alex replied. "You know as well as I do that our scents will draw the Ferals out. It'll make them aggressive."

"Not only that," Chuck added, "but our scent will linger. Ferals will be showing up in the area for days. Easy pickings for you vampires at night."

Firefly frowned. "It's too big a risk. There are hundreds of thousands of Ferals hiding out in this city. If one of you gets cut, the blood could draw hordes of them. Too many to handle."

"And how's that different from any of our other missions?" Alex asked. "Dangerous is what the GMT does. Or did you forget?"

Helen held up a hand, halting the conversation. "It doesn't matter what we think. It's been decided. Move on, Firefly."

Alex tried to keep the look of annoyance off her face. She didn't like how that woman talked to Firefly.

"You got a spot picked out for us?" Alex asked Firefly.

Firefly nodded and set a large tablet on the table. It displayed a map of the city with a spot on the west side marked with a green star. He tapped the star and the map zoomed in. "It's an old office building we scouted a month or so ago."

"You already cleared it?" Ed asked, clearly disappointed.

"Yeah, but..." He looked a little embarrassed. "We're pretty sure they come back a few nights after we clear out the buildings." He clicked a series of buttons on the screen. "I've synced the location on your devices. It's not far, and it has a big, open lobby, where you'll be able to draw them out and fight them in the open."

"Good." Alex turned to Owl. "We have what we need?"

Owl tapped on her own tablet for a moment. "We've got it."

"Then let's head out. Firefly, thanks again."

He nodded wearily. "Happy hunting."

Patrick did a mock salute. "You kids have a good sleep. While you're napping, we'll be battling the undead."

Firefly smiled. "Sure you don't want to stay for breakfast?"

Patrick turned to Chuck.

"He's kidding," Chuck confirmed.

Patrick forced a little laugh. "Ha, good one, Firefly."

THE MORNING LIGHT fell over CB's face and he woke with a groan.

He spoke without opening his eyes. "What time is it?"

"It's five a.m., sleepyhead. I figured I'd better wake you before I left."

The sound of Jessica's voice brought a smile to his face. They'd both been working so hard lately that their time together had been rare. CB tried to savor the early mornings and late nights when they saw each other, even if it was usually just in passing. He opened his eyes and saw Jessica standing next the window, one hand still on the shade she'd just opened. Backlit by the morning light, she looked stunning.

"You figured right," he said. "Now take off your clothes and get back in bed. You can wake me up properly."

She walked to the bed and leaned down, kissing him gently on the lips. "That sounds much better than what I had planned. Unfortunately, I don't think the Council would appreciate me showing up for this morning's meeting without a finished report."

He sighed. "I guess that means we're going to be responsible grownups today."

"I'm afraid so."

"Just like yesterday. And the day before."

"I'm almost caught up with my backlog, though, so mornings of you wrapped up in me are on the horizon."

CB smiled. "Good. I need something to look forward to."

She squeezed his arm and kissed him again. This time their lips lingered, threatening to ignite a passion that neither of them had time to indulge that morning. "I'll see you at the meeting."

After Jessica left, CB allowed himself another few moments in bed. He briefly considered going back to sleep, but as soon as Jessica had mentioned the Council meeting, his brain had begun spinning through the tasks he needed to accomplish that day. The list seemed endless. There was the GMT mission to Puerto Rico. He was supposed to speak to a group of new badge recruits. And then there was his special project, the one he couldn't talk about.

It looked like it was going to be yet another full day.

He was climbing out of bed when his radio chirped. He glanced at the clock. 5:05 AM.

"CB, here."

"It's Russell, sir. Sorry to call so early."

CB sat up a bit straighter, suddenly on high alert. Russell oversaw the night shift at GMT headquarters. He was an experienced and capable man who wasn't prone to calling his boss unless he absolutely had to do so. "What is it, Sergeant?"

"I think you need to get down here, sir."

CB's heart was beating faster now. The GMT had left for Puerto Rico a couple of hours ago. A million ways that their mission could have gone wrong competed for primacy in his mind. "Is it the GMT?"

"No, sir. It's... It's the access key card to the weapons supply room."

That gave him pause. There were plenty of possible problems on his radar, but the weapons supply room wasn't one of them. "What about it?"

"Carl lost it, sir."

He drew in a deep breath and exhaled slowly. "God-dammit. Okay, change the codes and have Linda make the new cards right away."

"We did that, sir. But..." There was a long pause. "Carl

lost the card three days ago. And he didn't tell anyone until an hour ago. We're going through the inventory, and there are definitely some weapons missing."

CB slammed his fist on the mattress. "I'll be there in five minutes."

THE BUILDING FIREFLY had selected was a large structure with a glass canopy over the entrance. Most of the glass had been knocked out long ago, and trees grew up through what had once been an elegant entryway. They'd landed the away ship outside the building and approached on foot.

Owl pointed toward an area just west of the building. "Check it out. Solar panels. I'll bet we could salvage some of those."

Alex squinted toward where Owl was pointing. It took her a moment to spot the panels through the thick vegetation. Due to the limited space on *New Haven*, it generally wasn't a good idea to bring back extra items from field missions, but Jessica was always on the lookout for solar panels. If they came back with some, it would be another mark in favor of the missions. "Good find, Owl."

"Guess you're more than just a fancy haircut, after all," Patrick said.

Alex paused in front of the entrance to the building. This place had clearly been the scene of a battle during the infestation. A barricade had been constructed out of rusted-out cars, and a mesh curtain made of tarnished silver hung over the doorway. Several makeshift towers stood on either side of the door, each with a fifty-caliber gun mounted on top.

It was also clear that these defensive measures hadn't

been enough to save the humans inside. Next to the door, a hole the size of a pickup truck had been knocked through the wall. That would be the GMT's way in, and a quick way out, if things went badly.

"We're going to take this slow," Alex told the team. "I'm looking at you, Ed and Patrick. We have no idea how many are in here. Watch each other's backs. We'll stay near the exit and draw them toward us."

The team slowly walked through the hole and into the building, pausing just inside and letting their eyes adjust to the dim interior. After a moment, Alex was able to see the wide open area that had served as a lobby. The ceilings were at least thirty feet high and the floor was littered with shell casings. Like so many of the places where they'd been on the surface, this building must have been the site of a major battle. It would likely be the site of another battle very shortly.

"There," Chuck said quietly. He pointed to a dark mound in a far corner of the lobby.

Ed turned to Alex. "What's the plan, Alex? Can we light that guy up?"

"Hold on." Alex surveyed her team, making sure everyone was in position and ready. "Watch the blind spots and be ready to go out the way we came in if they start to come too fast. On my mark and don't be shy. We want to wake up his friends."

Patrick grinned. "About time. I'm sick of all this sneaking around. I'm ready for a fight."

"Well you're about to get one. Patrick, do the honors."

Patrick opened fire, spraying a quick burst of ammunition into the sleeping creature's head.

The sound of gunfire faded, and all was silent.

A howl came from Alex's left, quickly followed by another.

"There!" she shouted, pointing to the open elevator shaft from which the howl had come.

Chuck was closest to the shaft. He squeezed off a round the moment the first pair of Feral eyes appeared through the open elevator door. It was quickly followed by a second, which he dispatched just as efficiently.

"Save some for the rest of us," Ed complained.

Patrick smirked. "Oh, you decided to join the fight? I figured you'd be back on the ship, reading Shakespeare."

"Good wombs have borne bad sons," Ed grumbled.

Patrick looked at Alex. "Did he just insult me? Using Shakespeare?"

"Heads up." Alex looked toward the large staircase leading down to the lobby and saw a Feral bounding down the steps on all fours. She raised her pistol and waited until it was halfway down the steps, then dropped it in one shot.

The team killed three more Ferals in the lobby, two on the steps and one in the elevator shaft. When they'd waited a full five minutes without an attack, Alex led them slowly up the staircase, deeper into the building.

"Make sure you're keeping track of your kills," she told them. "And no exaggerating, Patrick. We need an accurate count for Firefly."

They spent the next hour moving through the lower two levels of the building. Most of the Ferals they came across were sleeping, but a few, roused by the combination of human scent and gunfire, attacked the team. By the time they finished their search of the second floor, they'd taken out a total of thirty-one Ferals.

"Not a bad morning's work," Owl said.

Ed nodded toward the staircase. "We could do a lot

better if you'd let us keep going, Captain. There are twelve floors of sleeping Ferals above us. Easy pickings."

Alex suppressed her own desire to keep hunting and shook her head. "The last thing we want is to be trapped on an upper level and have them all wake up. That's not a good scene. Trust me."

"Amen to that," Owl muttered.

Alex knew they were both thinking of the nuclear facility in Texas, where they had woken an angry horde of Ferals. They'd paid a dear price for their carelessness that day, one that Alex had never fully gotten over.

"Besides," Alex continued, "our primary objective is to draw the Ferals. We've made our presence known. Come nightfall, this place is going to be crawling with them. It's up to Firefly to clear them out."

6

LATER THAT AFTERNOON, Alex knocked on the door to Brian's office.

"I heard you were looking for me."

His eyes lit up when he saw here. "Ah, Alex! Yeah, one second."

He looked at the two chairs in front of his desk, both covered in mechanical equipment. After considering for a moment, he picked up the junk from the chair on the left and set it on top of the already full chair on the right, where it perched precariously.

He gestured to the now-empty chair. "Have a seat."

Alex did so, cautiously eyeing the stack of old parts on the other chair. "Someday, we're going to find you under a pile of rubble, and you'll have no one to blame but yourself."

"Probably," he said cheerfully. "At least I'll die happy, buried in my work."

"You're a seriously weird guy."

"True. Lucky for you, I put that weirdness to good use. I managed to get access to those Horsemen Project files."

Alex raised an eyebrow. "Managed, how?"

"Well, I wouldn't call it hacking exactly but..."

Alex raised a hand, stopping him. "Forget I asked. It's probably better I don't know. I'm a captain, after all."

"Fair enough. Look." He angled his monitor so she could see it. "The name of the project is an old biblical reference to the Four Horsemen of the Apocalypse. There were four horses, each representing some type of catastrophe."

"I'm guessing that one of the horses is black."

"Yep. From what I can tell, these were four projects designed to defeat the vampires during the last days of the infestation. The black horse represented famine. *New Haven* was a result of that program. So was Agartha."

"Why famine?" Alex asked.

"That was the root of the plan. Hide the remnant of humanity in the sky or under a mountain until the vampires starved to death. It looks like there were a whole bunch of settlements developed as part of that program."

"How many?"

Brian scratched at his chin as he brought up the file. "It doesn't give a number or any specific locations. My thought is that they didn't want the other settlements compromised if one city was taken and the vampires got hold of these files."

"So there could be another city like Agartha?"

"Anything is possible, but I doubt any more could have survived. We would have seen another city ship, if one existed, and the only reason Agartha survived was because of Jaden and his crew."

That made sense to Alex. If there was another city, it would have to be very well hidden. "Okay, what are the other three horses?"

"The red horse represents war. That was the military

operation against the vampires. It's a pretty big file, but it's mostly just a record of things that didn't work. We tried conventional weapons and set up fronts and defensive positions around the world. None of them were effective. The spread was too fast, and the enemy was too strong. Jaden might have more information on Red Horse. We know he was very involved in those efforts."

"So, Red and Black, we already knew about. What are the other two horses?"

Brian shifted in his seat. "This is where it gets weird. All the information on White Horse and Pale Horse are gone. They've been completely wiped from the records. Other than the file names, I have nothing."

The gnawing sensation Alex had been feeling since she had first heard the phrase Project Black Horse was growing now. "What's the biblical significance of the white and pale horses?"

Brian's face was grim. "Conquest and death, respectively. I could speculate on what those projects were, but it would just be guesses. Maybe Jaden could provide some insight?"

"I'll ask when I see him next. In the meantime, keep working on finding out anything you can. I think we should keep this between us, for now."

"What about CB? Shouldn't we bring him in on this?"

Alex thought about that a moment. "No. CB's a bit of an overworked dick right now. Let's do a little more digging before we bring him in on it."

"There is one more thing I found," Brian said. "The Four Horseman headquarters was at a military base called Fort Buchanan."

"Yeah? Where's that?"

"Just south of San Juan, Puerto Rico."

ALEX WALKED into CB's office and found Carl, a senior badge, sitting across from CB, staring down at his hands and looking like he'd just gotten the dressing down of a lifetime.

CB's face was beet red as he shouted into his radio. "I want an update every fifteen minutes until we find that lost card and figure out who has it."

Alex hesitated in the doorway. More and more lately, it felt like every time she spoke to CB she was distracting him from something that he felt was more important. She kept waiting for the perfect time for them to have a real conversation, for things to be like they'd been in the old days, but that opportunity never seemed to arrive. It felt like it had been months since they'd talked for more than five minutes. The good conversations these days were the ones when CB was only rushed and didn't bite Alex's head off.

"Everything okay, CB?" she asked, as he set down the radio.

"No. Everything is a bit of a mess right now. I have a problem that I'd like to solve before the Council meeting."

Alex took another step into the office. "What's up? Anything I can help with?"

"Not unless you can hire me some badges who actually keep track of dangerous equipment."

"Shit." She looked at Carl. "What did you lose?"

Carl didn't look up when he answered. "A few guns from the storage locker. I mean, technically I didn't lose any weapons. I lost a key card. Now, some pistols are missing and—"

CB shot him a look that could have wilted an entire garden. "I don't want to hear a goddamn thing come out of your mouth unless it is an answer to who took those weapons."

Alex crossed her arms and leaned against the door frame. "At least it's only a couple of pistols. It could have been much worse."

CB turned his steely gaze on her. "Sorry, you think it's no big deal to have missing weapons on a ship loaded with sensitive equipment? Equipment that keeps us from plunging to our deaths? Not to mention an unarmed civilian population."

"I didn't say it's not a big deal. I just meant, it's not like there is a bomb on the ship or anything."

CB's glared at her. "Was there something that you wanted, or can I get back to this?"

Alex felt the all-too-familiar sting of her boss being too busy for her. Yet again. Time was, he would have set aside everything to talk about GMT business with her. She tried her best to look at it in a positive light. After all, giving her more autonomy meant that he trusted her to deal with the day-to-day. It wasn't easy to keep that perspective, though. Not that long ago, he'd been willing to be declared a traitor and hunted through the ship to protect her. Now, she couldn't get his full attention for five minutes.

"I was hoping to discuss some ideas about the ground mission with you before we meet with the Council," she said, "but I can tell you aren't in a planning mood."

"No," he answered, turned in his gaze back on Carl. "I'm in a fix-stupid-problems-caused-by-incompetent-employees mood."

"Fine. I'll see you at the meeting." She started to leave, then stopped. "If I were you, I'd talk to the Gecko sisters from sanitation. They're stupid enough to think stealing guns from the badges could be a good idea, and if I'm not mistaken, they play in a Saturday night card game with Carl."

As she walked off, she heard CB shouting into his radio, "Send someone to talk to the Gecko sisters."

GENERAL CRAIG SCRATCHED his chin as his stared at the figures displayed on the tablet in front of him. "So, you're telling me the Feral kills quadrupled the night after the GMT's mission."

"Yes, sir," Alex confirmed. "Not only that, but Firefly's team was able to make more than one-hundred-fifty kills over each of the next three nights. All on the same block where we ran our mission."

The City Council had agreed to meet with Alex and CB to review the results of the GMT's first mission in Puerto Rico. As far as the Council was concerned, they were just there to review data, but Alex was secretly hoping to get approval for another set of missions on the island before the meeting was over. So far, things were going well, but she knew that there would be objections yet to come.

Horace, *New Haven*'s former chief pilot and newest City Council member, grunted in approval. "That's damn impressive. But I'm not sure it's a good idea to approve more missions without talking to Jaden."

"I'd second that," Ambassador McCready said.

Murmurs of agreement came from around the table.

This was the one objection that Alex had known she would get, and she was ready for it. "With due respect, sir, I'll point out that we *have* talked to Jaden. He agreed to a trial run to gauge the results."

"Which we've done," Horace interjected.

"I'd argue that a single mission isn't much of a trial," Alex countered. "We don't know if future missions will bring about similar results. Are we able to replicate this? Or even do better next time? Jaden will expect hard data, and in order to bring it to him, we'll need to carry out multiple test runs."

All around the table, she saw the City Council member's faces change. If there was one thing they cared about these days, it was impressing Jaden. Which was why she'd taken that tact.

General Craig turned to CB. "What do you think, Colonel?"

Alex fought to keep the smile from her face. She almost had them. She could feel it. With CB's buy-in, the whole thing was a lock.

"I don't think it's a good idea," CB answered.

Alex drew in a sharp breath in surprise.

"We have a plan," CB continued, "and there's a team of vampires carrying out that plan. There's no reason to risk the GMT on this."

Alex knew she should probably keep her mouth shut, but she couldn't help it. "There's very little risk. We'll focus on drawing the Ferals out."

CB turned and met her eyes for the first time. "Can you honestly look me in the face and say there's very little risk in any surface mission?" He turned back to General Craig. "Two years ago, we pushed too hard for Resettlement, and it almost cost us the lives of everyone on this ship. This time, we need to exercise patience."

"You're not wrong. Still, it would be nice to have more data to bring to Jaden." Craig thought a moment before continuing. "I recommend to the Council that we approve two more trial missions. Then, we discuss it with Jaden before approving anything further."

The rest of the Council quickly agreed to the plan.

Five minutes later, Alex was headed out of the Hub when she heard CB calling to her.

"Alex, hold up!"

She briefly considered ignoring him, but he was still her commanding officer.

"Hey, look, about in there..." he started as he fell into step beside her.

She couldn't deny that it hurt, not having CB back her in front of the Council. Just another sign that he was growing more and more out of touch with what was really happening with the GMT. "You don't have to apologize."

"I wasn't going to." He sighed, and she saw the weariness in his eyes. "Look, we're not always going to agree, and that's okay. You made your case and I made mine. The Council voted your way. Now, we move forward."

She nodded slowly. "Yeah, I guess you're right." They walked in silence for a moment before she spoke again. "Any luck with the missing pistols?"

"Turns out you were right about that, too," he said with a smile. "The Gecko sisters had them in their quarters."

Alex chuckled. "Good. Now that the crisis is over, you can finally get some rest and stop being such an asshole."

"There's always another crisis. And I'll always be an asshole."

"No argument there."

His face grew serious. "Hey, you seem pretty dead set on getting back to Puerto Rico. Is there some reason, other than killing Ferals?"

For a brief moment, she considered telling him about what she'd learned about the Horsemen projects and the headquarters south of San Juan. She'd looked into Fort Buchanan, and it was nothing but rubble, now. However, if the Horsemen projects were headquartered on the island, there might be more information for her to find there.

But right now, it was just a hunch, and CB had enough to worry about. Besides, if he knew she had ulterior motives, he might be even less likely to back her with the Council the next time around.

"Nope. Just trying to do my part for Resettlement."

"Okay, then." He clapped her on the shoulder. "Looks like you've got a mission to prepare for, Captain."

7

"ALL RIGHT, lady and gents, we are approaching San Juan, Puerto Rico, the oldest city in the former United States territories."

Owl's voice came through the GMTs' headsets as they prepared for landing and for the mission that would soon follow. Since the Council approved two more missions to the island, the GMT hadn't been able to contact Firefly, but Alex wasn't worried. Radio communications were spotty at best from *New Haven* to the surface. That was the very reason that Firefly carried a tracking device. He didn't want to miss his bi-weekly delivery of blood and bullets just because his team was on the move.

"The port of San Juan is the second largest in the western hemisphere," Owl continued. "The largest telescope in the world is located in Puerto Rico. Let's hope the Ferals don't learn to use that, or they'll be able to spot *New Haven* with no problem."

Alex checked the location of Firefly's tracking device on the map on her tablet. He was in a residential area in the north section of the city, a section the GMT had yet to visit.

She just hoped he'd be able to point them to a location where they could draw out the Ferals.

"The old part of the city was surrounded by a massive wall which was twenty feet thick and forty feet tall in some places. The San Juan Gate was the only point entry into the city back in the seventeenth century, and it was closed every night at sundown to protect the city from invaders."

"Heh, maybe the pre-infestation people weren't that different from us, after all," Ed said. "Had to protect themselves from bad guys at night."

Owl set the ship down next to a long, ugly building that appeared to be made of concrete.

"What is this place?" Chuck asked as they stepped off the ship.

"According to the records, it was a shopping center," Owl said.

It didn't take the GMT long to locate Firefly. He was huddled in what must have been a clothing store back in the day. There were thirty or so vampires passed out on the floor, but Firefly was awake, his arms crossed as he waited for them to enter the darkness of the store. He wasn't the only vampire awake. Helen stood at his side.

"Great, vampire bitch is up," Patrick muttered.

"Vampire hearing!" Owl reminded him quietly.

Alex greeted Firefly with a smile. "I didn't figure you'd be awake."

"We weren't." The grogginess was clear in Firefly's voice.

"You heard us coming?" Chuck asked.

Firefly nodded. "That ship of yours isn't exactly silent to vampire ears. Luckily, I wasn't all the way out yet. I usually sleep like the dead. So to speak."

Helen stepped in front of Firefly. "What are you doing here? Does Jaden know you changed the schedule?"

Alex sighed. She'd known plenty of people like Helen back in her badge days. People so rules-oriented that they'd never dream of going outside the chain of command, even when the situation and logic called for a little rule bending. Add to that the fact that Helen seemed to consider humans a lesser species and Jaden a god, and her obsession with the GMT doing things Jaden's way began to make sense.

Still, Alex forced a friendly smile onto her face. They were there to fight Ferals, not Agartha vampires. "I need to talk to Firefly, Helen. You can go back to sleep."

Helen crossed her arms. "I asked you a question. What are you doing here?"

"Fine, you want to listen in, be my guest." She turned to Firefly. "The GMT is going to be running more test missions. That first one went well, but we need a larger data set before we make a long-term strategy."

Firefly nodded slowly. "Not a bad idea. The results last time were pretty great. I set a personal best for most vamps decapitated in one night after your mission."

Alex shot him a grin. "You know what they say about personal bests."

"Made to be broken," he replied.

Helen looked back and forth between the two, eyes narrowing. "I'm sorry, but did Jaden approve this plan?"

"He approved a trial," Alex countered. "The *New Haven* City Council decided the trial's not over yet."

Helen gave Alex a condescending smile. "Oh? The men in the city in the clouds have a pretty good read on what it's like down here, do they?"

"I filled them in," Alex said. "Look, we're going to do this thing. We're going to run a few more missions. Next time we meet with Jaden, we'll give him a thorough report. Then we'll decide how to proceed. Together."

Helen's lips pulled back in what was almost a snarl, and Alex caught a glimpse of white teeth. "You know how long Jaden planned for Resettlement?"

"He's made that quite clear," Alex replied.

"I don't want you running around the island, causing trouble, unless Jaden knows about it and has approved it. Let the adults run things. You're like a child."

"And you're like an incredibly old lady. Scratch that, you *are* an incredibly old lady." Alex took a step forward. She knew she was starting to lose her cool, but she didn't care. "We don't need your permission. Firefly, I'll check in with you every day and let you know where we've hunted. Then you can camp in those areas and kill the Ferals at night, like last time."

"Alex, listen to me." Helen's voice was hard as gravel. "You've earned a certain measure of leeway. I'll allow a lot of things from you. But disrespecting Jaden isn't one of them."

Alex drew a sharp breath, taken aback by the woman's words. "I'm sorry, did you just say you'll *allow* me?"

Helen ignored the comment. "Jaden is the savior of the human race. You and your city would not exist, if it weren't for him. The things he did to make that possible... you have no idea. When I get orders from him, I'll follow them. But I'm not allowing any silly plan you and your Council of idiots concocted in cloud city."

Chuck put a hand on Alex's shoulder. "Captain, maybe we should—"

Alex shrugged the hand off. "Listen, you old hag, we are going to kill Ferals today. That's why we're here. It's what we do. And we're damn good at it. You have no say in the matter."

"The last time you humans came up with a Resettlement plan, the Ferals took you out in what? Ten minutes? You run around this island, and you might unite the Ferals and get us all killed."

Firefly, uncomfortable, said nothing.

"That was different," Alex answered. "We're not trying to spend the night down here. I'm done with this conversation." She turned to Firefly. "Let's talk somewhere private."

Alex walked deeper into the old store, toward a corner with no sleeping vampires, and Firefly began to follow.

Quick as a snake, Helen's hand shot out and she grabbed Firefly's arm.

Firefly's head whipped toward her, and he showed his teeth. "I wouldn't do that."

Helen didn't flinch. "You are not going with her."

The GMT stood frozen, watching.

Alex understood that whatever was happening here was more than just between Helen and Alex. This was a battle of will between two vampires. A challenge to Firefly's leadership. As advanced and wise as the true vampires often seemed, there was something animalistic about them, too, and it came out even more strongly in the daytime, when their humanity faded a bit due to daysickness.

Firefly looked at Helen's grip on his arm, then back to Alex. Then to Helen's hand. His jaw set, and Alex knew he was about to act.

He spun, twisting his arm from Helen's grip, but Helen was ready. As Firefly twisted his body, she grabbed his other shoulder and spun him the rest of the way around. She grabbed his arm again, pinning it behind his back in a hammerlock.

She held him like that for a long moment, her teeth inches from his neck. She spoke softly, but her voice carried easily to the GMT. "Listen close, young one. Jaden thinks you have potential, which is why you're here. But make no mistake. I let you call the shots on day-to-day decisions, but when all is said and done, I'm in charge. You *will* do as I say."

Firefly's jaw tensed, and Alex made a mental note to talk to him about that tell. Helen didn't seem to notice. He leapt into the air, spinning his body in a forward flip, pulling Helen along with him on his back. In mid-air, he flung her forward, and she flew fifteen feet through the air before crashing into the ground.

No sooner had she landed than she was back on her feet, sword drawn.

Alex drew her pistol without conscious thought. In her periphery, she saw her teammates had done the same, with one exception.

Chuck stepped forward, hands raised. "Whoa, everyone. We're not enemies. Let's take a deep breath and—"

Helen rushed forward, and slammed an open palm into Chuck's chest. He flew back, crashing into Patrick, sending them both to the ground.

Alex starred in disbelief, her mouth open. Helen had just attacked a member of the GMT.

Before Alex could move, Firefly had his sword to Helen's throat. He spoke in a calm voice. "Put it away, Helen."

Helen glared at Alex a moment, but then sheathed her sword.

"That was way over the line," Alex growled.

"Yes, it was," Firefly agreed. "You have our apologies."

Alex glanced over at Chuck and Patrick, both of whom were climbing to their feet, apparently unhurt. "Let's just get to the task at hand."

"Actually," Firefly said, "I think that's enough action for one day. I agree with Helen."

"You've got to be kidding me." Alex stared at her friend in disbelief.

"Talk to Jaden about all this. I'm sure he'll be fine with it. We just need to do this by the book, you know?"

Helen didn't smile, but the victory was clear in her eyes.

Alex glared at her. "You'd think after hundreds of years you wouldn't have such a hard-on for paperwork. How about this? I'll get Jaden's sign off, and you stop attacking your allies."

Back on the away ship, they were strapping in when Ed shook his head sadly. "That wasn't our worst mission, but it was definitely in the top five."

Alex didn't trust herself to say anything quite yet. She was too busy fuming. It wasn't only that superior-acting vampire that was bothering her, it was also that she was going to have to go back to the Council and tell them she hadn't completed the mission. That she'd had her hand slapped by the vampires and that she needed to get Jaden to sign a permission slip before she could do her job.

It was infuriating. And insane. This was Resettlement. It was going to take guts and smarts.

"Hey, Alex," Owl said through her headset. "Look out the starboard window."

Alex turned, and scanned the horizon. It took her a moment, but when she saw it she drew a sharp breath.

"You seeing what I'm seeing?" Owl asked.

"Affirmative."

East of the city, a column of smoke was rising into the sky from somewhere near the base of a mountain.

Owl's voice came through her headset again. "What is that?"

Alex considered that a moment. She didn't have an

answer, and they suddenly had a free day on their hands. "I don't know, but there's only one way to find out."

―――――――

OWL LANDED the ship in a small clearing at the foot of the mountain. The mountainside was covered with a thick blanket of trees and vegetation. A river snaked down its length, feeding a small lake next to the ship. In most circumstances, it would have been beautiful. It was difficult to take in the natural grandeur with the smoke billowing into the sky from a spot halfway up the mountain, and the knowledge that they were going to have to trek through the jungle to get there.

Alex took in the scene for a moment. The mountainside was fairly steep, but climbable. She hoped that if they stuck near the river, they'd be able to find a way up.

Patrick groaned as he followed Alex's gaze. "You know we have a ship, right? We could fly up there."

Owl shook her head. "No way we could land in that thick vegetation. If you want to get there, it'll have to be on foot."

"And what if I don't want to get there?"

Alex scowled at him. "Now's probably not the best time to mouth off to me. I'm sorta itching to kick somebody's ass."

Patrick held up his hands. "Sorry, Captain. Just letting off a little steam."

"You and everyone else." She sighed. "Okay, let's do this."

They started their climb, following the river up the mountain. It was nearly midday, and while the thick canopy of trees provided some protection from the sun, the humidity had their shirts soaked with sweat in less than ten minutes.

"Stay alert, people," Alex said as they moved deeper into the jungle. "There's some sun getting through, but not enough to make me comfortable."

A few minutes later, Ed gestured to a mound of dirt under a tree, confirming Alex's suspicions. Not fifty yards ahead, they found another. Then a third. Alex ordered the team to give the mounds a wide berth. The Ferals should have been in a deep sleep at that time of day, and they wouldn't be able to come out of their mounds without catching fire, but that didn't mean they weren't dangerous. It was all too easy to imagine a Feral hand snaking out and grabbing an ankle, then hauling the unlucky GMT member down.

The closer they got to their destination, the more mounds they saw. Alex thought about what it would be like to be here at night, trapped in the jungle with hundreds of starving Ferals.

Chuck moved close to Alex and spoke in a quiet voice. "This is a remote area. And look at all of the Ferals sleeping here. There have to be way more vamps than we thought on this island for this to make sense."

Alex considered that a moment. "Maybe there is something drawing them to this area. Maybe it's the same thing that started that fire."

"Could be. Hopefully, we will get some answers soon."

Patrick spoke much more loudly. "Speaking of the fire, how far away are we? I'm sweating my ass off."

"Let's try not to wake the Ferals, guys," Alex ordered.

Owl checked her tablet. She replied in a hushed tone. "We've got about a thousand yards to go. It is just over the next ridge."

Patrick nudged his brother. "I don't know if I can make it

to the top. I need some motivation. Give us some of that sweet Shakespeare."

Ed thought for a moment. "'Be not afeard; the isle is full of noises...'and stanky-ass brothers."

Owl laughed, but Patrick just frowned.

"That isn't in there."

"Yes, it is." Ed paused a moment. "I mean, I put my own spin on it, but it's in there."

By the time they reached their destination, the fire had mostly gone out, but the effects were clear. A thirty-foot area of the forest was charred and smoking, as if from an explosion.

Owl took a step into the clearing. She gestured toward something. "Check it out."

A metal hatch lay twisted on the ground, a few feet away from the opening it must have been covering.

"Looks like somebody wanted to get down there pretty badly," Chuck observed.

The team moved to the edge of the opening and peered down into the blackness.

"Looks like some kind of pre-infestation bunker," Alex said.

Patrick shook his head. "Why were we the only ones who went up towards the sun? Digging down seems so dumb. Ferals can dig. Up ain't so easy."

"Same goes for humans," Chuck said. "Any dummy with a blasting cap or a shovel can make a hole. It takes funding and know-how to build a ship that never has to land."

Alex reached into her pack and pulled out her daylight. She attached it to a rope, turned it on and lowered it down the shaft. When it finally touched the ground forty feet below, they waited, but they didn't hear screaming. At least they knew there were no Ferals directly at the bottom of the shaft.

"We're going down there, aren't we?" Ed groaned.

Alex clapped him on the shoulder. "Yep. And now, you get to go first. Thanks for volunteering."

Ed knew better than to argue. He just set his jaw and started climbing the ladder attached to the side of the shaft. Alex went close behind him, followed by Owl, Chuck, and Patrick.

Alex reached the bottom and turned in a circle, illuminating the area with her headlamp. They were at the end of a long, narrow tunnel. "Well, the good news is, there's only one way to go."

She started down the tunnel, then froze as she saw something huddled ten feet ahead. She almost fired, but she stopped herself. Something about the way the creature was sitting seemed unnatural. Instead, she drew her sword and approached, slowly and cautiously. When she was four feet away, she discovered why it wasn't moving—its head had been removed from its body. The creature was definitely a Feral, and it had been killed in the recent past.

Alex turned to her team and spoke softly. "I don't know who did this, but they might still be here. Stay focused."

At the end the tunnel, they came to four doors. Alex motioned for Chuck and Patrick to enter with her, while Owl and Ed watched their backs in the tunnel.

Alex opened the first door and the three of them entered, quickly clearing the room, ensuring that no one was hiding there. No one was, but that didn't mean that it was empty.

"Jesus," Patrick muttered. "It's like we were already here."

The room appeared to be a small kitchenette and dining

area. Three long tables, two of which had been flipped over, dominated the space. The chairs, many knocked on their sides, were scattered throughout the room. But the thing that caught Alex's eye was the Ferals.

There were ten of them, all dead. Their heads lay piled in the corner like dirty laundry. The floor was sticky with the Ferals' thick, inhuman blood.

"What the hell's going on, Alex?" Chuck asked.

Alex didn't have an answer. They moved back into the tunnel to the next door.

The room turned out to be a locker room, with two showers and three stalls with toilets. It was free of dead Ferals and looked unlived-in compared with the battle-torn room they'd just left.

The third door led to the largest room they'd seen yet. It was some sort of laboratory. The numerous work stations in the room held computers, centrifuges, and microscopes. Alex suddenly wished that they'd brought Brian along. He might have been able to shed some light on the type of work that had been done here. To Alex, it was just science.

"Alex," Chuck said softly, motioning her over.

She looked where he was pointing and saw a computer on its side, its tower ripped open. A hard drive lay next to it, smashed to pieces. "Check the other computers."

As they did so, Alex felt a change in the air. Whoever had done this wasn't just killing Ferals. Every hard drive in the lab had been purposefully and thoroughly destroyed. She was suddenly aware of silence in the lab, and she felt it pressing on her like a weight.

The clang of something hitting metal sounded throughout the lab, and Alex flinched, her hand going to her gun.

"Sorry," Patrick whispered. "I kicked a table."

Alex's heart was still racing as they moved to the fourth door. She tried to calm herself before opening it. If the people who had killed the Ferals were still down here, this was where they'd be.

She pulled the door open and stepped inside.

This room was clearly sleeping quarters. Six sets of bunk beds lined either wall, and a footlocker stood at the end of each set. There may have been other things in the room too, but Alex didn't notice. Her eyes were fixed on the beds.

Four of them were occupied.

The figures in the four beds didn't move as Alex's light fell across them. They didn't breathe, either. If Alex hadn't known better, she might have thought they were corpses.

Chuck stepped beside her and whispered. "I recognize them."

"Me, too," Alex answered.

Griffin. Daniel. Janet. Stanley. She'd met them all before, both on the island and back in Agartha.

These four vampires were members of Jaden's recon team.

8

JADEN'S EYES opened moments after sunset. After he finished his meditation and climbed out of bed, something caught his eye, stopping him. His two swords hanging on the wall. It was impossible for him to look at them without seeing the centuries of battles reflected in their blades. He'd long ago lost track of how many lives his swords had taken, or how many they'd saved.

He smiled as he took them off of the wall, his plan for the night set. He strapped them onto his back and went to work.

He was walking toward the vampire training facility when George stopped him.

"Ah, Jaden, glad I ran into you."

Jaden gave his friend a pat on the back. Ever since he'd picked up his swords, he'd been in a great mood. "How are things on the day crew?"

George gave him a rundown of the happenings that day, and their progress on the ship. They were waiting for some parts, which Natalie and her team would find for them that night.

"Excellent," Jaden said. "Listen, how about that other thing? The communication system?"

George shook his head. "It's a non-starter. At least, right now."

That soured Jaden's mood. He was sick of relying on the GMT for all communication between Agartha and the island. It wasn't that the GMT was untrustworthy, or that he didn't think they'd deliver the messages accurately. It was simply a matter of directness. He was tired of being two steps removed from the process of Resettlement. Besides, there were some things that he'd like to communicate to his team that the GMT simply couldn't know.

"It's a matter of logistics," George continued. "Puerto Rico is twenty-seven hundred miles from here, and there's a nice stretch of ocean to consider. For communication over that distance, we'd need infrastructure, and it's going to be a long while before we can build that."

"What about the existing infrastructure from the old days?" Jaden asked.

George considered that a moment. "Maybe, if I went on a cross-country trip and spent a year and a half inspecting the fiber networks to determine what's still functional. Then another couple years to fix what isn't. Assuming I can avoid being eaten for, what, a thousand nights outside?"

"All right, I get the picture. Global communication isn't going to happen right now. Which means we need that ship more than ever."

Jaden got to the vampire training facility just as the seven vampires on the patrol team were gearing up to head out. Rudy, the team leader, raised an eyebrow when he saw Jaden. "Hey, boss. What's up?"

Jaden glanced at the tablet in Rudy's hands and saw a list of supplies that they would be hunting. "You're headed to an airport in Colorado Springs. Hunting hydraulic equipment, I see. I thought I'd tag along."

Rudy didn't look thrilled at the prospect. "It should be pretty routine. Nothing we can't handle."

"I'm not going for you," Jaden said. "I'm going for me. It's been a while. The last time I had a real fight was the battle of Denver. I need to leave the bunker every once in a while. Remind myself what we're fighting for."

Rudy still didn't look psyched about the idea, but he just nodded.

The team of eight vampires headed for the main exit. A vampire named Toby was manning the door. He shut down the auto-turrets and opened the outer blast doors. As soon as the vampires were clear, he'd turn the defensive weapons back on.

The run to Colorado Springs was one of the most pleasant hours in recent memory for Jaden. The summer air was warm, even in the dead of night, and a gentle breeze carried the smells of the mountains to him. He took it all in, and it reminded him how unnatural it was to live in the city that they'd carved out for themselves in the mountain. Everything was musty and stagnant in Agartha, at least to his vampire senses. Even their advanced ventilation system couldn't compete with fresh air. Out here, Jaden could smell the individual trees, all similar, but each possessing a unique scent, which he could differentiate if he concentrated.

He watched his fellow vampires bound through the mountains, scurrying up steep inclines and bounding down them again. This was how they were meant to live. They should run free.

This was why Resettlement was so important. Once

they'd paid their debt to the humans, they could be free once again.

Jaden caught sight of Colorado Springs up ahead, and the team slowed to a walk, not wanting to draw the attention of the many Ferals roaming the area.

As they walked, Rudy moved next to Jaden. "Are you out here for fun tonight, or are you expecting trouble?"

"I always expect trouble," he said with a smile. "That's probably why I've been around so long. The only question is whether we'll find any fun. Care to place your bet?"

"Um, not really," Rudy answered. "The plan is to grab the stuff on the list engineering gave us and get out of here. No trouble or fun required."

Jaden clapped him on the back. "Sometimes, you need to look for the fun. We just ran down a moonlit mountain toward a ruined city filled with monsters. If you can't see the fun in that, you really need to take a step back."

"I'll try Jaden, but for now I think we should focus."

Jaden's eyes grew a bit more serious. "Focus should be the default."

The team moved through the city in a tight, defensive formation. They hadn't gone far before they came upon three Ferals, moving slowly through the streets. The creatures wandered aimlessly, sniffing the air occasionally, searching endlessly for a meal that would never come.

Rudy started to move past the creatures, but Jaden signaled for him to wait.

Jaden walked to the nearest Feral and stopped a few feet in front of it. The creature stopped and sniffed the air, its eyes cautiously on this stranger. Jaden squatted down, his hand on his sword, and the two stared into each other's eyes.

The creature clearly didn't know what to think of Jaden.

It was on the verge of attacking or fleeing, but it had yet to decide.

Jaden stared intently into the face of the Feral. The grey, wrinkled skin stretched over the misshapen face. Razor sharp teeth sticking out from its mouth. Lonely, long strands of hair falling to its shoulders and behind its pointed ears. The two vampires stared at each other, one eternally young, with strong muscles and perfect skin, and the other, a monstrous thing that looked even more hideous by comparison.

The beast tilted its head, deciding how to proceed. It tensed its arms and began to raise the claw of its right hand.

Jaden moved as quickly as fire, pulling a blade off his back and springing forward. As he moved, the blade sliced cleanly through the Feral's neck. By the time he landed, Jaden had his other blade drawn. He plunged the tip of the sword into the second Feral's heart.

The third Feral was fifteen feet down the road, and as the second Feral died, it drew in a deep breath, clearly preparing to howl and alert the thousands of creatures in the city to the danger. It never got the chance. Before it could release the breath, one of Jaden's swords flew through the air and sank into its neck to the hilt, severing the vocal cords.

The injured Feral charged toward Jaden, moving at an impressive clip considering the weapon in its neck and its off-balance, loping gait. When it was ten feet away, it leapt into the air.

Jaden moved aside, dodging the creature. As it flew by, he grabbed the hilt of his sword and pulled it free of the Feral's neck, leaving the head dangling, attached only by the spine and the remaining flesh on the back of its neck.

Still, the creature didn't seem to notice the injury. It

stumbled toward Jade as thick, inky blood poured out of its neck and down the front of its body. Jaden finished the job with a flick of his sword, and the Feral's head fell to the ground.

The battle had lasted less than ten seconds.

The patrol team watched in awed silence as Jaden pulled out a cloth and cleaned his blades. It had been two years since the vampires had seen Jaden in action, and, though they were all great warriors, it was clear they still had a lot to learn from their leader.

"I guess you found the fun," Rudy said. "Is this why you're really out here? You're keeping your skills sharp?"

Jaden kept his eyes on his blade as he spoke. "The billions of Ferals on this planet are trapped souls. These creatures are the shell of the old world. When we kill them, we aren't just protecting ourselves, we're freeing them." He slid his first blade into the scabbard on his back and began cleaning the second. "Never forget, the fall of mankind occurred because one of our own went rogue. The end of the world was caused by a single vampire."

Rudy grunted in disagreement. "It started with one. But it wasn't quite that simple. Not in the end."

Jaden didn't answer for a long moment. "I suppose not. Things are seldom simple. Still, we are the greatest weapon of mass destruction the world has ever known. And that weapon is littered all over the planet, now."

"What are you saying?" Rudy asked. "Are we too dangerous?"

Jaden shrugged. "Too dangerous. Not dangerous enough. I really don't know. The world needs us now, but I question our actions in the past. And I will do whatever it takes to make sure they aren't repeated."

"So you just left them there, sleeping?" CB asked.

"Waking them didn't seem like a good idea," Alex replied. "And we couldn't really wait around until sundown."

Though the sun shone on *New Haven*, for Alex and the residents of the city-ship, it was the middle of the night. After returning to *New Haven*, going through the decontamination process, and doing the official debriefing, she was now sitting with CB in his office. Both of them were dead tired, but as far as Alex could remember, it was the first time she'd had his undivided attention in weeks, and she wasn't going to waste it.

"I hate to say it, CB, but Jaden's up to something. There's something he doesn't want us to know."

CB's face betrayed no expression, but she saw the concern in his eyes. "It doesn't look good, I'll give you that. What we need to do now is take a deep breath and think about this before we do anything rash."

"I'm not saying we bust into Agartha, guns blazing, but we have to do something. It's pretty damn clear that the recon team is doing more than just scouting for Ferals."

"Agreed. But Jaden's earned the benefit of the doubt, hasn't he? I'm sure there's a logical explanation. It's in his best interest to make sure humanity survives, and we know for a fact he's been working hard to make sure that happens. If we die, so does he."

"Then why are his vamps tearing up secret computers on the island?" Alex drew a deep breath. On the one hand, she knew CB was right. Jaden had saved her life on more than one occasion. He'd been the one to push for the new

Resettlement plan when the *New Haven* City Council was gun shy after Fleming's death.

"I don't know," CB allowed, "but our first step in finding the answer is to ask him. He's been pretty forthcoming so far. We owe him the opportunity to explain himself."

Alex ran her hands over the rough fabric of her pants, taking another deep breath. The Alex from two years ago, the Alex who'd tried to smuggle daylights out on a mission, probably would have stolen a ship and flown down to Agartha to confront Jaden immediately. Thankfully, she'd learned a little patience since those days. CB was right. The best course of action was to sit down at a table with Jaden and straight up ask him what they wanted to know.

"Okay," she said. "Let's go to the Council in the morning and get approval to head to Agartha. We can talk to Jaden tomorrow night, and hopefully put this all behind us."

CB scratched at the stubble on his face a moment before answering. "Our next scheduled meeting with Jaden is in, what, four days? I think we should wait and talk to him then."

Alex grimaced. She wasn't sure her patience extended quite that far. "Why wait? Don't you want answers now?"

"Of course, but let's think this through. To get approval for a special trip, we'd have to tell the Council exactly what's going on. I'd rather we don't get them involved until we have to. Besides, if the Council knows, so does McCready."

"Ugh, I forgot about the ambassador."

"The last thing we need is to create political tension between our two cities for no reason. We'll tell the Council, but not until we give Jaden a chance to explain himself." He gave her a weary smile. "Now, get some rest. You look as tired as I feel."

Alex left the meeting partially satisfied. On the one hand, CB had listened and taken her concerns seriously. With everything he had going on, that wasn't always the case these days. Mostly, she agreed with his decision. Yet, something about his wait-and-see attitude didn't sit right with her. He'd seemed mildly concerned at her news, but not panicked. They now knew for a fact that Jaden was hiding something from them. Shouldn't that be a bigger deal?

Instead of going to her quarters, Alex headed toward Sparrow's Ridge. Due to the wide variety of schedules on *New Haven* and the fluidity of the concepts of day and night, Tankards never closed.

She found Owl and Brian waiting at their regular table, just as she'd known she would. While she trusted every member of the GMT, Owl and Brian were the two people she trusted most, aside from CB. They were also the two people who seemed to understand the gravity of the situation. These two took Jaden's secrets just as seriously as Alex did.

Alex smiled when she saw there was already a beer waiting for her.

"What did he say?" Owl asked, as soon as Alex sat down.

"He listened, I'll give him that. He understands our concern, but he wants us to take it slow." She recounted the details of the meeting, including CB's reluctance to talk to the Council.

"I can't blame him, there," Brian said. "They do have a record of being a bit reactionary."

Alex wasn't so sure. While the Council did tend to overreact, she couldn't quite see them turning on Jaden. They loved the vampire and sought his council at every turn. If anything, she could see them dismissing the evidence against Jaden, rather than overreacting to it.

"Listen, I need both of you to do some research for me," she said.

"Research I can do," Owl said with a smile.

"We need to find out everything we can about Puerto Rico, and Jaden's connection to it."

"That won't be easy," Brian said. "There aren't a lot of records on vampires. We didn't even know Jaden existed until you knocked on his door in Agartha."

"Agreed, but maybe there's something in the records about Puerto Rico that we can tie to him. He's clearly searching for something. There's information on the island he doesn't want us to have. We need to put that in context."

Owl nodded. "I don't like this at all. As my mom used to say, 'Secrets, secrets are no fun. Secrets, secrets hurt someone.'"

Alex had just taken a big sip of beer, and she nearly spit it out as she laughed. "Cool, we'll just confront Jaden with your mom's nursery rhyme, and I'm sure he'll come clean."

Brian chuckled. "CB does have a point, though. Jaden has earned our good will. We'll research, but I'm betting there's a logical explanation for what he's doing."

Owl nodded sagely. "Trust but verify."

Alex laughed again. "Jesus, Owl, you're a walking cliché tonight."

"I prefer to think of it as the wisdom of the ages." She turned to Brian. "I'm not doubting you, but what possible innocent explanation could there be?"

Brian thought a moment. "Maybe there's something dangerous on the island. Something that could destroy us. Maybe he wants to get rid of it before we have the chance to misuse it."

"So he's humanity's daddy, who has to make sure we don't play with the dangerous toys?"

"Maybe he's looking for something he lost?" Brian tried again.

Owl shook her head. "And the best way to find it is smashing hard drives? That's pretty weak." She took a sip of beer. "I know he's saved our asses a few times, but I still find it difficult to fully trust one of the vampires who was around when his kind nearly destroyed the human race. What if this whole Resettlement thing is a ruse to get us out of the sky, so he can enslave *New Haven*?"

Alex frowned. None of the possible explanations Brian and Owl had presented sounded likely. "There are way too many maybes in this conversation. Right now, we are just guessing, and it'll drive us crazy if we keep it up. We need hard facts and information. I want you both to dig up everything you can so I can be somewhat informed when I head down to Agartha. Next time I meet with Jaden, I intend to find the truth."

9

FIREFLY WOKE TO A FAMILIAR FEELING: hunger.

He felt the hunger as got out of bed and as he dressed. He felt it as he opened the door to his room and the artificial light in the hall hit his eyes. Hunger was his constant companion.

He and his troops received fresh supplies of blood every two weeks, and today was night twelve. The GMT brought enough blood to keep the vampires on the island from going feral, but not enough to allow any lasting relief from the hunger. The reasoning was sound; a packet of blood was like a nuclear weapon. A few spilled drops could result in thousands of Ferals attacking their location. It had to be handled with extreme caution, and it couldn't be left sitting around. When the GMT brought the supply, the vampires drank immediately and gave the empty blood packets back to the GMT to take with them when they left.

Firefly hoped that over time, his body would adjust to only eating once every other week, or that maybe his system would learn to be more patient, and stop constantly demanding to be fed. The hunger was like a pulse, constantly pounding deep within him, thrumming to be satisfied.

It was always worse the last few days before the supply came. Panicked thoughts crept into his head. What if *New Haven* crashed into the ocean, or the GMT was killed on another mission? Then the blood would never come. What if the people of *New Haven* had finally decided to punish him for his role in the first disastrous attempt at Resettlement? The torment of starvation would grow until it consumed him, transforming him into an unthinking monster.

Even now, after a year without one late supply, such thoughts were difficult to overcome. He took a deep breath, and it calmed him a little. His body seemed to respond to such unnecessary things, soothed by a reminder of what it had been like to be human. He had to keep it together for two more days, for his troops, if not for himself. Then the blood would come, he'd be briefly sated, and the cycle would begin again.

A thought occurred to him. If Jaden approved the plan for the GMT to come more frequently and run missions on the island, perhaps the blood would be resupplied more frequently, too. He had brought the issue up to Alex, telling her that two weeks was a long time to go without feeding, but there was no way for her to understand how hard it truly was. The Council had decided that *New* Haven's repairs were the priority. As long as the blood supplies were frequent enough to keep all of the vampires healthy, that was enough for them.

Helen spotted him standing in the doorway and gave him a nod. She was squinting, clearly as affected by the electric lights in the hall as he was. "I still don't understand why we need these damn things. Running the generator is a waste of resources, and we can see just fine without them.

"Good morning to you, too," Firefly said with mock cheerfulness.

"Don't give me that. I know you're as hungry as I am." She gently shoved his chest, pushing him back into the room.

"I've explained it before. My troops and I are new vampires. Walking around in the dark twenty-four, seven is a little off-putting. Especially considering we spent our lives on *New Haven* and rarely saw darkness. Electric light is comforting."

"Yeah, well the hum is driving me nuts." She stepped into the room and shut the door behind her. "I need something to take my mind off the hunger. Take off your clothes." She pulled her shirt over her head without waiting for a response.

Firefly paused. "I... I really don't have time for this tonight. The troops are waiting for orders, and I need to meet with the team commanders." He maneuvered around Helen and made his way toward the door.

Helen put a hand on his chest, stopping him. "I told them that they could relax for a bit while we talk. They are just as hungry we are. You think they really care if we chase Ferals around the city tonight?"

Firefly looked down at her hand and the strong, but gentle way she was touching him. As much as he didn't want to look, his eyes were drawn to her bare chest. Her body was eternally young. Perfect. Beautiful. It awoke a different kind of hunger within him, and the thirst for blood faded slightly.

"You do remember that you threatened to kill me," he said. "I am never sleeping with you again."

Helen smiled up at him.

And then she was in motion. She spun behind him, wrapping one arm around his chest. Her other hand caressed his stomach, then moved confidently downward, inside the waist of his pants, and lower still.

Her lips brushed his earlobe. "You sure about that?"

Firefly knew he'd lost this battle and all that was left to do was give in and enjoy the ride.

The two of them emerged from his room a half hour later. Helen smirked at Firefly as she walked out the door. "I guess *never* came early this year."

Firefly swallowed hard, trying the push back the bile of regret that rose in his throat. He always hated himself a little after he was with Helen. Sleeping with someone he could barely stand having a conversation with... Not his proudest of accomplishments.

But then, hating himself was something Firefly was starting to get used to.

He closed the door to his room and headed out to find his team.

THAT NIGHT, Brian and Owl gathered in Alex's quarters to discuss what they'd been able to learn about Puerto Rico. While Alex would have much preferred them to be sitting behind some beers at Tankards, she figured it might be wiser to do this in private. Though she didn't want to admit it, she was already beginning to plan for the possibility that they would have to continue these clandestine meetings for some time to come.

"We have a lot of records on the island," Owl explained. "The problem hasn't been finding information; it's been sifting through it to find something useful. I could probably spend months reading all the information, but most of it is mundane stuff from before the invasion. The rest of it, we already know. It was the last human stronghold and was kept free of vampires longer than any other known location. There were naval mines placed in the sea around the island and anti-aircraft guns around the perimeter. It seems the strategy worked for a while, but..."

"Yeah," Alex finished. Like all other strategies against the vampires, it had failed in the end. "What about the bunker we found? Any information on that?"

Brian shook his head. "I dug deep into the military records. There was Fort Buchanan, and a few other, smaller military outposts, but nothing in the location where you found the recon team. Whatever it was, it was either non-military, or too secret to be kept in the official records."

"Which means there could be others," Alex mused.

"The secrecy makes sense," Brian said. "Think about it. During the infestation, anyone could be bitten and turned. And then any information in their heads or on their hard drives was suddenly property of the vampires. I'm guessing the human leaders shared as little as possible."

Alex frowned. "So you're telling me that you didn't get anything?"

Brian leaned forward, an excited sparkle in his eye. "Not exactly. The ship's database didn't have any official records on Puerto Rico, other than the general data that Owl mentioned. As we discovered, most of the information on the Horsemen programs was erased."

"I'm not hearing anything new."

"Maybe most people would stop there. Lucky for you, I'm not most people. I searched through the personal logs of the first generation who lived on New Haven."

Owl's mouth dropped open. "Hang on, you can search our personal logs?"

"Not legally, no."

Alex laughed. "What's in your logs, Owl? Sounds like Brian should check that out, next."

He held up a hand. "Relax, I didn't look at your stuff. In fact, I haven't figured out a way to look through the logs of living residents. They have those locked down tight." He glanced at Alex. "Not that I've tried. Anyway, point is, once someone dies, the protection level changes. People with high access can review the records, if needed."

"Or someone who can mimic that access," Alex added.

Owl still didn't look too comfortable. "So if you wanted to read someone's personal log, you could just kill them first?"

"No." Brian tilting his head back and forth, considering the question. "I mean, yes, you could. But that's not the point."

"Tell us what you found," Alex said.

"One of the engineers in the first days of *New Haven* was quite the record keeper. He and his wife were going through a rough patch, and he was not shy about putting the details in his log."

Alex leaned forward. "This is getting juicy."

"It seems the source of their marital strife was their professions. See, he'd helped build *New Haven*, and he believed living on the ship was the only chance for survival."

"Good call," Owl said.

"His wife disagreed. She wanted to stay and fight. Turns out, she was a scientist working on another secret program. A program called Project White Horse."

"Oh, shit," Alex said, smiling now.

"The logs were focused more on the details of their

marriage than on Project White Horse, but I was able to suss out a few details. See, the reason the wife didn't want to leave was that Project White Horse was working on a weapon she believed could change the course of the fight against the vampires. And, according to her, they were close to finishing it."

"Did the logs says what the weapon was or what it did?" Owl asked.

Brian shook his head. "Like I said, it was light on details. I've been trying to figure out what it could be, but…"

"Yeah," Alex agreed.

Owl ran a hand through her pink hair. "So the question is, is Jaden trying to hide something about Project White Horse? And if so, why?"

Alex met her friend's eyes. "Why is he trying to hide a weapon that hurts vampires? I think the answer to that is pretty clear."

Brian shook his head in disbelief. "We've been so focused on wondering whether we should trust Jaden that we've missed obvious. He doesn't trust us."

The three of them sat in silence for nearly a minute. Then Alex stood up.

"We're going to Agartha tomorrow night. We'll see what we can get from Jaden then. In the meantime, keep looking. I want to be armed with as much information as possible."

"Secrets, secrets, hurt someone," Owl said softly.

Alex didn't respond, but she wondered if that were true. And, if it were, who would end up getting hurt before this was said and done.

FIREFLY AND HIS team walked through the empty streets of

San Juan, their swords at the ready. A warm breeze blew from the harbor and through the streets. The palm trees that grew through the massive cracks in the pavement rustled in the breeze, filling the otherwise quiet night with pleasant sound.

During his first few weeks on the island, Firefly had imagined they'd have no problem hunting down all the Ferals. The biggest challenge then had been to pick off a reasonable number without killing too many at once. They had been afraid of setting off a wave of rabid Ferals. But that wave had never come, and the Ferals had started to hide. Firefly could feel the mental connection the Ferals shared enough to understand there were still hundreds of thousands of them in the city. The downside was that they could sense him and his team as well. They'd learned that Firefly and his troops meant death, not food. Thankfully, their mental connection was a far from perfect method of communication.

The other thing that concerned Firefly was that he and his fellow vampires still didn't fully understand the way that the Ferals behaved. Sometimes they were docile, not even putting up a fight, as Firefly's soldiers walked right up to them. Other times, they attacked at the mere sight of the intelligent vampires.

Though tonight, calling his troops intelligent vampires felt like a stretch. They were hungry and lethargic, and probably would have preferred to spend the night in the hotel. Instead, they were out patrolling the streets yet again, and weren't all too happy about it.

As they walked, Firefly's headset chirped.

"Alpha, come in, this is Echo."

Firefly recognized the voice as Henry, team leader of the Echo squad.

He touched his radio to reply. "This is Alpha. Go ahead."

"We found two Ferals. They're fighting each other in the middle of the street. Permission to take them out?"

Firefly hesitated. He didn't like any team engaging in battle without at least one other team backing them up. Situations could go bad quickly. "What's your location?"

"Five blocks south of the hotel. In an open area, by some low-rise buildings."

Firefly immediately recognized the location. It was a spot he'd been intending to clear for a while. "We are only a few blocks to your west. Give us a minute. We're on our way."

"No need, Captain." Henry sounded annoyed at the suggestion that they couldn't handle two Ferals. "We got this."

"Negative." Firefly felt a bit annoyed, himself. Henry knew the rules. No team engages alone. "Wait for us. That's an order. Firefly out."

He motioned for his team to pick up the pace and they ran the few blocks to Echo's location, not going all out, but moving quickly and quietly through the silent street.

The low-rise housing complex was comprised of fifteen three-story buildings. From the way they'd deteriorated faster than most of the other buildings, Firefly had to assume they hadn't been built of the highest quality materials to begin with. There were few windows left and some of the buildings had holes large enough for Ferals to pass through in their walls.

In the center of the complex, there was a large courtyard. Firefly felt a bit of relief when he spotted Henry and the rest of Echo squad huddled in the courtyard, waiting. The situation was exactly as Henry had described. Two Ferals circled each other, occasionally lunging forward to nip or scratch at each other. What could cause two Ferals to come to blows, Firefly did not know. It's not like there was blood to fight over. Whatever the reason, they were concentrating on each other and seemed oblivious to the forty soldiers gathered near them.

Henry shuffled his way to Firefly's side. "Permission to engage now?"

One of the Ferals jumped forward, sinking its teeth into the other's forearm. Then it leapt back and the two continued circling each other.

"Permission granted."

Firefly's team Alpha spread out so that they'd have the entire courtyard covered if any other Ferals tried to join in the fight.

Echo spread out too, forming a circle around the Ferals. Henry signaled to two of his soldiers, and they crept forward. The fighting Ferals still hadn't seemed to notice anyone but each other.

Henry signaled again, and the two soldiers dashed forward, their swords raised. They attacked in unison, each taking out a Feral with a single sword stroke.

As the two Feral heads hit the ground, team Echo seemed to relax, backing away.

Then, a deep angry howl came from one of the buildings. The sound had only just registered in Firefly's ear when four more howls answered, each from a different low-rise.

"Shit," Firefly muttered, his hand going to his radio.

More howls joined the cacophony, until the ground shook.

"All teams to the low-rises five blocks south of the hotel, now!" Firefly shouted into his headset. "We're under attack!" Then he turned to his team. "Prepare for combat!"

10

FIREFLY LOOKED FRANTICALLY DOWN the courtyard for some way of escape. The howls were coming from every direction, and he knew they wouldn't stand a chance once the Ferals started pouring out of the buildings. From the howls, he knew they were already outnumbered, and that wasn't even considering the Ferals in the surrounding blocks—maybe farther—that would be drawn by the howls and the waves of distress the ones in the low-rises were putting out.

They wouldn't stand a chance in this open courtyard, where Ferals would be able to attack from all angles, including from above.

"We need to get inside!" he shouted. He motioned toward the nearest building, hoping that both the Alpha and Echo teams would hear him in the midst of the chaos.

Firefly led the charge, rushing toward the nearest door. When he was ten feet away, the door burst open, and Ferals charged out. He hefted his sword. "Get in formation and take them out! We need this building."

Team Alpha fell into formation like the well-trained soldiers they were. They shifted into a tight circle, covering all directions and slowly making their way toward the building, cutting down the Ferals who emerged.

Firefly glanced to his left. Team Echo was in a similar formation, also cutting their way through the dozens of Ferals pouring from the building. Both teams were taking care of business, but Ferals were charging out of the surrounding buildings, too. They sprinted at the soldiers. Still, Firefly stayed focused. They had to make it to that building.

A scream came from Firefly's left, and he saw one of the Echo soldiers stagger forward, a Feral on his back, a claw sunk into each eye. Three more Ferals fell on the soldier as he collapsed to his knees.

"Stay in formation!" Henry shouted to his team. They tightened the circle, closing the gap that had been created by their fallen brother.

From the corner of his eye, Firefly saw something above. A Feral leapt off the building and plunged toward team Echo.

"Henry!" Firefly shouted. But it was too late to give any real warning.

The Feral slammed into Henry, knocking him to the ground. He let out a pained grunt as five more Ferals converged, viciously attacking with claws and teeth. In seconds, he was torn apart.

Firefly felt a pang of grief welling up inside him, but forced it back down. There was no time for that now. He didn't have time to consider that Henry had just died under his leadership for a second time. The flurry of activity around the two fallen soldiers had created a gap in the Ferals.

"Everyone, get into the building now!" he shouted. Then

he led the charge, ushering his team through the last of the Ferals between them and the door.

Team Alpha rushed inside, and Echo followed close behind. But more and more of the Ferals from the surrounding buildings reached them before they made it through. Firefly watched in horror as six more Echo soldiers fell on their way into the building.

Firefly glanced through a window and cursed. There had to be five hundred Ferals in the courtyard now, and more still coming. This was the thing he'd most feared during his year on the island: the drought of Ferals suddenly becoming a flood. They'd been outnumbered since day one. Perhaps it was inevitable that this would happen.

Just like it had happened before. Fort Stearns. The first Resettlement.

No. He clenched his teeth and gripped his sword. It wasn't going to happen like last time. He was going to get his people out of this, whatever it took.

"Get to that hallway!" He gestured to a corridor about eight feet wide. The enemy's numbers would be far less overwhelming if they could narrow the battlefield to eight feet.

The remaining thirty soldiers ran to the hallway, filling it until every door was covered by multiple vampires.

Ferals attacked from both ends of the hallway, but the Resettlers held fast. Using the tight space to their advantage, they cut down every Feral that reached them.

Firefly knew they couldn't keep this up forever. He spoke into his radio. "We're trapped in the third building from the north end of the courtyard. All teams converge on us, but be careful. There's a hell of a lot of them."

Ferals swarmed the building and entered the apartments on either side of the hallway through every window, then attacked the hallway from every door. The combined teams Alpha and Echo kept a tight formation, taking all comers until the bodies of fallen Ferals piled up, filling the apartment doors. As the bodies accumulated, the flow of Ferals began to slow.

Shouts from outside reached Firefly's ears, and he hoped that meant the other teams had arrived. Then Hector's voice came through his headset. "We're trying to draw them away from the west side of the building, Captain. We'll let you know when you have an opening."

"Roger that," Firefly said, "and many thanks. I'll owe you a blood packet when this is over."

A loud crash came from his right, interrupting the conversation. He spun toward it and saw that a Feral had broken through the thin wall between the hallway and the apartments. The closest soldier was ready, and she stabbed the Feral in the heart before it ever finished climbing through the hole.

But just then, another Feral came through the wall on the other side of the hallway. And a third.

"They're attacking from every direction!" someone shouted.

"Stay tight," Firefly growled. "Keep in formation and they can't—"

A cracking sound from above cut him off.

He took a step back. "What the hell?"

Another crack, much louder than before, and a hole appeared in the ceiling above them. A Feral jumped down, landing on the soldier. It attacked viciously, sinking its teeth into the soldier's neck and ripping out her throat.

Dust tumbled down on Firefly as another hole appeared

in the ceiling. A Feral jumped through and Firefly slashed at it, removing its head before it landed.

All around them, Ferals were coming through the walls and ceiling. Their defensive corridor was turning into a killing ground, and it wouldn't be long until the building came down on their heads. They had to get out of there, now. Firefly just hoped Hector and the other teams had drawn enough of the Ferals away.

"Get to the courtyard!" he shouted. He was on the other end of the hallway, and he walked backward as his team retreated, fending off the Ferals who began to fill the hallway.

"We can't make it, Captain!" someone called. "There's too many of them!"

Firefly glanced to his left and saw a hole in the wall, leading to one of the apartment buildings. "Follow me!"

He dove through the hole and into an apartment. He saw two Ferals and charged, removing one's head and stabbing the other in the heart. Just ahead he saw a glassless window, and he ran toward it. He had no idea what was waiting for them in the courtyard, and he wanted to be the first to face it. Leaping, he dove through the window, hit the ground, and somersaulted to his feet.

The courtyard was less densely populated than the last time he'd seen it. Apparently, the other teams had successfully drawn away the majority of the Ferals. A few teams had stayed behind and were dispatching the Ferals still in the courtyard.

As teams Alpha and Echo regrouped, the Ferals still inside the building came for them. Most didn't bother with the doors and windows, instead tearing new holes in the exterior walls in their frenzy. The building groaned and shook.

Firefly cupped his hands to his mouth and yelled. "Anyone still in there, get out fast!"

The building groaned again. Teams of soldiers gathered around the building, killing the Ferals as soon as they exited.

Then there was a groan so deep that Firefly felt it in his bones, and the building collapsed on itself.

After five more minutes of fighting, every Feral in the courtyard was dead.

Firefly felt numb. "Team leaders, take a count."

As they did, he gathered team Alpha and did a count of his own. He'd lost six members. Echo had lost eight. Fourteen vampires dead, all in a matter of minutes.

Barbosa, a member of the Echo team, tapped him on the shoulder. "Captain, I think Hargrave was in there when it collapsed. He might be buried in the rubble."

Firefly nodded slowly. "Everyone, gather around. We need to look for survivors."

A howl came from nearby, as if in answer to his words.

Helen appeared and stood in front of him. "We need to go. Now."

"We're not leaving anyone behind," Firefly said.

"You don't know that there's anyone in there. If we stick around, everyone's going to die." Her voice softened a little. "Don't you think we've lost enough today?"

He hesitated a moment, then nodded. He turned to his troops "We're leaving. Stick with your teams. Each team go in a different direction and move as fast as you can. We'll meet at the shopping center on the south side of town before dawn."

Barbosa stared at him is disbelief. "We can't just—"

Firefly grabbed him by the shoulders. "You are in charge of Echo Team. Get your soldiers to safety. We will come back to search for survivors tomorrow night. Now, go!"

The vampires sprinted out of the courtyard and into the city, the sounds of angry howls at their backs.

CB LEANED over to Alex as they walked through a long corridor in the heart of Agartha. "There's one word I want you to remember today, and that word is tact."

"Tact?" Alex tried to keep the annoyance out of her voice. There were a lot of things on her mind as she prepared for her meeting with Jaden, and tact wasn't one of them.

"Exactly. Remember, Jaden isn't our enemy. This isn't an interrogation. It's going to take diplomacy. And, yes, tact."

"Said noted diplomat, Colonel Brickman."

CB chuckled. "You've got to admit, I've gotten better on that front. I sit through three City Council meetings a week, and I want to put at least one person's head through the table at every one of them. All I'm saying is, we need to present the facts and see how he responds. We're not here to pick a fight."

"When have I ever picked a fight?" She couldn't even say it with a straight face.

"I'm serious. I have enough on my plate. I don't need you causing trouble between us and Jaden. We want answers, but keep it civil."

They reached the conference room and found Jaden, Natalie, and George already seated at the table. George immediately popped out of his chair and shook their hands. Natalie and Jaden did so more slowly.

Probably the effects of daysickness, Alex realized. After

her recent encounter with Helen, she wasn't looking forward to dealing with more cranky vampires.

"How's life in the sky?" George asked as they all took their seats.

"Same as always," CB replied. "Sunny."

Natalie shot CB a look. "I'm sorry, but could we move on to business? I should have been asleep an hour ago."

"Of course." CB pulled his tablet out and set it on the table. "These are the numbers since our last conversation."

Jaden picked up the tablet and studied it for a moment. "Hmm. The numbers are trending even lower than before. Except this bump at the end." He looked up at Alex. "I take it that was your trial run?"

Alex nodded. "We ran a quick mission and took out maybe six Ferals. As you can see, it worked exactly as we'd predicted. The Ferals were drawn to that area for days, and Firefly's team cleaned up. A pretty successful trial, I'd say."

Jaden grunted noncommittally.

"We'd like to continue the test," Alex continued. "I'd like to propose that the GMT run missions every other day for the next month."

Jaden raised an eyebrow at that. "That seems a little excessive. Adding a regular human element could drastically change things on the island. We don't know how the Ferals will react."

"I'm not talking about a full-scale invasion. These would be quick easy missions, and we'd be out well before dusk."

Jaden handed the tablet back to CB. "I understand what you're saying, and I know the slow process isn't your ideal scenario. But we have a small team of vampires down there, and I'd like to do everything we can to ensure they stay alive to complete their mission. Having the GMT down there could make the Ferals more aggressive. Even if we lose one team member for every twenty thousand Ferals killed, we won't have enough vampires to clear the island."

CB answered before Alex could. "That makes sense. We appreciate your input. What would be a more reasonable frequency for the mission?"

Jaden thought a moment. "How about once a week?"

"Once a week?" Alex couldn't help herself. "We're still trying to clear the island, right? That's still the plan of action?"

"You do like action, don't you Alex?" Jaden said, looking her in the eyes. "I was able to survive that dangerous part of my youth. I truly hope that you are able to, as well."

"I remember a certain GMT that saved you and your vamps in Denver," she replied. "Action isn't always a bad thing. Maybe you should listen to us. Youth and passion have their place in the world, too."

"Watch yourself," Natalie said, a growl in her voice.

Alex glanced at CB and made a mental note to hold their next meeting at night. She and CB could just sleep down here and leave in the morning. It would beat the hell out of dealing with these cranky vampires again.

Jaden still sounded calm. "We've both helped each other, and I do respect the passion of youth. And I want us to keep talking about this stuff. Let's stay on task and agree to open communication, moving forward."

Alex shifted in her seat. This was her opportunity, and she wasn't going to waste it. "In that spirit, I need to ask you something. The last time the GMT was on the island, we sort of ran into your recon team. The thing is, they weren't doing recon. We found them in an old bunker of some sort. They'd torn apart a lab and destroyed the computer systems. What were they looking for, Jaden?"

CB gave Alex a warning glare.

Jaden thought a moment before answering. "As you know, the only communication between me and the vampires in Puerto Rico goes through you, so I can't tell you exactly what they were doing. I simply don't know. I instructed them to gather any and all intel they discovered. If they destroyed something, I'm sure they had a reason. Next time you meet with them, ask. I'd like to know the answer, too."

Alex looked at CB, and he gave her an almost imperceptible shake of the head. Still, she knew she need to press Jaden, just a little. "Is it possible they were searching for something related to the Four Horsemen Program?"

If Jaden was surprised, it didn't show. "It's possible. What do you know about the Horsemen?"

"Not much really," Alex answered. "I know Agartha and *New Haven* were part of Project Black Horse. I'm guessing you can fill in some of the other gaps."

"Yes. I believe I can."

Jaden still looked stone-faced, but his companions were less adept at hiding their feelings. Something close to shock was displayed on Natalie's face. George looked like a man trying to understand a language he didn't speak; he clearly had no idea about the Four Horsemen Program.

"You're right about Black Horse," Jaden began. "It was one of the last resort plans for if we were unable to stop the third wave. Obviously, I wasn't thrilled with the idea of starving the vampires out, but I went along with it once I realized it was the only way. Until then, I had been most involved with Project Red Horse."

"That represented war, right?" Alex asked.

Jaden nodded. "The military used every conventional means at their disposal. Unfortunately, they were fighting an unconventional war. The other true vampires and I did what we could. We fought alongside the human armies and carried out our own strategic strikes. It wasn't enough."

His voice was flat as he spoke, but Alex could see the pain in his eyes now. He was recounting the greatest failure of his incredibly long life.

"Project White Horse—conquest—was a plan to create an effective weapon against the vampires. They kept most of the details from me, what with me being a vampire and all. But I'm told the project had great potential. Many of the greatest minds of the day worked on that one. Sadly, there simply wasn't enough time to make it happen. The world died before the project produced any results."

"That leaves Project Pale Horse." CB spoke softly, almost as if he was reluctant to speak at all. "The pale horse is Death. What was that project?"

Jaden sighed. "If what the recon team is doing had anything to do with the Four Horsemen Program, I believe it's related to Project Pale Horse. As you said CB, the pale horse is Death. This was a last resort for if all else failed, including our two cities. It was the nuclear option. Literally."

"Nuclear?" Alex asked.

"Yes. At the time, many countries possessed enough nuclear weapons to destroy the world, some many times over. When it became clear this was a fight for humanity's survival, many of the world's leaders fled to Puerto Rico, the last stronghold. Project Pale Horse gathered all the world's nuclear controls in one location. If all else failed, they could be used to destroy the vampires. Then those gathered in Puerto Rico would try to survive the nuclear winter that would follow."

"Holy shit," Alex muttered.

"Thankfully, that option wasn't used." Jaden paused a

moment. "I'd like to ensure it never can be. The recon team knows my feelings on the matter. I believe there's a chance they discovered nuclear codes or the launch protocols. They certainly would have destroyed that information if they ran across it."

"Rightly so," CB said.

Alex shook her head. "I can't believe humans once had the power to destroy the world."

Jaden smiled. "Yes. There were worse threats than vampires back then. I hope I've addressed your concerns, Alex."

Alex thought for a moment. She'd been expecting a big secret to be exposed, but maybe CB had been right all along. Maybe the explanation was just that simple. "Yes. You have."

"Good." Jaden handed CB back his tablet. "Was there anything else?"

11

THE GMT CLIMBED off of the away ship and out into the bright morning sun of Puerto Rico.

"Again," Owl said to Alex, "I'm really sorry. I feel like I've let you down."

"Would you let it go, already?" Patrick said with a groan.

Owl glared at him. "I will not let it go, Patrick. It's my job to provide interesting and inciteful facts about our destination. Today, I failed in that task."

"It's not your fault," Alex said. "How were you supposed to know they wouldn't be in San Juan?" She stopped in front of the building and put her hands on her hips. "We're sure this is the place?"

Owl consulted her tablet. "This is it."

The GMT was on their regular supply run to Puerto Rico. Much to their surprise, when they got into range of Firefly's tracker, they found he was not in San Juan at all, but in a city to the south, called Bayamón.

The tracker had led them to a large manufacturing building, not the type of place the Resettlement team usually holed up for the day. Owl had landed the away ship beside the building in a large open area that had once been a parking lot.

As Owl put her tablet in her pack, Patrick nudged Chuck and pointed to Owl's wrist.

"You see that?"

Chuck shook his head. "Yep. I'm guessing there will be more of those."

Alex had seen it too: a brand-new tattoo—the outline of an Owl. She thought it looked pretty cool and she wasn't about to judge. Still, Owl did seem to be going through something lately. She was trying her hardest to stand out, and this was just the latest example.

Alex led the way through the front door of the building, her hand on the butt of her pistol, just in case. Patrick and Chuck came with, while the others stayed outside waiting for the all-clear signal to bring in the new supply.

"You awake in there?" Alex called. "We've got some refreshments for you."

The response was immediate. "We're here. Come in."

Alex stepped into the large, mostly open area of the building and found the vampires eagerly waiting. The last time she'd been down to the island at that time of day, only Firefly and Helen had been awake. Now, with the promise of blood so close, every one of the vampires was awake and standing, looking at the GMT members as they entered.

She radioed for the rest of the team to bring in the fresh supply, and a moment later, Ed and Owl rolled the rover in through one of the bay doors. A large, sealed metal crate was loaded on the back.

As they unloaded the crate, Alex once again noticed the oddness of this location. The building was full of old, rusted machines and conveyor belts, and the roof had seen better days. Shafts of sunlight came down through holes in several parts of the roof. It seems like a dangerous place for vampires to hole up.

Ed nodded to Firefly. "What seest thou else in the dark backward and abysm of time?"

Firefly looked at him oddly. "What are you talking about, Ed?"

"It's Shakespeare. It means, why are you staying in this jacked-up old factory?"

"I don't think that's what that means," Chuck said.

Alex crossed her arms. "Still, it's a valid question. Why'd you clear out of San Juan? Don't tell me you ran out of Ferals."

"No." Firefly stared at the floor as he answered. "Things... They haven't gone well since last time you were here. I'll tell you all about it, but can we get the blood handed out first? My people are hungry. Hungry enough that you all smell a little too sweet."

"Is he kidding again?" Patrick whispered.

Chuck shook his head. "I don't think so."

Owl pried the crate open and Firefly's team leaders went to work handing out the blood packets.

Firefly walked among his hungry soldiers, talking in a loud voice. "Remember to put your empty packets back in the crate. If you spill even a drop, make sure to follow the clean-up procedures." Only after everyone else had their packets did Firefly grab one for himself. Then he nodded to the GMT. "Let's go into one of the offices in the back. I'll tell you about what happened."

He led them toward a corner office, drinking from the pouch as he walked. The blood pouches were all equipped with a valve that fed into a tube that the vampires could use as a straw. Brian had devised the system to minimize the risk of spillage, and so far it had proven effective.

By the time they reached the office, Firefly had finished his meal. Alex could immediately see the change in him. Before he'd had a grayish, ashen hue. Now he looked almost human.

"So, what happened?" she asked.

Firefly took a moment, again staring at the floor, then answered. He told them about the fight at the low-rises and how he'd lost fourteen soldiers.

Alex put her hands on his shoulders. "I'm so sorry, Firefly. Are you holding up?"

"I... I'm not sure, honestly. Still trying to process everything." He looked up, meeting her eyes. "I've been thinking about it ever since, and I'm pretty sure the attack was a trap."

Chuck tilted his head in surprise. "Is that even possible? I mean, are Ferals that intelligent?"

"Remember Denver?" Alex asked. "We've seen them pull off some incredible things."

"There were just so many of them," Firefly continued. "There's no way they just happened to be in those buildings. And two Ferals randomly fighting each other, with no blood in sight? How often have we seen that?"

"Never," Owl answered.

Firefly nodded. "The thing that cemented it for me was the next night. We went back to look for survivors and we saw it again a few blocks over. Two Ferals fighting in an open area, next to a couple buildings."

"Damn," Ed said.

Alex drew a deep breath. "Jaden agreed that we should run more missions down here. Maybe we can find out where these big groups are sleeping during the day. And I'll tell Brian what happened. He might be able to put together some tech to help us out."

"Thanks," Firefly said. "Much appreciated."

Chuck glanced at the gathered vampires milling about outside the office. "What about Helen? I haven't seen her. Did she make it through the fight?"

"Yeah, she's fine." Firefly sighed. Clearly his emotions were a bit mixed on the issue of Helen. He turned to Alex. "She's hanging out with the recon team. And she's pretty pissed at you for some reason. They all are."

"Shit," Alex muttered. She told Firefly about what they'd seen in the bunker. "They never woke up, though. Would they have been able to smell that we'd been there?"

"For sure," Firefly said. "They probably would have been able to pick out your individual scents, too. Especially yours, Patrick."

Patrick's eyebrows shot up. "Hey! Are you trying to say I have a...scent?"

Firefly cracked a smile. "Don't worry, you smell delicious."

"Wait, what?" Patrick's expression changed from surprise to nervousness.

"I should probably go talk to them," Alex said, with a sigh.

She made her way to an office on the other end of the building and found the five Agartha vampires finishing their blood pouches. "Hey, sleepy heads. You're a little more awake than last time I saw you."

Helen gave her an ice-cold look when she walked in. "Well, at least you're woman enough to admit what you did."

Alex leaned against the doorway, trying to look more relaxed than she felt. She was suddenly aware that these five could kill her at any moment and there would be little she could do to stop them. "I've got nothing to hide. I did my job. We saw something unusual, and we investigated it."

Griffin, one of the other vampires, gave her a sharp look.

"Your job is to be a delivery service. You bring blood and bullets. We do the real work. Try to remember that."

Alex's fingernails dug into her palms as she tried to keep her cool. "Funny, that's not what Jaden said. He's approved our plan to run more GMT missions on the island."

"You're not serious," Helen said.

"I am. And I know you're big on doing everything Jaden says, so I guess we won't have a problem." She paused a moment. "Jaden also told me about your little side project. What you're looking for."

Silence hung in the air for a long moment. Then Griffin said, "What did he tell you?"

"I think you know. The Four Horsemen Program. The last ditch solution to destroy the vampires. Everything."

Another long silence. It felt good to see Helen with her mouth hanging open, speechless for once.

"So," Alex said, "did you find it?"

The vampires looked at each other. Finally Griffin spoke. "No. That bunker was much too small. They may have done some work on the formula there, but we need to find the lab where they actually produced the sample. Jaden was very clear about that."

For a moment, Alex could hardly breathe. It took everything in her power to keep her face blank. She just hoped her eyes didn't betray the panic she was feeling.

"Well," she said, "I guess the search continues, then. Enjoy your breakfast."

With that, she turned and left the Agartha vampires.

She wanted nothing more than to run to her teammates and tell them what she'd learned. But, as Ed had demonstrated when he'd admitted not knowing Shakespeare, vampire hearing was an incredible thing. She couldn't risk it. So, she waited until they were back on the away ship, her heart racing.

Then she joined Owl in the cockpit.

"What is it?" Owl asked. "You look—"

Alex grabbed her arms. "He lied. Jaden lied."

"What?"

"The recon team. Jaden lied about them. They are searching for something on this island, but it sure as hell isn't nuclear codes."

12

OWL WAS quiet for a long time as she guided the away ship toward San Juan. "If Jaden's team isn't looking for the nuclear codes, what are they looking for? Project White Horse?"

"That's my guess," Alex answered. "White Horse was developing an anti-vamp weapon. I could see why Jaden wouldn't want that getting out."

If that was the answer, it raised a lot of questions. Namely, why? Was Jaden just being cautious, destroying the weapon so that it didn't fall into the wrong hands? Or was there something more behind it.? Was Jaden planning something that would cause *New Haven* to have to defend itself against him?

Thinking about it made Alex's stomach hurt. This had all seemed so perfect. A group of vampires who'd saved the GMT in their darkest hour. Twice. Maybe she should have known it was too good to be true.

And if Jaden did turn out to have bad intentions, what the hell could the GMT do to stop him? They'd barely survived Mark and Aaron, two idiots with the combined patience and intelligence of Ed and Patrick. What chance did they have against Jaden, a master warrior and strategist? Not to mention his army of loyal, intelligent vampires.

"What do we do now?" Owl asked.

Alex thought a moment before answering. "For today, we do our jobs. I don't want to worry the rest of the team, and I certainly don't want to raise any alarms with Helen and the recon vamps. Let's keep this between us and run the mission. We'll talk to CB and Brian when we get back home."

Owl nodded. She looked a little relieved to have permission to put this out of her mind for a while. She consulted her tablet, then gestured to a group of buildings below them. "That's it."

They were heading to the location where Firefly had seen the second set of vampires fighting the previous night. It was another set of low-rise buildings surrounding a courtyard, similar to the place he and his troops had been ambushed. If his theory was correct, the Ferals were setting another trap for the Resettlers here. That meant there were probably hundreds of Ferals sleeping in these buildings.

"We need to do a sweep," Alex told the team. "Confirm that this is where the Ferals are sleeping. But do it carefully. We want to find them, not engage."

"What's the plan after that?" Chuck asked "I don't think we can clear out a building that's wall-to-wall Ferals. I mean, we're good, but not that good."

Alex smiled. "All we need to do is give the building a skylight. The sun will do the heavy lifting."

They split up and began searching the surrounding low-rises. Alex and Ed headed for one of the closest buildings and eased the front door open a crack, just enough to see inside. It only took one look for Alex to confirm dozens of slumped, sleeping bodies in the hallway.

The team reconvened in the center of the courtyard. They had all seen Ferals, but Patrick had struck the motherlode.

"They were shoulder-to-shoulder in there," he said excitedly. "I'm talking a couple hundred, at least."

"Okay." Alex turned to Chuck. "Looks like you're up."

Chuck swallowed hard and reached for his pack of explosives.

He spent the next hour rigging the building Patrick had searched, working slowly and carefully. Luckily for him, the glass was long gone from the windows. This allowed him to easily climb into the apartments, staying in the sunlight near the windows. He placed charges in alternating apartments, attaching them to the ceilings, close to the wall shared with the hallway where the Ferals slept.

Owl watched nervously as he worked. "You realize, if he drops something and wakes up the Ferals—"

"Yeah," Alex answered. She wasn't overly worried, though. Chuck had come into his own as an explosives expert over the past couple of years. She had faith that he could do the job quietly and with precision.

Finally, Chuck rejoined the rest of the team in the courtyard, his explosives bag much lighter than it had been an hour before. "I've rigged it so the explosion should blow the building outward. That way, there will be less rubble between the Ferals and the sunlight."

"We get to watch, right?" Patrick asked hopefully.

Alex looked at Owl. "Can you get us to somewhere safe?"

Owl smiled. "I gotcha covered."

Five minutes later, they were in the away ship, hovering five hundred feet above the building.

"All right, Chuck," Alex said, raising her binoculars to get a closer look at the low-rises. "Do your thing."

Patrick giggled with delight as Chuck pressed the remote detonator.

Chuck had done his job well.

The explosion ripped through the building, tearing it apart from the inside. Debris flew through the air, exploding outward from the center of the building. As Alex watched, she realized it wasn't just rubble; it was Ferals. Dozens of them. The second and third floors must have had as many Feral in them as the first.

Fires leapt up within the building as sunlight hit the suddenly exposed Ferals. The creatures' bodies caught fire midair, bursting into flames before they even hit the ground. Flaming arms, legs, and torsos flew through the air.

Not all of the Ferals were killed in the blast. Some were blown clear of the building. Alex estimated she saw fifty of them frantically scrambling, trying to find a safe harbor from the sun even as they burst into flames. Some tried futilely digging under the rubble of the collapsed building. Others ran for the nearby buildings. A few landed closer to other buildings, and those dove through windows and doorways, getting inside as quickly as possible.

Alex watched as one Feral struggled to its feet and sprinted thirty yards to the nearest building. As it ran, it caught fire, and the flames spread. Before long, it was leaving a fiery footprint in the dry grass with each step. The creature reached the building a moment too late, collapsing against the door in a burning pile.

Even from five hundred feet up, they heard the howls, first from the burning Ferals and then from those in the surrounding buildings. Alex wondered if their mental connection allowed them to feel some measure of their fellow creatures' pain, or if they'd just been woken by the sound of the blast.

After a few moments the last of the Ferals stopped moving, and all that was left of the building was a lingering cloud of dust and smoke.

"Holy shit," Ed muttered. "That was insane."

Chuck pointed toward the building just north of the one that had exploded. "I don't think it's over yet."

Alex raised her binoculars again, looking toward where Chuck was pointing. Sure enough, smoke was billowing from the windows. "I guess too many fiery Ferals made it to that building. They set the damn thing on fire."

They continued watching, and soon Ferals were jumping out of windows and running out the doors. Some were already on fire, and the rest were as soon as the sunlight outside hit them. Much of the grass around the buildings had caught fire now, and some of the other buildings had smoke seeping out of their windows.

Within a few minutes, most of the complex was on fire. All around, Ferals were frantically trying to bury themselves under the dirt or make it to one of the other buildings, which only served to spread the fire farther.

Screeches of pain and terror cut through the air. The smoke reached Alex's nose, and she took in the grotesque combination of burning wood, rubber, hair, and flesh. The smell was nauseating.

"I never thought I could feel sorry for Ferals," Owl said through their headsets, "but this is pretty messed up."

"Are you crazy?" Patrick asked. "This rules. They burn, while we hover safely in the sky. Talk about some efficient vampire hunting."

"Have I given fire and rifted Jove's stout oak with his own

bolt,'" Ed said sagely. "I think that applies to our current situation."

Patrick shook his head. "I think you have no idea what you are talking about. I certainly don't."

The team watched a bit longer. The spread of the fire seemed to stop at a ring of small houses outside the low-rise complex. There were no more Ferals fleeing the buildings. It appeared that the rest of them had either found shelter or burned.

"I hope you were keeping count of the dead Ferals, Captain," Chuck said with a smile. "You know how CB is about getting accurate numbers for the City Council."

Alex shook her head. "I guess we'll never get a true count on that mess, but I bet there were five hundred Ferals in those buildings." She lowered her binoculars. With everything that was going on, it felt good to do some old-fashioned Feral killing. "Owl, take us back to Firefly's location. We need to let him know what happened here so he doesn't investigate the smoke tonight. I have a feeling the Ferals are going to be mighty agitated this evening."

"So, what do you think?" Alex asked.

She was sitting across from CB in his office. She'd just recounted everything that they'd learned on that day's mission. He'd listened silently, a stoic expression on his face.

"What do I think?" He paused a moment and rubbed his eyes. "I'm concerned."

Relief flowed through Alex. A large part of her had thought that maybe CB was going to blow her off again. It felt good to finally be taken seriously. "Good. I'm concerned too."

"Don't get me wrong," he continued. "That was good work. Innovative thinking. I'm not trying to undercut that."

"I don't need kudos right now, CB. There is bigger stuff going on we need to address."

He nodded. "Okay, just making sure you knew I appreciate your good work. But this thing with Firefly... I mean, losing that many vampires? We can't afford any more nights like that."

"Yes, that was tragic," Alex agreed. "But I think he's learned from that mistake. The Ferals won't catch him like that again."

"Let's hope not. Anything else?"

Alex blinked hard. "Anything else? We're not going to talk about Jaden's recon team?"

CB rubbed his eyes again. Alex wasn't sure if she'd ever seen him looking so tired.

"Yeah, sorry. I agree that it looks bad."

"It doesn't just look bad. Jaden lied to us, CB. He lied."

"Let's not jump to conclusions. We'll ask him about it next time, and—"

"Why?" she asked, her voice growing louder now. "So he can make up another lie? At some point, we've got to stop giving him the benefit of the doubt."

CB leaned forward and looked her in the eyes. "Okay. So he lied. There's something in his past he wants to hide. But it's just that. Past. We have to worry about the future. Don't you think we have enough on our plates without chasing down some conspiracy theory?" He took a deep breath. "I promise, we will look into it. But now is not the time."

Alex couldn't believe what she was hearing. Part of her felt like she might be going crazy. It was like she were shouting 'Fire!' and everyone was ignoring her, calmly waiting as the flames drew closer. "Are you kidding me? You want to wait? Until *when*? Until Jaden's had a chance to destroy all the evidence of whatever he's trying to hide?"

CB's expression hardened. "I'm done talking about this, Captain Goddard. You have your answer. Now, I've got work to do. Do you understand?"

Alex answered through gritted teeth, barely choking out the words. "Yes, sir."

She turned on her heels and marched out of the office, tears of frustration forming in her eyes.

13

—————

"So, you make all of the weapons for the GMT?" Susan leaned forward as she spoke, her low-cut top allowing quite the view.

Brian swallowed hard. "Yes. Well, I design all of them. And I make a lot of the prototypes. But, you know, a lot of the parts are scavenged. By the GMT, I mean. On their, you know, missions."

He silently cursed. Why was it that no matter how often he did this, he never got better at it?

The two of them were having dinner at a small restaurant in a nicer section of Sparrow's Ridge. It was Brian's second date this week. Susan did something in the medical department, though Brian wasn't entirely clear on what. She was in her mid-twenties, had curly red hair, and seemed very interested in Brian.

Susan swirled her water glass, making the ice clink against the sides. "That's amazing. What are you working on now?"

Brian felt himself ease up a little. Finally, a topic of conversation with which he felt comfortable. "I'm working on an exciting project at the moment. It's a power relay circuit for a special set of lights that I created. Of course, I designed it with a solid-state relay, for obvious reasons, but I realized that there's a much better way. I've been using a gamma ray transmission signal. It allows me to make the relay eighty-five percent smaller and more efficient." He let out a laugh. "Can you believe that?"

"Uh-huh," Susan said, a bemused smile on her face.

"There are also no moving parts, so it will work better in the field. Of course, the interference issue was something I needed to get past, but I got there." Brian looked up and saw the vacant look in Susan's eyes. "I'm sorry, I always get carried away talking about that stuff."

"No, it's... I mean, you're so smart. Can you show me around your lab sometime?"

Brian frowned. "Uh, no. The lab is for authorized personal only. Besides, it's a sterile environment. I wouldn't want you to risk bringing in a static charge or an outside contaminant." He leaned forward and spoke in a low voice. "This one time, a lab assistant came in without hitting the static discharge. Can you believe that? What a mess that was." He shook his head and laughed at the memory.

Susan's face fell. "Sorry. I didn't mean to risk a discharge, or whatever. I just thought it would be cool to see the stuff you make."

"Oh." Brian felt his face grow hot and knew he was blushing. "I didn't mean... I just thought, you know, it's actually pretty boring for most people. And with the protocols—"

A hand clapped him on the shoulder, and he almost jumped out of his seat. He looked up and saw CB staring down at him.

"Hey, Brian. Sorry to interrupt, but I need a word." He turned to Susan. "If you'll excuse us a moment, Miss..."

"Oh!" Brian said, suddenly remembering his manners. "This is Susan. Susan, this is Colonel Brickman."

Now it was Susan's turn to blush. "Oh my gosh, I know who you are CB. It's a pleasure to meet you." She reached up and shook his hand.

CB gave her a charming smile "The pleasure is all mine. Sorry about the interruption, but I need a word with the smartest man alive. This city would fall out of the sky without him."

"Yeah, of course," she said. "Whatever you two need to do."

CB led Brian to a quiet corner of the restaurant.

"Everything okay?" Brian asked.

"Maybe. Sorry to interrupt your date. Though, I was watching for a moment and you deserved to be interrupted. That was some awkward conversation, my friend."

Brian frowned. "So, you had nothing going on and you figured you'd come insult me?"

"No," CB said with chuckle. "Listen, I wanted to get to you before Alex does."

Brian looked concerned "Why? What's wrong?"

"She just left my office, and I think she's a little pissed. I'm afraid she'll do something rash." He paused a moment. "We both know she'll probably come talk to you. I need you to let me know if she is planning on doing something crazy."

Brian shifted his feet uncomfortably. "Honestly, CB, it sounds like this is between the two of you. I'd rather stay out of it."

He put his hands in his pockets, not meeting CB's eyes.

CB stared at him a moment. "So, she's already planning something."

"I didn't say that," Brian stammered.

"You didn't have to. It's all right. I'll take care of it." He nodded toward the table where Susan was sitting. "Get back to your date. She's a looker. You're lucky she waited this long."

"Wait." Brian looked CB in the eyes. "Alex isn't planning anything crazy. Maybe once upon a time she would have, but she's grown. She'll listen to orders. But I also think you owe her the respect of taking her seriously. We aren't out in the field. She is. She has the best intel. And the best instincts."

CB nodded slowly. "Thanks. I'll keep that in mind. And while we're giving advice, can I give you some?"

"Of course."

"When you get back to your date, listen more than you talk. Trust me, the night will go much better for both of you."

"THESE RESULTS ARE PRETTY STAGGERING," General Craig said the next morning.

They were gathered for the City Council meeting. Alex sat at the foot of the long table, CB close by in his normal seat. He was staring at Alex, but she didn't meet his eye. He'd tried to pull her aside before the meeting, but she'd deftly avoided him. She knew what he was going to say, and she didn't want to hear it.

"Yes, sir," CB said. "Captain Goddard and her team were able to hunt out the nest, based on the info Firefly gave them. The GMT exposed the hostiles to sunlight."

"Exposed them, how?" Horace asked.

Alex leaned forward, her elbows on the table. "We

planted a bunch of explosives and blew the shit out of the building they were hiding in, sir."

A few members of the Council chuckled. After everything she'd done for *New Haven*, the Council tended to give Alex a little more leeway than most. Many people would have gotten a stern warning for cursing during a Council meeting. Alex got a laugh. She was going to test just how far that goodwill extended today.

"And Jaden agreed to the GMT running more missions?" General Craig asked.

"Yes, sir. One a week."

He nodded slowly. "Good. As long the plan has Jaden's approval, we can keep moving forward. Anything else on Resettlement?

CB answered quickly. "No, sir."

"Actually, there is one more thing," Alex said. "When we were down there, we found some troubling evidence that Jaden is hiding something from us. He—"

"That's enough, Captain," CB said sharply. He turned to Council. "I apologize for that. There was a little confusion, but I managed to clear it up. No need to trouble the Council with it."

"With all due respect," Alex said, "this is more than a misunderstanding. There's been a willful attempt to—"

"Shut your mouth, Alex," CB growled. "That's an order. You've wasted enough of the Council's time."

Alex hesitated. For a moment, she considered continuing. Every eye at the table was fixed on her. Anger coursed through her body, and she felt a vein pulsing on her forehead. But from the look on CB's face, she knew he was serious. If she spoke again, he'd bench her from the next mission. Maybe the next few missions. And there was no way she could find the information she needed about Project White Horse from up here.

She drew a deep breath before speaking. "My apologies. Nothing else, General."

She sat quietly, her teeth clenched, for the rest of the meeting. When it was over, she hurried out before CB could speak to her.

SOMETIMES, when life became too much, Alex took out her frustrations in the gym. Other times, she took the less healthy route and put in a long session at Tankards. Today, it seemed like neither of those was going to make her feel better. Getting drunk would probably result in a hangover and a few regrets. If she went to the gym, she'd probably end up breaking Patrick's arm in the sparring ring. Neither of those outcomes were particularly appealing. She wanted to get away from everything having to do with the GMT, CB, and Jaden. Just for a little while.

So she found herself standing in front of the door to the quarters of someone she hadn't spoken to in six months. She hesitated for just a moment. Then she knocked.

The man who opened the door looked haggard. A comb clearly hadn't touched his head that day, and a rag stained with what looked like vomit was draped over his shoulder. He stared at her a moment, blinking hard, before speaking.

"Alex." A slow smile crossed his face. "It's been too long! How've you been?"

She couldn't help but smile back at him. "Hey, Wesley. You mind if I come inside?"

"Of course not." He stepped aside and waved her in. "Excuse the mess."

"Mess? Looks more like a war zone." Alex stepped around toys strewn all over the floor and made her way to the living room.

Wesley hurried over and moved a pile of clean diapers so she could sit down. He still limped a little, a permanent reminder of his GMT past.

"So, where is that little cutie?" Alex asked.

"Napping. Finally." He cleared off the chair across from the couch and took a seat.

"Oh, sorry," Alex said, lowering her voice. "I hope my knocking didn't..."

Wesley waved the thought away. "Are you kidding? Pretty sure I could strap her to my back in a gun fight and she wouldn't wake up." He raised his voice to almost a yell. "Isn't the right, Charlotte?"

Alex cringed a little, but there was no response from the bedroom area. "Vanessa's at work?"

Wesley nodded. "She's pulling a double, so it's the single dad life for me, tonight." He paused a moment. "So what brings you by?"

She thought a moment, not sure how to answer. "Do I need an excuse? Look, I'm sorry it's been so long. A visit was overdue. Work's been...crazy."

Wesley gave her a crooked smile. "I completely understand. I've been picking up a few shifts a week with the badges. I had to write a ticket for loitering last night. So my life's been pretty crazy too." He chuckled. "Seriously though, I get it. When you're in the GMT, everything's life and death. It's tough to pay attention to anything else."

Alex was surprised at how good it felt to see her old friend. In truth, Wesley hadn't been a member of the GMT all that long. He'd joined after Simmons died. A month after Fleming's death, he'd met a chef named Vanessa. It had been a surprise when the two had married a few months later, and an even bigger surprise when Vanessa had gotten pregnant soon after. Wesley had promptly resigned from the GMT.

At the time, it had seemed like an incomprehensible move to Alex. But now, seeing him in his quarters, his young daughter sleeping in the next room, maybe she finally understood.

Though they'd worked together for a relatively short period of time, it had been an intense one. Wesley had been there when they'd discovered Agartha. He'd been there for the Battle of Denver. And he'd been by her side on the ship as they flew to *New Haven* for the final confrontation with Fleming. Seeing him like this, living a normal life, it gave her hope. Not that she wanted it, at least not right now, but it was good to know that a different kind of life was possible, even for someone like her.

Wesley leaned forward and looked her in the eye. "I know you didn't come here just to see Charlotte. What's really going on? Is everything okay with Resettlement?"

"Yeah, it's...it's fine."

Wesley wasn't part of the GMT anymore. He didn't have security clearance, and she couldn't go more into depth than that.

"Is CB okay?" he asked. "I ran into him a couple weeks ago, and he looked beyond stressed. I worry about that guy."

"I do too, sometimes. He's fine, I guess. Workaholic. An infuriating boss at times."

"Same as always, then."

"I guess so," she said with a laugh. "Remember how mad he used to get at Drew?"

Wesley laughed. "I wonder how many times I heard him threaten to resettle Drew's shotgun up his ass if he didn't fall in line. Now he's got the Barton brothers. That's like having two Drews."

"I almost think two is better than one. Ed and Patrick are like puppies. They spend most of their energy driving each other crazy." She shook her head, still laughing.

Wesley was quiet for a long moment. "You know, when I told you I was leaving, you gave me this look. Like you couldn't understand what you were hearing. You couldn't believe anyone would ever leave that job, especially for something as trivial as having a baby."

Alex felt herself redden. "I was an idiot. I'm sorry."

"No, you weren't. See, that's what makes you so good at the job. You can't imagine not doing it. It's your life." He paused a moment. "And in a way, you were right. I do miss it, sometimes. Standing back-to-back with CB in the basement of some ancient NSA building, pumping Ferals full of bullets. I never felt so alive."

"It does have its moments," Alex agreed.

Wesley nodded to the stack of diapers. "So does this." He paused. "You know when I knew it was time for me to hang it up with the GMT? It was after Fleming died, when Jaden was first pitching us on his plan for Resettlement."

Alex swallowed hard. There it was again. Jaden. Seemed she couldn't have a conversation without him popping up.

"I got this feeling in my stomach," Wesley continued, "and I realized something. For the first time in my life, I was starting to believe that humanity had a future. That we weren't destined to fly around on this damn ship until something broke too badly for us to fix it. I saw a path forward."

Alex tilted her head. "I don't get it. Why'd that make you want to quit?"

"See, that's the thing. I didn't *want* to quit. I wanted very badly to be part of the fight for Resettlement. But then I met

Vanessa, and we started talking about kids. And I asked myself, if I really believe in the future, am I better off creating life than trying to end it? I think if you believe in something, you have to sacrifice for it. So I sacrificed the one job I'd ever loved." He paused. "Let's be honest, I wasn't the difference maker. I knew you and the GMT and the vampires would build us a new home. So, I decided to concentrate on raising someone worthy of living there."

"Damn," Alex said with a smile. "When you put it that way, maybe I should find a young stud and try my hand at this parenting thing."

Wesley shook his head. "No way. The GMT needs you. I want my daughter to see Alex Goddard leading humanity back to the surface. And I want to tell her I used to fight by Alex's side."

Alex fought to push back the tears rising in her eyes. "I don't know, Wesley. The way things are going, I'm not sure that's going to happen."

"You'll figure it out." By the sound of his voice, he had no doubt. "I don't know what's bugging you, but back when I first met you, you probably would have stolen the away ship and headed down to do whatever needs to be done. Instead, you came to see an old friend. I call that progress."

"That or indecisiveness." Alex picked up one of the clean cloth diapers, holding it by the corner. "So, is there a class that teaches you how to do this parenting stuff? I wouldn't have any idea."

"Trial by fire," Wesley answered. "Like my first mission with the GMT. But much more dangerous. This one time I was getting ready to change Charlotte and—"

A knock at the door interrupted him.

"What the hell?" He stood up and walked toward the door. "Two visitors in one day. This is going in my diary."

Alex had her back to the door, but she recognized the voice immediately.

"Hey, Wesley," CB said. "I need to talk to Alex."

She stood up slowly, her arms crossed. "How'd you find me?"

CB stepped instead, a weak smile on his face. "I checked the gym first. Then Tankards. And your quarters. None of the GMT had seen you since this morning. This was the next logical place. Is there somewhere we can talk?"

Alex wanted to tell him to beat it, but instead she nodded slowly. "My quarters aren't far."

They said their goodbyes to Wesley and headed for Alex's quarters.

As they walked, Alex said, "Look, CB, I think—"

"Not here," he said gruffly. "Wait until we get inside."

When they'd reached her quarters, Alex shut the door. They stood in the kitchen area.

CB looked at her, his face unreadable. "Listen, about this morning..."

Alex held up a hand. "I apologize. I shouldn't have gone over your head like that. But I need you to really listen to me. I know what I'm talking about here. This isn't just some conspiracy theory. Jaden lied. He's purposely hiding information from us. Something is not right."

CB looked her in the eyes. "I know."

Alex raised an eyebrow. "You know? You know, what?"

"I know that Jaden's lying. I've been investigating him for the last six months."

14

THE LONELY NIGHT had fallen over Agartha.

"As you can see, we're planning to put the tech from *New Haven* to good use," George said to Jaden as they walked. "Colleen got back from her month on the ship today and she got right to it. The new lights she's building from their design are twenty percent more efficient. That'll make a big difference in the agricultural department."

They were walking through Agricultural area, where the vertical farming setup provided enough food for all the humans in Agartha in a surprisingly compact space.

"Good," Jaden said as he walked. "And what did Marian report?"

George shook his head. "Their defenses are a bit behind ours. She's recommending we share the plans for our defensive turrets. It wouldn't take too much adaptation, and it would really up their defenses."

Jaden nodded. "Good plan. Let's do it. The sooner the better."

George tilted his head in surprise. "Is there some kind of

threat to *New Haven*? I mean, it's not like Ferals have their pilots' licenses all of a sudden."

"No," Jaden agreed with a smile, "but it's one of the last two human cities. They need to take their defense seriously. Honestly, it worries me that they haven't built stronger defensive weapons since their launch. I know humans only worry about what's right in front of them, but just because they have never been attacked doesn't mean that they never will be."

George stopped in front of a tray of lettuce and turned to face Jaden. "How would that even happen? We're the only other people on the planet, and I know that we aren't going to attack them."

Jaden plucked a small leaf off of the plant next to him. A bead of water stood on the leaf. He tilted the leaf, and the water began to roll toward the edge. "I hope that is true."

"You hope what's true? That we aren't going to attack New Haven, or that we are the only other people on the planet?"

The bead of water reached the tip of the leaf. It hung there for a moment. Then it fell. Jaden's other hand shot out, moving alongside the falling drop, then arching underneath it. Somehow, he caught the drop on the tip of his index finger. He rotated his hand, letting the water roll down the back of it. Then he put his hand next to the leaf.

He stared at the leaf as the drop once again made its way back down its center. "Both. In my experience, time is a loop. What you think is past will come around again." The droplet reached the end of the leaf once again. This time Jaden let it fall to the ground. "Thanks for the report, George. Have a good night and remember to send *New Haven* those turret plans."

With that, Jaden took his leave and headed for the

training facility. He was hoping to get some sparring in, but he found Natalie waiting for him.

She spoke with no greeting or preamble. "The *New Haven* exchange people brought back a report from Ambassador McCready. Alex Goddard was in the Council meeting today. She was hell bent on discussing the idea that you're keeping secrets. Something about your recon team, apparently. She didn't get far before CB shut her down."

"Hmm." Jaden sat down on a bench near the sparring mats.

"Hmm? What's that mean?"

"It means I'm concerned, but not overly so."

"This is serious," Natalie said, her hands on her hips.

"Perhaps. Alex might be suspicious, but she doesn't know much. Otherwise, CB wouldn't be shutting her down. Besides, we have the trust of the Council, and Alex answers to them."

Natalie raised an eyebrow and looked Jaden in the eyes. "You know that girl answers to no one. She will search until she gets the answers she's looking for."

"I know," Jaden said, with a smile. "That's what I like about her."

Natalie sighed and sat down next to him. "Send me to the island. Let me handle it. This will take some finesse, and finesse isn't exactly Helen's strong suit."

"Unnecessary," Jaden said. "But I do appreciate the offer. Look, this is nothing to worry about. It is unlikely that anything is left on the island."

"And if something is left? This is not the kind of thing we should leave to chance."

"So you will remove the chance if you go to the island? I think that we need you here. You are right though; this should not be taken lightly."

"What is the plan then? How do we keep them happy, but in the dark?"

Jaden thought a moment. "Happiness and survival rarely go hand in hand. Keeping them in the dark will be hard, but not impossible. As long as we can help them create a safe place on the surface, I think everything else will be forgiven."

ALEX COULDN'T BELIEVE what she'd just heard. "What? So all this time, you've just been gaslighting me?"

CB gave her a guilty half-smile. "I've been suspicious of him for a while."

She wandered absently to her couch, her mind reeling, and sank into it. "And you didn't think maybe that was information you should have shared with me?"

"Don't think I didn't want to. I'm sorry I lied." CB's face grew grim as he sat down across from her. "Alex, I don't think you've fully considered just how dangerous this is."

She raised an eyebrow. "Calling out an immortal warrior with super powers? No, I hadn't considered that it might be dangerous."

"Okay, fine. Maybe you have. But I've spent the last six months agonizing about it. Thinking about the ways it could go wrong." He shifted in his seat. "Every time we've met with Jaden, it's been on his territory. Not only could he kill us in seconds if he wanted to, but he could simply decide we shouldn't be allowed to leave. He could keep us prisoner. Hell, he could turn us into vampires and force us to obey."

Alex leaned back in her seat a little, surprised. "Damn. You don't really think he'd do any of that, do you? I mean, yeah, he's lying, but he's not out to get us or anything."

CB looked toward the floor. "I... I honestly don't know."

"Damn," she repeated. This was a pretty hard turn from CB not even wanting her to question Jaden. "And here, I thought you were just being an asshole for the last six months."

"Well, I was," he said with a grin. "But I was also trying to protect you. I knew you needed to meet with Jaden on a regular basis. He's a master at reading humans, and... No offense, but you have the worst poker face on *New Haven*."

"Hey!" Alex said.

"It's not an insult. You're passionate. But I knew you wouldn't be able to hide it from Jaden, once you knew."

Alex opened her mouth to protest, but she stopped. Even she had to admit that it was true. "So, you've been keeping this to yourself for six months?"

"Jessica knows," CB said. "Her contact with Jaden is limited and she's one hell of a good liar. Other than that... Yeah, just me."

"What made you suspicious?"

"It started when we were planning for Resettlement. I suggested to Jaden that we use the GMT to scout possible Feral locations from the sky. With the away ship, we'd be able to cover a large area fast, and then his vampires could move in and investigate further at night. He immediately shut down the idea. He was very insistent that his team on the ground would do a better job."

"Did you consider that maybe he just has a bias toward trusting vampires over humans?"

CB smiled. "Ah, how the tables have turned. Now you're trying to convince me I'm the crazy one."

"Not at all. Just thinking it through."

"Of course, I considered it. But then I began to notice other things. Little things at first. Ambassador McCready mentioned that the five vampires on the recon team were all part of Jaden's inner circle, along with Natalie. It seemed odd to me that he would send an army of inexperienced vampires he barely knew to do bulk of the work, and five of his most trusted allies as scouts. Then I noticed that very few of the nests Firefly and his team discovered were the result of the recon team's efforts. I started to wonder if maybe they were up to something else."

"Why not bring up your concerns to the Council?"

"I did." CB paused, his face darkening. "I even made sure to do it privately when Ambassador McCready wasn't around. I was told in no uncertain terms that Jaden was our ally, and I wasn't to spend my time investigating conspiracy theories."

Alex smiled. "Sounds familiar."

"Yeah. Worse yet, word got back to Jaden. He took me aside and tried to ease my mind the next time I was in Agartha. Still, the inconsistencies were piling up. I knew I'd have to handle this quietly." He sighed. "I've come to the realization that the Council will side with Jaden over us, unless we bring them concrete proof that he's lying."

Alex rubbed her hands against her eyes. All this time, she'd been working to prove her theory to CB. She'd thought if only she could make him understand, things would be better. While it felt good to have him on her side, the sinking feeling in her stomach told that her this hadn't solved anything. "So what do we do?"

"First of all, we keep it quiet. No more confronting Jaden or blowing up at Council meetings."

"Hard to stick to a secret plan when you don't know there is one."

"Fair enough. Look, I've had a few of the people in the exchange program sneaking around Agartha for the last six months. They have been trying to gather information on Jaden's plans, but they haven't found much. I'm convinced that you're right. If we're going to find the truth, it's going to be on the island."

Alex nodded her agreement

"We need to move quickly," CB continued. "I'll do what I can to run interference with the Council. We need to find whatever Jaden's searching for before he does."

"We can search the island, but we need some more info. Right now, we don't even know what we're looking for."

"Agreed." CB thought a moment. "I think it is time to bring Firefly in on this. He has a better chance of figuring out what the recon team is up to than we do. Hopefully he can still be trusted. In the meantime, I'm going to have Brian dedicate all his time to finding more information. That and developing more effective weapons." He looked down at the floor. "Just in case."

Alex swallowed hard, hoping it wouldn't come to that. "Yeah. Just in case."

IN SOME PLACES, the ground still smoldered. The smell of burnt flesh covered the area like a blanket, and ash hung in the air. Firefly cursed his vampire senses and tried to remember not to breathe.

They'd waited three nights after the GMT's attack on the low rises before coming to the area. He just hoped they'd waited long enough for the Ferals to have calmed down.

"You have to admit, it's an effective technique," he said, his eyes scanning the neighborhood. All of the low rises had burned; all that remained of most of them was rubble and ash. The wet, humid atmosphere and damp vegetation had kept the fire from spreading further.

"Maybe we should just burn the whole island down," Hector mused. "The plants would grow back in a decade or so. We could start fresh."

Helen stood next to Firefly. She let out an annoyed grunt. "We tried something similar early in the third wave of the infestation. Even in areas we bombed, some vampires survived. They dug down into the ground and waited. When the human cleanup teams moved in, the survivors fed on them." She glanced at Hector. "We're a resilient species."

Firefly looked at the rubble again and wondered how many Ferals were still alive, buried under there either by choice or circumstance, waiting for the chance to strike. "Still, the GMT did manage to kill a hell of a lot of Ferals without losing a single solider. Maybe it's time you started giving Alex a little more respect."

"She's a foolish child," Helen snapped. "Just like you are."

Hector shifted uncomfortably. Clearly, he didn't like anyone talking about his captain that way, but he wasn't about to go up against Helen either.

"Gee, tell me what you really think of me," Firefly said.

Helen gave him an appraising look. "The difference is that you will learn over time. Alex's human life is far too short to make any real progress, but you have the potential to develop into a real warrior, if you can learn patience." Her eyes softened a bit. "I was a child, like you, once. Growth takes time. And mentorship. This..." Her hand indicated the gathered vampires. "This isn't how it's meant to be done. We rarely turned vampires, so that we could ensure that we developed them properly. Most of these vampires will be lucky to survive the Resettlement effort."

"Believe me, we weren't fans of being murdered and turned into vampires, either. But here we are. Let's make the best of it." He forgot himself and took a breath, instantly regretting it as he tasted the bitter ash. "All right, wise one. Enlighten this poor child. What should we be doing to clear out these Ferals?"

Helen frowned. "There are two keys to learning an enemy. Patience and observation. I'm still in the midst of the process. I believe our best method would be to use the humans to lure them out. Even if it meant sacrificing one or two of them, it would help."

Firefly frowned. He would never allow that to happen. But he was learning something from Helen: study your enemy before acting. Patience and observation. So he kept his mouth shut.

Something deep in his stomach suddenly felt like it was wriggling. Like a mass of creatures was squirming inside him.

Helen must have seen the horrified expression on his face. "You feel it, too."

"We need to go." He recognized the feeling: it was the collective consciousness of Ferals. And, based on the intensity of the feeling, not a small number of them. He turned to the rest of the team and shouted, "Let's go! Now!"

Firefly led the way out of the city, Helen and Hector on either side of him. It wasn't long before they heard the Ferals behind them. They sprinted, leaping over rusted out cars and crumbling barricades. Firefly was operating on instinct, letting his reflexes make decisions that were happening too fast for his mind to full process. He felt his team moving behind him, running through the city, a pack. And further back, he could feel the horde.

The occasional howl reached his ear as he ran, always

answered by more howls in the distance. He knew the horde pursuing them was growing larger as they ran, gathering new Ferals to their cause with each passing block.

"It's another trap," Firefly shouted. "They were waiting near the burned-out buildings. They knew we'd be back."

"Yeah well, we slipped out of it this time," Hector replied.

"Let's not get ahead of ourselves," Helen said.

Firefly glanced over his shoulder. Though he knew what he'd find there, it was still a disconcerting sight. Hundreds of Ferals were half a block behind them, many bounding on all fours, teeth bared.

"Look out!" Hector yelled.

Just ahead, a pile of rubble blocking their path. He leaped, and his feet just cleared it. Behind him, he heard Ferals crashing into the rubble, but plenty of others landed safely on the far side of the obstacle.

Firefly tried to focus on the road ahead. He needed a plan. If they lost this race, he and the twenty vampires with him would die. Yet, he couldn't risk leading them back to the base, either. These mindless creatures would follow him until they collapsed. He had to find a way to lose them, and soon.

"Head east," he yelled to his team. "We're going to the lake. Let's see if these bastards can swim."

As they got farther toward the east side of the city, the buildings grew closer together. They had to duck through narrow alleys and race down winding streets. Still, when he looked back, it was clear they were putting more distance between themselves and the Ferals.

Helen saw it, too. "We need to split up. We can pair off and scatter. They won't be able to track us all."

Firefly only considered it for a moment. "Negative. We're

staying together. Some pairs would get picked off. If it comes to a fight, I want as large a group as possible."

Helen gave him a look of something like pity, mixed with annoyance. She looked like she wanted to argue. She turned, ducking into an alley and disappearing.

"So much for team work," Hector said.

Firefly frowned, but he didn't answer. Helen was all too willing to risk the army she considered baby vampires in order to protect herself and the others she thought of as higher beings. For the past year, he'd tried to work with her and learn, just as Jaden had told him to, but now, he finally understood where her true loyalty lay. He and the other Resettlers were just a tool for her to use. He was done being a tool.

They were almost at the edge of the water now. He risked another look back and saw that the horde had fallen farther behind.

"Follow me," he shouted to his team.

Then he jumped, diving through the air and into the cold, black water of the lake.

His body moved fluidly and gracefully through the darkness. He felt an instinctual momentary panic at not being able to breath, but he pushed the human feeling aside. He was a new thing now, an eternal thing, and it was time he got used to it.

He felt his team behind him, following through the murky waters and down toward the deepest part of the lake.

15

CB SMILED as Jessica sat down at their kitchen table and looked at the meal in front of her.

She raised an eyebrow. "You made this?"

"Yep."

She tentatively poked at a piece of asparagus with her fork. Then she lifted it to her mouth and took a bite. Her eyes widened.

"Not bad, huh?"

She finished chewing and gave him a sharp look. "Colonel, do you mean to tell me you are this good at cooking, and you've been hiding it?"

"Firefly may have taught me a thing or two back in the day." He paused, realizing that she was right. He'd never really cooked for her. Quick meals here and there, sure. But he'd never taken the time to prepare a great meal. He felt shame at the realization. They'd been married for well over a year. "I'm sorry. I've been so caught up with work."

She smiled and stabbed another asparagus. "I get it. Saving the world is a full-time gig."

"Still, it's no excuse. I'm going to do better. I promise."

"Fine," she said with a smile. "A couple more meals like this, and I think I can let it slide."

They ate is silence for a few minutes, enjoying the food and each other's company.

Then Jessica spoke again. "I'm glad Alex knows."

CB nodded. Jessica had been pushing to bring Alex in on the Jaden situation for a while. CB understood why. Keeping secrets from his team, and from her in particular, had weighed on him in a way he'd never expected. He and Alex had grown close over the years. In many ways, she was his legacy, the future of the GMT. He'd come to understand that she'd be running things long after he was gone. So keeping something from her—especially something that big —had gnawed at him, changed him until he wasn't sure he liked who he saw in the mirror anymore. So, yeah, having that weight off his chest was freeing. He finally felt like his old self again. And Alex was already proving valuable. They'd met with Brian that morning to brainstorm possible weapon ideas, and they'd met with the rest of the GMT a little later to devise a strategy that would allow them to help clear the Ferals, while also searching for the answers to Jaden's mystery.

Still, it wasn't all sunshine and roses. Along with the freedom came an implied timeline. Alex wanted action.

"I'm glad she knows too," he said. "But the long game approach isn't going to work anymore."

"Maybe that's a good thing. Whatever Jaden's doing, it's clear his focus isn't fully on clearing the island. The sooner you can get this cleared up, the sooner everyone can put their full efforts toward the important stuff, right?"

"Agreed. It's just... this whole thing is baffling. Jaden's been nothing but helpful since we met him. Hell, his best friend died in a fight to save us."

"I hear you. Whatever he's hiding, either it's something little, maybe something from his past. Or..."

"Or it's not," CB finished. "And if it's not, it could change everything. I feel like I may be a little out of my league when it comes to ancient vampires. I don't think I can trust him, and I'm worried that he is so many steps ahead of us that we will never see anything coming until it's too late."

"Don't sell yourself short. You're pretty good at this whole art of espionage thing. Plus, you have a team behind you. What can I do to help out?"

"For now I'll take another kiss and a night of being normal."

She paused for a moment. "That's why you did this, isn't it? You wanted one night of normalcy."

He leaned forward and took her hand. "I don't know what's going to happen. Maybe there's still a simple explanation for everything. But if not, if things go badly, it could happen very quickly. I've given up a lot for my job. We both have. But for one night, I want to forget all that."

"Sounds pretty good to me."

He slid his hand up her arm, but she put her hand over his.

"Slow down, Colonel. I see that look in your eye, and there will be plenty of time for that. But there is no way I'm letting this food get cold." She pointed at his plate with her fork. "Eat up. You're going to need lots of energy for what I have planned for you this evening."

"MAYBE HIS TRACKER IS BLOCKED," Alex said as they flew through San Juan, traveling fifty feet above the ground. "Is that possible, Owl?"

"Possible," the voice in her headset answered. "He'd have to be somewhere deep underground, though. He knew we were coming, right?"

They were on their first mission to Puerto Rico since discussing the Jaden situation with CB. It was to be a trial run of their new approach: get some Ferals riled up as quickly as possible, then spend the rest of the day tracking down leads in the hopes of finding what Jaden was after. Before they could do any of that, they needed to locate Firefly and coordinate the area in which he wanted them to work. The task should have been simple, but his tracker wasn't showing up on their reader. It was as if he'd simply disappeared.

The team stared out the windows of the away ship, looking at the city below.

"Still think we need to rile up the Ferals, Captain?" Patrick asked. "They look pretty riled already."

Alex grimaced. It appeared their previous efforts to unsettle the Ferals had worked a little too well. Starting at the location where the low rises had been and heading south, there was a path of destruction nearly one hundred yards wide. The vegetation that grew throughout the rest of the city had been trampled, and rubble filled the streets.

"How many Ferals would it take to do that?" Chuck asked, his voice filled with awe.

"More than I want to run up against," Owl answered.

Ed shook his head sadly. "Hell is empty and all the devils are here."

Patrick rolled his eyes. Despite their growing distrust of Jaden, Ed was still very much into Shakespeare.

They flew in silence for a few more minutes.

"We're almost at the edge of the city, Captain," Owl said.

"Keep going," Alex answered. "Those Ferals were chasing something."

They continued south, and eventually the trail of destruction grew thinner. Then it disappeared altogether. Apparently, the Ferals had either given up the pursuit or lost their prey.

Owl finally picked up the tracker's signal thirty-five miles south of San Juan. She set the away ship down in front of a small, solid looking building.

Alex frowned when she saw it. Seemed like an odd place to hide a bunch of vampires for the day. "You're sure it's coming from in there?"

"I'm sure. The signal's weak, though. Very odd."

They walked inside and found a lobby with a row of counters partitioning the main area from the back.

"I know what this is," Owl said.

Ed sighed. "Of course, you do.'

"It's a bank." She led them through the sunlit lobby and toward a door behind the counters. "This is where the signal is coming from. I'll bet it's the vault. Where they kept all the money."

Alex walked to the door. "Firefly! You in there?"

The voice that answered sounded muffled. "We're here, Alex."

"Okay, we're coming in. Stand back. It's pretty sunny out here." With that, she pulled the door open. She was surprised by the weight of it, and as it swung open she saw it was nearly a foot thick. "No wonder the signal had a hard time getting through."

Firefly grinned when he saw them. He was huddled in the vault with fifteen other vampires. "This place saved our asses. We had a run-in with a serious horde."

Ed frowned as he entered the vault and saw the walls

lined with steel boxes. "This is it? I was expecting piles of gold and stuff."

"We saw the horde's trail of destruction," Alex said. "There must have been thousands of them. I was a little worried you didn't make it. Where are the rest of your troops?"

Firefly shook his head "Alive, I think. We were the only ones in the path of the horde. I radioed everyone else to move away from the city. I didn't try to meet up with them since I wasn't sure we'd lost the Ferals. There were thousands of them. Last night was a big wake up call for me. The Ferals are not just getting harder to find and kill; they are figuring out ways to kill us."

Owl lowered her gaze. "This was our fault. When we set off the fire in the city, it must have unified the Feral."

Firefly shook his head. "Killing the Ferals is what we're here to do. No one is at fault. There is no way that any of us could have seen this coming."

There was a brief pause while everyone considered that. Finally, Alex spoke "Is Helen here?"

"No, she split off during the escape from the horde. She may have been killed, but I don't think I'm that lucky."

Alex looked at Firefly. "Is there somewhere we can talk?"

They went to a small office next to the vault, carefully shielding Firefly from the sunlight. When they reached it, Firefly took a seat on the desk.

"So, what's up?"

Alex thought for a moment. This was going to be tricky. Firefly was a vampire now, and Jaden was technically his commander. But she also wasn't sure how they would be able to do this without him. "Listen, I'm not sure how to say this, but I have reason to believe Jaden is up to something on this island. Something other than killing Ferals. The recon team—"

"They're looking for something," Firefly said. "The recon team won't tell me much, but I've overheard a few things here and there. They have a secret mission. I don't know anything about it, but it's real."

Alex tilted her head. "Talk."

Firefly nodded. "Jaden told me something when I first started working with him in Agartha. Something about how the world ended. He said the humans were working on a powerful weapon. They came close to completing it, very close, and if they had, the world would look very different today."

"What was the weapon?"

"He wouldn't tell me. He said it was so dangerous that we needed to limit the amount of people who even knew of its existence. He said most of his original vampires who were there at the time didn't even know the details. I... I think that's what the recon team is looking for. Jaden wants the weapon destroyed."

Alex stared at Firefly for a long moment. He was basically confirming what they already knew. But could she trust him? What if he was just playing along, giving her information he knew she already had?

But no. She couldn't believe that. Firefly had worked against her in the past, but he'd learned from those experiences. In the end, she had to trust someone. And she was going with Firefly.

"You think it's nuclear?" she asked.

"No. The way he talked about it, it's something else. Something new."

"We need to find that weapon before he does."

Firefly stared at the ground for a long moment. "What if

he's right? What if the weapon's too powerful? Maybe a thing like that shouldn't exist."

"Firefly, look at me." She waited until he did, before continuing. "That's not his call. If there's something that could help us get the people down here faster, we need to know about it. Every year, every month, every day we're living up on *New Haven* we're risking the inevitable. Someday, something's going to break so bad we can't fix it. Maybe Jaden's willing to take that risk and draw Resettlement out for the next three generations. If that's what we have to do, fine. But if there's another way, we deserve to know about it."

Firefly stared at her for a long moment. "I agree. I might be a vampire, but I'll always be GMT. What do you need me to do?"

16

SUNSET WAS ONLY a couple of hours away, and Alex knew they needed to finish up soon. They'd spent the majority of the day flying over the island, making sweeping passes from east to west and back again. Their goal was to use their airborne perspective to find any location that could potentially house a base or lab. Anything that looked strangely protected or stood out from the structures around it. In theory, they should be able to find these locations from the air much more quickly than a grounded team could, even a grounded team of vampires. They would mark the location of each of these suspected sites, and either Firefly and his team of trusted vampires would investigate during the night, or the GMT would check it out during their next day trip.

Alex had been a bit worried that they wouldn't find anything. Unfortunately, they were having the opposite problem. It wasn't that there weren't enough suspicious locations. There were actually far too many. It was clear from this low flight that the island had been in serious defensive mode before it fell. While they didn't find any central military hub, they did see hundreds of small fortifications, many of them in the jungle, or in small villages.

"There's one," Chuck said.

"Got it," Owl answered, marking another spot on their shared digital map.

This particular location was just a few small houses, with oddly large turrets built on their roofs.

Chuck sighed. "This is really a needle-in-a-haystack situation. We don't know what we're looking for. It could be anywhere on the island. Where do we start?"

Alex kept her eyes on the structure below. "If this was easy, Jaden would have found the weapon a long time ago. Still, it would be nice if we had something to point us in the right direction. Maybe Brian can find something in the records."

Patrick grunted his disapproval of that plan. "Why don't we start in the towns on the east side of the island and work our way west?"

Chuck shook his head and stared at Patrick "We aren't going to do that, because it would take the rest of our lives. Look at how many buildings there are, man. Searching every possible location in every town would take decades. Not to mention the fact that what we're looking for could be a bunker we can't see through the vegetation."

Ed frowned. "Okay, if you're so smart, how do we find it?"

Chuck nodded toward Alex. "Like the captain said. We get more intel. We need to know what we are looking for. It could be something big, like a missile, or it could be data on a computer. Until we have a clue, this is pointless."

Patrick nodded. "Right. So it sounds like we should do exactly what I said and start on the east side of the island. Seems like a better way to find intel than waiting around hoping Brian pulls something out of some ancient files. Or we can go the Chuck route, and relax on the ship, with our thumbs up our asses."

Chuck stood up and took a step towards Patrick.

Alex held up a hand. "Everyone, relax. We can do both. We have to kill Ferals anyway, right? Otherwise the Council and Jaden will get suspicious and stop these missions. We'll start on the coast and clear out some of the tiny villages, seeing what we can find along the way. Meanwhile, we'll hope Brian gets us some more information."

"T-minus two hours to sunset, Captain," Owl said.

"All right. We've seen enough for today. Let's get the map back to Firefly. He and his team can start checking some of the buildings we noticed."

The team stopped by the bank where Firefly and his vampires were holed up, and transmitted the data to him. The vampires agreed he'd start at the west side of the island, and the GMT would hit the east side on their next trip.

By the time they made it back to *New Haven*, Alex was beat. It was amazing how a day of sitting on the away ship, looking out the window and documenting what they saw could wear her out. It was a different kind of tired than she felt after a tough mission fighting Ferals, a less satisfying type of tired. Still, when the ship landed, she was ready to get through the decontamination process as quickly as possible and turn in for the night.

She was surprised when she stepped off of the ship and saw Brian standing there, an intense look in his eyes.

"Alex," he said. "I found something."

"Something good or something bad?" His tone had her a little nervous. Granted, he was always prone to being excitable, but this was beyond his usual intensity.

He looked at her for a long moment. "I'm not sure how to answer that. Get Owl and CB. We need to talk, now."

THEY MET in Brian's office in the lab, the three of them gathered around his desk, lit only by a single lamp in the otherwise darkened office. This was one of the few places on the ship that didn't face an exterior wall and the constant exposure to direct sunlight. Based on the serious look on Brian's face, Alex was glad for the privacy.

"You remember the log entry I told you about?" he said. "The one with the guy whose wife worked for Project White Horse?"

"Yeah, sure," CB said. "Don't tell me you found her logs."

"No such luck. Seems she wasn't the type to keep logs. That, or hers were somehow deleted. Either way, I hit a dead end."

"Damn." Owl shook her head. "Just our luck."

"I figured she was still our best lead, though, so I started looking for anything else I could find on her." He shook his head. "Their file organization system was all over the place. It took me three hours to even understand how the naming convention related to the root architecture, and that's not even considering the version history, which was beyond—"

"Brian." Alex held up a hand. "Can we skip to the good part?"

"Sorry. Once I figured out where to look, I was able to find this woman's personnel file. It had her listed as an engineering assistant, which wasn't much help. Then I looked a little deeper and found her background file." He turned and brought up a file on his computer, then angled the monitor so everyone could see it. It showed a form. He tapped a spot near the top. "Check it out."

It took Alex a moment to figure out what he was pointing at. When she did, her breath caught in her throat.

Pre-New Haven Occupation: Virologist

"Virologist?" Alex said. "As in viruses?"

Brian nodded. "Remember when I told you what the white horseman represented?"

"Conquest," Alex answered.

"Yeah. But I did some more digging. Turns out that's just one interpretation."

CB tilted his head in surprise. "What's the other interpretation?"

"Pestilence."

"Oh, shit," Owl said. "You think—"

"I do," Brian answered. "I don't know for sure but... Look, I suspected maybe the weapon was biological in nature. Now, I think it was a virus. A virus that only targets vampires."

"My God," CB said, putting a hand over his mouth.

Alex sat back in her chair, her eyes wide. "Imagine it. Drop a virus from the away ship. Come back a few days later and the area's cleared. No need for a single bullet to be fired."

"You're thinking too small," Brian said. "Remember the virologist's husband's logs? He said that if her weapon succeeded, the fight would be over in a matter of days. If he's right, this virus would have to be tough as hell and extremely infectious."

Alex and CB exchanged a look. She saw the same hope in his eyes that she felt in her own. "You're telling me there may be a way to wipe out the Ferals? Like, all of them?"

Brian hesitated. "I'm not ready to say that, for sure. But it seems that's what the members of Project White Horse thought. Obviously, it didn't work out like they'd anticipated, or we wouldn't be having this conversation."

"But if we find what they were working on, maybe we

could finish it," Alex said. "I mean, not me, but you and the other smart people."

Brian shifted in his seat uncomfortably. "I wouldn't get my hopes up too high, but... Yes, there is a chance."

Alex turned back to CB. "We head back down in two days. Hopefully, Firefly will have his troops back together and we can get them to help us with the search, now we know what we're looking for. A lab of some kind."

They sat in silence for a moment. Finally, CB spoke. "I'm still not sure why Jaden is hiding this from us. Something about it isn't right."

"It seems straightforward to me," Owl said. "This is a weapon that kills all vampires. He is a vampire. It makes sense that he doesn't want his species to go extinct."

Alex looked up sharply, taking in the significance of those words "Do we want that? I mean, of course we want all of the Ferals gone. But what if it means Jaden and the Agartha vampires die, too? And Frank? And Firefly and the Resettlers?"

The room went quiet again as they felt the weight of the question.

CB sighed. "First thing's first. Let's see if this weapon even exists. Then we'll worry about whether or not to use it."

"FIREFLY, I think we've got something."

Firefly paused when he heard Mario's voice coming through his radio. It was likely another false positive, but there was hope. For the past two nights, Firefly and his team had been carrying out the mission. Not the mission Jaden had sent them on, the mission of Resettlement, but the mission of the GMT.

At first, when Alex had told him what they were looking for, Firefly had been reluctant. He hadn't wanted to bring his whole team into this Alex versus Jaden situation. After all, they'd gotten into this mess by signing up for the Resettlement project back on *New Haven* two years ago. Resettlement was what they cared about.

On the other hand, he couldn't exactly not tell them. Firstly, because it would be unfair to them. But also because they were his one true advantage. The recon team knew more about this weapon they were looking for than he did, and the GMT could search by air. But Firefly had one thing they didn't: sheer numbers.

With nearly two hundred vampires, Firefly's troops could cover much more ground than either the recon vampires or the GMT. In fact, they'd covered quite a bit of ground in just the last two nights. And Firefly needn't have been worried about his soldiers getting on board with this new mission. It turned out that nobody much liked Helen, and—as former *New Havenites*—everybody practically worshiped the GMT.

Still, dawn was approaching, and they hadn't found anything yet. Unless Mario's discovery proved to be legit.

"Where you at?" Firefly asked, speaking into his radio.

Mario wasn't more than three miles away. Firefly grabbed his squad of twenty and they ran over, covering the distance in less than ten minutes.

He found Mario and his squad gathered near an old, dilapidated home.

Mario nodded when he saw Firefly. "Hey. Check it out."

Firefly squinted at the house for a moment, trying to figure out what made it different from the dozens of other homes around it. Then he spotted it. Exactly what Alex had asked them to look for: silver.

He took a step toward the house, but then his radio chirped again. This time, a female voice came through.

"Firefly," Helen said. "We need you back at the hotel. Now."

He sighed and briefly considered ignoring the summons. But something about her voice made him think this was more than her usual bossiness at play. "What is it, Helen? We're sort of in the middle of a mission, here."

"The Ferals can wait. Get back here. Now."

Once again, he thought about turning off the radio and ignoring Helen. But was that the right move? Especially now, when they may have actually found something?

He spoke into the radio. "We're on our way."

Firefly reached into his pack. There was no way they could lose this location. He had to mark it somehow. And he had just the thing. He pulled out the backup tracker from the GMT and set it near the door to the house, wedging it under a bit of vegetation.

Then he turned to his troops. "You heard Helen. Let's get going.

IT WAS two days later when the GMT headed down to Puerto Rico for their next mission and search operation. The team was quiet as they flew. Alex had decided not to fill in the rest of team on the details of the virus until they were sure. For now, they would continue their search.

The question that had been weighing on her more so was whether to tell Firefly. He'd been eager to help, but would that eagerness continue if he knew what they were really looking for? If he knew the weapon they were trying to find would kill him and all his soldiers if it were used?

For a brief moment, she wondered if maybe it would be better if Jaden's recon vampires found the virus first. They would destroy it, and the terrible choice would be taken out of Alex's hands. Resettlement would continue as planned. It would be as if none of this had ever happened.

But would it? Would she ever really be able to trust Jaden again? It would always be in the back of her mind that no matter how much lip service he paid to the idea of fighting for the future of humanity, he'd had the means to kill all Ferals in his hands and not even discussed the idea with them.

And then there was *New Haven* to consider. She thought about what Brian had said back when the power regulation system had failed: every person on the ship was one stroke of bad luck from falling out of the sky and dying on impact. Fleming had been right on that count. She wasn't going to be like him and throw caution to the wind in order to get the people to the ground, but if there a way to resettle safely, didn't they have to do it?

Owl set the away ship down outside of the old hotel where Firefly's signal originated.

As the team prepared to de-plane, Alex spoke. "Listen up. There's a pretty good chance Helen is going to be there with vamps. If she is, it'll look too suspicious for me to go off with Firefly alone. Owl's going to try to talk to Firefly privately, while I distract Helen."

"How are you gonna do that?" Ed asked.

Alex shrugged. "I'll probably just piss her off. Same as usual."

Chuck gave her a nervous glance. "Go easy. We don't want her ripping your head off."

"But we do want her distracted," Patrick said. "It's a fine line."

As the team stepped off the ship, Owl grabbed Alex's arm. "Be honest. You think we have a chance of beating the recon team to the virus?"

"You really doubt us?" Alex said with a smile.

"On an even playing field, no. But they live down here full time. They can hunt all night."

"And we can survey the island from the sky. Not to mention having Firefly as our inside man and Brian digging up information back home. I'd say that evens the odds a bit."

"Let's hope you're right," Owl said.

They stepped off the ship and Alex took a good look at the hotel. It was a large building, which Alex took as a good sign. Maybe Firefly had managed to round up all his troops. The team walked into the building and found it strangely quiet.

Owl glanced down at her tablet. "He's at the west end of the building."

They headed that direction, no one speaking, hands hovering over their weapons. Most likely, the silence was just due to the vampires sleeping, yet Alex felt a strange sense of foreboding. A terrible image flashed in her mind—finding the remains of Firefly's body torn to shreds by Ferals, the small tracker still attached to his tattered clothing.

She shook her head, pushing the image away.

They reached the end of a long hall, and Owl nodded toward the door in front of them, indicating Firefly was on the other side of it.

Alex hesitated. Waking a sleeping vampire was always

dangerous business, even when it was a friendly vampire. She knocked gently. "Firefly, are you in there?"

There was a moment of silence before he replied. "We're here. Come in, Alex."

The feeling of dread in her stomach grew stronger at the sound of his voice. Chuck shot her a nervous look. Apparently he noticed it, too.

Firefly didn't sound normal.

Alex drew a deep breath. With one hand on her pistol, she used the other to ease the door open.

The room was dim, and it took her eyes a minute to adjust. As expected, she saw the sleeping forms of dozens of vampires on beds arranged throughout the large room. Firefly stood in the center, his face draped in shadow.

There was another man standing to his left, but Alex couldn't see him well enough to make out who it was. She didn't recognize him until he spoke.

"Hello, Alex," Jaden said. "Come in. We have a lot to discuss."

17

ALEX STARED at Jaden with her mouth half open. The vampire was still draped in shadows.

She suddenly felt like a school girl who'd been caught looking at her neighbor's paper during a test. It was amazing how, even as a military commander who'd faced down hordes of Ferals and ran dangerous missions on a regular basis, a single look from Jaden could make her feel that way. Even when she wasn't plotting against him.

"Jaden," she said. "How'd you get here?

Jaden took a step forward into the light cast by her head-lamp, and she saw he was wearing a quizzical smile. "The same way that you did. On a ship"

"I didn't see any ship," Owl said. "You must not have docked it nearby."

"No. We plan to be here for a while, so we figured we'd better keep it in a more secure location."

A location he wasn't sharing with them, Alex noted. Was she just being paranoid, or was he purposely withholding information? "I didn't know your ship was functional. Why didn't you let us know that you'd be coming?"

"We finished ahead of schedule, and, well, I guess I couldn't wait. It's been a very long time since I've been more than a day's run from Agartha. It feels good. Besides, I've come to realize that this mission deserves my full attention. Natalie can keep things running back in Agartha." He paused. "Firefly told me about his losses. I blame myself. I should have been here from the start."

"Much appreciated, but we have it under control." Alex couldn't help herself. Saying that he was needed would have been like saying that they couldn't handle it without him. "We have a new strategy. It's going to allow for less risk and should also provide more results. I was going to go over it with you in our next meeting."

"Now you don't have to," Jaden said. He gave her a long look. "I know seeing me is probably a bit of a shock, but it almost seems as if you don't want me here."

There was a long awkward silence.

"No," Alex said. "Of course, we want—"

He waved his hand. "I'm kidding. I know how much you care about this fight. Why wouldn't you want an experienced warrior like me involved?"

"Of course, we do," Chuck quickly agreed. "It's going to be an honor to fight alongside you again."

"Well, I'll be fighting at night, and you'll be doing it during the day, but I appreciate the sentiment." He nodded toward the sleeping forms around him. "You mind if we find another room and talk a little business?"

"Let's do it," Alex answered. Her mouth felt dry, and she wondered if Jaden could tell that her heart was racing. Of course, he could. She thought back to what CB had said and realized it was true. She really did have *New Haven*'s worst poker face.

"Good." Jaden turned to his right. "Helen, care to join us?"

The female vampire groggily got to her feet. "Wonderful. It's the GMT. What's that stand for again?"

"Ground Mission Team," Patrick said, looking at her like she was an idiot.

"Huh. I always though it stood for Godawful, Moronic, and Tasty."

Alex smiled joylessly. "Helen. So glad you survived. I heard you ran away when Firefly's team was attacked."

"I made the tactical decision to retreat," she said as she finished standing. "Hardly the same thing. I didn't let my ego get in the way. It was the smart move."

"Call it what you like," Alex said, stepping forward. "But it seems to me the ones who listened to Firefly and stuck with their groups survived just fine."

Now Helen stepped forward, her hand on her sword.

Jaden let out a loud laugh. "Glad to see you two are getting along. I thought you might have this dynamic. Iron sharpens iron."

"Is that Shakespeare?" Ed asked, hopefully.

"Proverbs. But good try." He turned back to Alex. "You'll have to forgive Helen. Daysickness hits her even harder than most. She does have a sweet side, and she shows it at least once a century." With that, he led the way out of the large conference room. Firefly, Helen, and the GMT followed as he walked down the hall.

"So, you found the rest of your soldiers, Firefly?" Alex asked.

Firefly nodded. "Jaden helped us gather them last night."

"And the recon team?" Owl said.

Helen answered. "Still on the hunt. They'll reconvene

with us when you bring fresh supplies at the end of the week."

Jaden turned to Alex. "How about your team? How's your search going?"

The breath caught in Alex's throat. "What search?"

Jaden gave her a half smile. "The search for Ferals. I'm told your team is looking for hordes during the day. What else would you be searching for?"

"Nothing," Alex stammered. "I mean, good. We're killing lots of Ferals." She took a deep breath and concentrated on calming herself as she spoke. "The plan is for us to start on the east side of the island and work our way west. That way, if we disturb the Ferals, they won't attack the troops. After the Ferals in the city started setting traps, we figured it would be better to work outside the city for now. If we can clear the outskirts, maybe we'll have some room for Firefly's team to work without getting overrun."

"Seems sensible. Now that I'm here, let's make sure we're coordinating our efforts. Let me know exactly where you have been at the end of each mission so that we can avoid those places or send a recon team to observe how the Feral react to your presence. You were right Alex; good communication will make this much easier."

"Agreed," Firefly said. "Let us know where you hunt. And you always know where to find us if you need us." He looked Alex in the eyes, and there was an urgency in his gaze. "Just follow the trackers."

"Yeah, of course," Alex said, not quite sure what Firefly was getting at.

Jaden smiled. "Good. I guess you'd better get hunting. Report back at the end of the day."

Five minutes later, the GMT boarded the away ship for

their short flight to the east coast, to begin their work for the day.

As they climbed aboard, Owl nudged Alex. "Am I wrong, or did Jaden just get us to agree to tell him exactly where we were going each day?"

"Yep," Alex said with a sigh. "I just got taken to school by a really old man."

"So how are we going to search for Project White Horse if Jaden is here keeping tabs on us?"

Alex considered the question. If they shared with Jaden where they'd been, they were basically telling him the places the recon team didn't need to search. They were doing half his work for him. And it wasn't like he was going to tell them where the recon team was looking. But what was the alternative? Lie? It would be too easy to get caught, especially with the way that the Ferals got wound up for days wherever they'd been. "I don't know, Owl."

"Do you think he knows what we're up to?" Ed asked.

"Of course, he does." Chuck's voice sounded hollow. "Why else would he suddenly decide he needs to be here? Alex, I hate to say it, but maybe we should back off. Do our jobs and let things cool down a bit. The last thing we want is to make an enemy of Jaden and the Agartha vampires."

Alex thought about that, but only for a moment. "Waiting out an immortal vampire is not going to work. If Jaden does know what we're up to, he's playing it close to the chest. And no matter what he knows, there's not much he can do to stop us from searching the island during daylight hours. We need to stick to the plan. We keep searching for Project White Horse and as long as we don't find anything, we tell Jaden exactly where we've been. Once we find something, we will have to come up with a good cover."

Chuck sat down and strapped himself in. "I'll follow

your lead, but keeping things from Jaden is next to impossible. He's damn good at reading people, and from what I've seen, he always has a plan."

Alex couldn't argue with the logic, but it didn't change her approach. This was too important to give up on, even if it did risk their incurring Jaden's wrath.

Something was bothering her about what Firefly had said, and the pointed way he'd looked at her when he'd said it. "Firefly said we could find him by following the trackers. Why'd that need to be said?"

Patrick shrugged. "Why not? That's how we find him, right?"

"Wait," Owl said. "He mentioned trackers? Plural?"

"Yeah," Alex replied.

Owl pulled out her tablet. "Firefly has a backup tracker, but it isn't active. Unless..." She tapped the screen for a moment, then smiled. "Yes. That's it. The backup tracker is on. And it's nowhere near that hotel. He left it somewhere for us."

JADEN GROANED as he sat on the bed. He'd pushed the daysickness down as long as he could, but its effects were coming down on him hard and fast, now. Sleep would soon take him.

He spoke so softly that only Helen, lying in the bed next to his, would be able to hear. "I don't like it. Their frequent missions to the island could complicate things."

"The humans don't even know what they're looking for," Helen answered. "If they are looking, which I'm not convinced they are."

"Still, they could do damage. Imagine if they work a

horde of Ferals into a frenzy, and the Ferals unknowingly destroy the lab."

"Wouldn't that be a good thing?" Helen asked.

"No. I need to know it's been destroyed. And I won't be able to get a good day's sleep until I know that's happened."

"Really? I intend to sleep just fine. Starting now." Despite her words, Helen spoke again after a moment. "Here's an idea. Maybe we just tell them. Explain what we're after and ask for their help finding it."

Jaden chuckled. "Ask for help from humans? I never thought I'd hear you say that."

"I'm serious. They should be grateful, after all you've done for them. They'd help, if you asked."

"Perhaps. But humans are fickle. In most scenarios I would opt for full disclosure, but there's too much at stake here."

"It was almost two hundred years ago," Helen said. "We were at war. Don't you think they'd understand?"

"No. I am almost certain they would not. Now, go to sleep. Tonight, we hunt."

ALEX LED the GMT through the remains of what had once been a small town near the northeast coast of the island, following the signal of Firefly's tracker.

Unlike the city, Alex almost had to squint to imagine that this had once been a town. Much of the city had been protected from the stormy seas by a wall, but this small village had no such protection. Most of the small homes and buildings had been destroyed over the years. Still, signs of civilization remained. Large turrets stood facing the sea, spaced out every hundred yards. The sad pillars of death stood as another reminder of the immense effort that had gone into the futile attempt to stop the vampire infestation.

Looking at it, Alex felt a sudden wave of despair. If the pre-infestation people, with all their resources and vast numbers, couldn't keep the vampires off this island, what chance did their small team have? But what was the alternative? Keep flying until *New Haven* someday fell into the sea?

Chuck put his hands on his hips as they observed the town. "Well, the good news is, I doubt there are many Ferals in this little village. There's not much more than rubble left, here."

"Still, Firefly thought it important enough to leave his tracker here," Alex said. "Which means we have work to do."

"Yep," Ed agreed. "It's like Shakespeare said. 'This thing of darkness I acknowledge mine.'"

Patrick shot him a look. "That doesn't even make any sense. What does that have to do with searching a town?"

"It does make sense." There was confidence in Ed's voice now. It was clear that he was starting to think of himself as quite the Shakespeare expert. "We're taking responsibility for the terrible things that happened here. Even though we didn't have anything to do with what happened before, we're saying, what happens next is on us."

Owl chuckled. "Wow, maybe Jaden was right about benefits of studying Shakespeare. That actually makes sense."

"See?" Ed responded, giving his brother a pointed look.

The team followed the backup tracker's signal through the ruined ghost town. Owl led them, using the map on her tablet. They'd been walking for less than five minutes when she stopped on a corner that appeared to be no different from a dozen others they'd passed.

Chuck pointed at something off to their left. "What's that?"

"It appears to be where the signal is coming from," Owl said.

The small house was so covered with vines that it took Alex a moment to spot it through the vegetation. "Huh. Looks like a normal house."

But as she approached, she noticed some oddities. First, there were the bars over the windows, something that was clearly not the norm, considering they hadn't seen bars on or near any of the other homes. Then she noticed the front door. It had a strange, irregular black and gold coloring.

She took a step closer. "Is that... is it tarnish?"

The others gathered around, and Chuck approached the door and ran his hand across it. "I think so, Captain. I'm pretty sure this door is made of silver."

Alex took another look at the bars covering the windows. They were made of tarnished silver as well. "Seems like somebody wanted to keep vampires out of this place pretty badly."

"If you lived here and the world was being overrun with vampires, wouldn't you?" asked Owl.

Alex couldn't argue with that. At the same time, it wasn't like this house was bigger than those that stood around it. It didn't seem like the occupants were particularly wealthy. Either way, it deserved further investigation.

Owl bent down near the door and stood up a moment later, the small tracking devise in her hand. "This is it. Firefly wanted us here."

Alex stared at the door for a moment. "I can see why. Silver door. Silver bars on the windows. This is exactly the kind of place I told him to look for."

Patrick tried the door. "It's locked."

"Can you kick it open?" Alex asked.

In response, he gave the door a vicious kick. It didn't budge.

"Son of a bitch!" Patrick shouted, shaking out the leg he'd used to kick the door.

"Interesting," Alex said. "Chuck, you're up."

Chuck nodded and retrieved the cutter from his pack. He went to work, burning through the door, forging a circle around the handle and lock. He continued the circle, cutting into the wall next to the door to ensure that nothing on the wall was holding it shut.

When he was finished, he crouched down by the door and looked back at the team. "Ready, Captain?"

Alex checked that her team had their weapons ready, then nodded to Chuck.

Chuck gave the door a gentle shove and it slowly swung open. They waited in tense silence, but nothing inside the house moved. Chuck squinted at the section of wall he'd cut away. "Alex, check this out. The wall has a layer of silver mesh inside, up against a steel frame."

"Damn," Ed said. "Someone really did want to keep the vamps out."

Alex thought a moment. "Okay, let's move in. But take it slow. For all we know, this could have been a vampire holding cell. Could be Ferals trapped inside. On me, and stay tight."

The team slipped into the house, their weapons drawn. Slivers of sunlight cut through the dirty windows, illuminating particles of dust dancing in the air. But most of the house was dark, and there were plenty of spots for Ferals to hide. Alex moved slowly, working her way through the modest living room and into the kitchen. The thick layer of dust over everything was evidence that nothing had moved in the house for a long time.

Still, Alex pressed onward, careful as ever.

They reached a short hallway with three doors, all of them shut. The first led to a bathroom. The other two were bedrooms. As they finished checking the final bedroom, the team started to relax a little.

"Well, that's disappointing," Patrick grumbled. "I thought maybe we'd actually found something."

Alex wasn't ready to give up yet. There had to be a reason this house was so well protected. "We're missing something. And we're not leaving until we figure out what it is."

The team spent the next twenty minutes searching the house. They looked through drawers, cabinets, and behind pictures. They overturned every piece of furniture looking for something, anything that could possibly be related to Project White Horse. Before long, the house looked like a battleground, but they'd still found nothing.

Chuck shook his head. "I don't get it. Maybe it really was just some rich family who could afford to protect their house better than everyone else."

"A lot of good it did them," Ed said.

As they talked, Owl stepped out of the bedroom and paused. She walked into the bedroom next to it. Then back out and into the bathroom again.

She stepped out into the hall and put her hands on her hips. "This space doesn't add up."

"Uh, what now?" Patrick asked.

"Look." Owl paced down the hallway toward them. "The hall is twenty feet long. The bedroom is ten feet. The bathroom is five feet. I'm no math whiz, but it seems to me there's five feet of space missing between the two rooms."

Alex couldn't help but smile. "Nice work, Owl. Chuck, why don't you open the wall between the rooms and see what's in the mystery space."

Chuck pulled out the cutter again, a smile on his face. "I get to use the cutter twice? And it's not even my birthday."

He made short work of the wall, opening up a hole five feet high and four feet wide. When he finished, he kicked the cutout piece of wall inward and shined his headlamp into the hole. Then he waved Alex over.

The first thing Alex noticed was the silver mesh inside the wall, just like on the exterior wall. The small room was empty, but for a single item in the center of the floor: a tarnished, silver hatch.

The hatch had no handle or grip, but the hinges were visible.

Alex turned to Chuck. "I hope you kept the cutter warm. Open her up. It looks like we're going down."

18

CHUCK MADE the last the cut and the hatch door fell through the hole and into the darkness below. It was over a second before they heard it hit the ground with a loud clang.

After a moment, Chuck flinched, his hand covering his nose.

A moment later, Alex realized why. A foul odor hit her, and she, too, instinctively took a step back.

The team waited in silence as the smoke from the cutter dissipated. The howl they were all waiting for never came.

Chuck leaned over the hole, shining his headlamp down. "Looks like this goes about thirty feet down."

"Drop a daylight," Alex ordered. With the way this place was decked out in silver, it seemed unlikely there'd be Feral down there, but better safe than sorry.

Chuck activated his daylight and dropped it into the shaft. "I don't hear anything."

"Okay, let's make our way down."

The team descended the ladder attached to the wall and gathered at the bottom of the shaft. It reminded Alex of the hatch they'd found in the mountains. Same type of ladder.

Same hall at the bottom leading to an underground bunker. She just hoped they wouldn't find the recon team sleeping in this one.

The smell was even stronger now that they were at the bottom. Alex breathed through her mouth and hoped she'd get used to the odor soon.

They made their way down the hall and came out in a large, open room. The walls were lined with monitors and a dozen workstations, each with computers. The dust was even thicker than it had been upstairs. It looked to Alex like no one had been down here in a long time.

"Is this it?" Patrick asked. "Is this Project White Horse?"

Alex frowned "Too soon to say. Right now, it's a possible hostile environment. Let's make sure that there are no Ferals down here, then we'll start trying to figure out what this place is."

"Look at all this silver," Owl muttered as the made their way through the bunker.

Whoever had made this place hadn't been messing around. The desk, chairs, walls, floor and ceiling were all made of silver. The room would be deadly to any vampire with exposed flesh. Alex couldn't imagine a Feral surviving long down there.

A door at the end of the room led to another slightly smaller room. It appeared to be a storage area. Shelves lined the walls, and each shelf held a half dozen cannisters. Alex read the faded writing on the outside of some of them: rice, flour, beans. The door at the end of the room led to yet another room.

"Now we're talking," Chuck said as they stepped inside.

This room had clearly been a lab of some sort. Tables with beakers and test tubes filled most of the space. But the most interesting items were at the far end. There were five three-foot-by-three-foot glass cases, each with two holes with built-in rubber gloves, allowing the user to work with whatever was inside the case without exposing it to the open air.

Owl turned to Alex, her eyes wide. "This is it, right? It has to be."

"I don't know." As promising as this appeared, she didn't want to get her hopes up too high. And yet, she couldn't fully push aside the feeling that the plans for White Horse virus could be in this room. The secret to safe Resettlement could mere feet away.

Chuck turned, and as he did his elbow hit a metal tray, sending it clattering to the floor.

Everyone froze, their weapons ready.

After a few moments of silence, Patrick glared at Chuck. "Watch it, butter fingers."

"Let's keep searching," Alex said. "We'll circle back here once we've given the whole bunker a walkthrough."

The next room was a living area with couches and a small kitchen. They found a bathroom off of the living area with a standup shower, a sink, and a toilet. Like everything else in this place, it was designed to optimize the space and covered with plenty of silver.

"I think I found the source of that smell," Ed called out, standing in the doorway at the end of the room.

The team followed him into the next and final room of the bunker, the sleeping quarters. The space was dominated by three bunk beds. Five of the six beds were occupied.

Alex drew a sharp breath, thinking for just a moment that the recon team had somehow beaten them there. But the occupants of the beds were not vampires. They were the regular, old-fashioned kind of dead.

The five corpses were all laying in an identical fashion:

on their backs, arms crossed over their chests. It almost looked as if someone had arranged them like that. They all wore similar uniforms, though the way the cloth had rotted made it difficult to tell much about it. The rotting cloth had fused itself to the old leather that had once been their skin. The corpses were so deteriorated that it was difficult to tell much about them, including their gender.

They found the sixth corpse slumped over the lower bunk at the end of the room. An old gun lay on the floor next to it, and there was a clear exit wound in its skull.

"What do you think happened?" Patrick asked. "Maybe this guy went nuts and killed his buddies, then himself?"

Alex didn't answer. Instead, she bent down and picked up something next to corpse. A small leather book. She flipped through it and saw the pages were filled with small, messy handwriting. It was all formulas, drawings, and scribbled paragraphs of text.

She turned to the last page and saw it was empty except for two lines of text:

Time has run out. We've failed.

Forsusanandjacob.

Alex stared at the book for a long moment, her heart racing, wondering if they'd found Project White Horse. Then she took a deep breath and put the book into her pack.

She turned to her team. "We need to move quickly. Patrick and Ed, I want every hard drive in this bunker loaded onto the ship. Owl, you're with me. We'll search for anything else that looks like it might be important."

"What about me?" Chuck asked.

"I need you topside. You're going to rig the remains of every building on this block with enough explosives to blow it to hell."

Chuck raised an eyebrow. "Why?"

"I don't want Jaden seeing what was down here. Blowing up this building will draw his attention, but if we take out the block, we can tell him that we ran into trouble with Ferals." She turned to the rest of the team. "Let's get to work."

It took three hours to comb through the bunker and load everything that could possibly be important. Alex decided to err on the side of caution and take everything that even had a slight possibility of being useful. They looked under every mattress and through every food cannister. They even looked for hidden rooms or compartments. By the time they were done and back on the ship, there wasn't an inch of the bunker they hadn't been over at least twice.

Chuck waited until they were airborne, then detonated the charges. The block was obliterated.

"What do we do now, Captain?" Owl asked.

Alex grimaced. She wasn't looking forward to this next part. "We've got to get this stuff back to Brian. But first, we need check in with Jaden."

Patrick groaned. "Can't we just tell him we forgot?"

"No." Alex paused. "And Owl? Park someplace sunny. The last thing we want is Jaden coming aboard this ship."

———

IT TURNED out they didn't have much to worry about back the vampire hotel. It was late afternoon, and Jaden's daysickness was much stronger than it had been when they'd spoken to him that morning. It was all he could do to keep sitting up straight as they gave their report. He was in a hurry to have them gone so he could go back to sleep, and that was perfectly fine with Alex.

Back on *New Haven*, Brian was ecstatic to see the haul they'd brought. Alex was a little nervous about the support staff who saw all the hard drives, but she was careful not to get too specific while they were around. Besides, they knew enough to keep their mouths shut about what they saw at GMT headquarters. CB didn't take kindly to information leaks, and they knew they'd all feel his displeasure if any word of this left the hangar.

Brian got to work immediately, but he quickly hit a roadblock. The hard drives were encrypted. It was going to take him days, maybe weeks, to find a way past it.

That was when Alex remembered the notebook in her pack. "Try For Susan and Jacob. Capital F, the rest lowercase. No spaces."

CB and Alex watched as he keyed in the password and a wide smile crossed his face. "We're in."

The three of them sat in Brian's office, the curtains drawn. CB crossed his arms, a nervous expression on his face, as Brian began to sift through the contents of the hard drive.

"Holy shit," Brian said. "This is a goldmine. I'm not sure where to start. It looks like these might be the records of experiments, but there's thousands of them."

"What's that folder?" Alex asked, pointing to the one labeled Personal Logs.

Brian clicked it open. "It's video files. Sorted by years, it looks like." He turned toward Alex, his face pale. "There's over ten years of daily logs here."

"Ten years?" Alex asked. "You're telling me Project White Horse started ten years before the infestation?"

"Not according to the dates here. Looks like it started

about shortly before *New Haven* launched." He looked up suddenly. "And continued until nine years later."

CB frowned. "Bring up the last log."

Brian clicked his way to the last folder and opened the final file.

A video began to play.

A man's face filled the screen. He was pale, and the cheek bones stood out on his gaunt face, dark circles around his eyes. He stared silently at the camera for a long moment before speaking.

"This is..." he trailed off, his voice thick with emotion. "This is Dr. Carl Webber. This will be my final log. I don't imagine..." He paused, his eyes filling with tears, before swallowing hard and starting again. "I don't imagine anyone will ever see this. Or any of the logs we've made over the past ten years. The fact is, we failed."

He leaned forward, staring straight into the camera, the tears threatening to spill out of his eyes.

"I want to make one thing clear. We never gave up. The men and women here did their absolute best, right to the very end. There were so many times I thought we were going to crack it. It always seemed so close. Maybe if we could have stayed in contact with the other labs. But communication was too dangerous. The vampires may have been listening, so we had to work alone."

He paused, gesturing at something offscreen.

"We've been able to watch some of what's happening outside through our security cameras. That's what's passed for entertainment around here these many years. Once the humans were gone, the vampires began to fight amongst themselves. Then eventually, they started to change. They're monsters now." He chuckled. "More so than before, I mean."

He paused again and let out a deep sigh.

"I guess I'm probably the last human. Jill died late last night. She was the last, other than me. We were able to ration out the food supplies six months longer than expected, but it still didn't give us enough time." He blinked, and the tears finally ran down his cheeks. "Part of me wants to go outside. To feel the sun on my face one more time. Maybe I could even find some food and survive a little longer. But I know I can't do that. I've studied their biology and know how powerful their sense of smell is. And I've seen how they're mad with hunger. My scent would draw the vampires. They'd gather here at night and tear this place apart, even if it meant burning their hands off on the silver. I can't risk that. Our research is too important. I have to hope that someday, somehow, it will be found. Otherwise, the last ten years have been for nothing.

His body shook as he fought back the sobs wracking his body.

"If anyone finds this, please remember our sacrifice. I'm sorry that we didn't do better. I'm sorry we failed. I think I have just enough strength left to go and join the others. This is Dr. Carl Webber, signing off." He reached up and turned off the camera.

The three sat in silence, staring at the black screen.

"Jesus," Alex said. "Ten years in that bunker. Can you imagine? How would they even stay sane?"

Brian nodded toward the hard drives. "They had their work to focus on. Hope kept them going. I guess that was enough. The real question is, what does this mean for us? Is this what Jaden is looking for?"

"It may be," CB said. "We know that they didn't finish, but we can pick up where they left off. First, we need to go through this research and catalog their finding. He also said that there were other labs. If we can locate them, they might have more answers."

Brian nodded. "I'm on it. It's going to take forever to go through all this. I could really use some help."

"It would have to be someone we really trust," CB said. "I'll see if Jessica can help."

"And Owl," Alex said. "Between missions, at least. She's good at this stuff." She turned to Brian. "What about the silver?"

"What do you mean?"

"The house above the bunker had silver lined walls and a huge silver door. It was loaded with silver. Is there a way that we can detect that? Like a silver metal detector that we can use from the air?"

Brian thought a moment, then smiled. "That's brilliant Alex. I think that I can rig something up that will send you in the right direction. It may pick up other elements too, but it could still help narrow down your search."

"You're the best. Sorry if we just killed your social life for the foreseeable future."

"It's probably for the best. I'm sure that I would have killed it on my own, anyway." He paused. "It'll be interesting to try to detect silver. I spent so long working on the Silver Spray, but it's been a while."

"What's Silver Spray?" Alex asked.

Brian reached into his desk and pulled out a small cannister. "Weapon I was working on. It shoots a fine mist of tiny silver particles into the air. The idea was it would get in the vampire's eyes, nose, the pores of their skin. It would really mess them up. But it turned out to be incredibly time-consuming to make. And you have to be so close to it to use it that it's not a very practical weapon."

Alex pointed at the cannister. "That one work?"

"Yeah. It's the prototype. Only one I ever made, actually." She snatched it off the desk. "I'm taking it."

"Are you sure you...? Ah, never mind. I know I'm not talking you out of it."

Alex clipped the small canister onto her belt and turned to CB. "What now? Do we tell the Council about the hard drives?"

"Yes," CB said. "But not yet. I want all the information I can get before we tackle that. If we find a weapon to kill vampires, they'll understand why we need to keep this from Jaden, and why he kept it from us. Until then, let's keep this knowledge limited to the GMT."

FIREFLY STOOD on the roof of the hotel, arms crossed. "What are we doing up here, Jaden?"

The older vampire didn't answer. His eyes were closed, and a light breeze blew through his hair. His hands were relaxed by his side as he stood silent.

Firefly considered asking the question again but thought better of it. He'd learned that Jaden moved at his own pace. He'd speak when he was ready, and not a moment before. Instead, he sighed and looked out over the edge of the roof. The humid night air tossed the leaves of the plentiful plant life below. In the distance, Firefly heard the sound of waves.

"This place was once considered a tropical paradise," Jaden said. "You should take the time to appreciate it, now and again.

Firefly chuckled. "I've been here a year, and I can tell you it's not paradise. It's one big nest of Ferals, and every one of them wants to kill you." He paused. "Speaking of, I was hoping you'd be able to help us figure out a way to live through this clean-up process."

Jaden opened his eyes. "You're quite dead already, so I can't help you there. Still, I do think we'll succeed in clearing the island. Whether any of us survives, remains to be seen."

"So what's the game plan? Is there a faster or safer way to get rid of all of these damn Ferals?"

Jaden turned to him and smiled. "Right now, my plan is to make a plan. That's why I'm here."

Firefly shifted on his feet uncomfortably. "Well, if you're in brainstorming mode, here's an idea. Let's make better weapons. You know Brian McElroy on *New Haven*?"

"I'm familiar with him, yes."

"The guy's a genius when it comes to this stuff. We should have our people work with him. I'll bet he could come up with a crazy new Feral-killing device, or something."

Jaden paused a moment. "There's an old saying: it's the poor carpenter who blames his tools."

"Yeah, I've heard that one. It may be true, but it's the idiot carpenter who doesn't use the best hammer he's got when there's a nail that needs driving."

Jaden gazed down at the street below them. "The memory of humanity is so short. Before humans had to fight vampires, they fought each other. Each war was worse than the last. They built bigger and better weapons that killed more people more quickly and efficiently. If not for our kind, I believe that they would have succeeded in wiping themselves off the planet." He turned and looked at Firefly. "To answer your question, I don't think that stronger weapons are the answer. Call me old fashioned, but I like to know who I'm killing."

Firefly considered that a moment. "I don't need to fight toe-to-toe with those beasts to feel good about killing them. Look, we're not talking about nuclear weapons, here. A tool to kill Ferals isn't going to destroy the world."

Jaden put a hand on Firefly's shoulder. "The best of intentions often lead to the worst outcomes. Trust that we will find a way to rid the surface of Feral without going down that path. We have a unique opportunity to start over. Let's do it right." He paused. "Come on. Grab your team and let's go for a run. I want to see how the Ferals are reacting in the area where the GMT hunted today."

Firefly said nothing, but inside, he was a mess of conflicted feelings. Of course, he'd been delighted when he'd learned the GMT had hunted in the very spot where he'd left the backup tracker. And he wouldn't mind seeing what was left of the place after the GMT was done with it. Still, he wasn't sure he wanted Jaden snooping around the area. Not that there was much he could do about it.

Jaden left Helen in charge of the troops at the hotel when they headed out with Firefly's group of twenty soldiers. They quickly made their way to the coast and ran south along the shoreline, the ocean at their side. The shore was littered with the remnants of the war that had happened here. They dodged rusty tanks and old, ruined missile turrets. As they ran, they passed a few small groups of Ferals, who scattered at the sight of them, but didn't try to attack.

When they got within a few miles of the town, Firefly began to smell the ash. The residue from the explosives left a bitter taste in his mouth. Soon, the town came into sight, and Firefly stopped his team.

He turned to Jaden. "The Ferals have been waiting for us in hordes anytime there's a major disturbance like this one.

We should probably give them a few days to cool down before we get any closer."

Jaden ignored the comment. He was staring toward the town. "Be quiet for a moment and listen."

Firefly bit back his reply and did as he was told. He closed his eyes and listened. At first, it was just the usual mix of nighttime sounds on the coast. But after a moment, he began to identify specific sounds. First, the obvious ones. The waves. Insects buzzing. Then he began to pick out more details. Rustling leaves. The flap of a bird's wings high over-head. And then something else. Shuffling feet.

Firefly's eyes snapped open. "I hear it. There's something moving up ahead."

Jaden raised an eyebrow. "Good, but I didn't mean for you to listen with your ears. Try to sense the vampires around you. Listen with your mind."

Firefly felt his face redden. "Sorry, where I come from, listen implies ears. I'll try again."

He once again closed his eyes.

At first, he could just feel the vampires close to him. He felt their unease at this exercise. And he felt an infectious sense of calm coming from Jaden. Then he pushed his mind, tried to stretch it further, and he felt something else.

It wasn't the first time he'd experienced it. It was a raw animal instinct, mixed with pain and rage, and it made his guts squirm. It was weak, but definitely there.

"There are Ferals here," he said. "I can sense them."

"Good," Jaden said. "The skill will improve the more you use it. Keep practicing." He turned toward the town. "I only sense a few Ferals. I think we're safe to investigate."

Without waiting for a reply, he started trotting toward the town. Firefly motioned for his team to follow.

The smell of charred wood and explosives grew stronger

as they entered the town. They quickly made their way to the block the GMT had destroyed, keeping a tight formation and watching for Ferals.

When they reached the edge of the destruction, Jaden stopped, and the rest of the soldiers followed suit.

"Do you see them?" Jaden asked.

"Yes." Firefly spotted about twenty Ferals wandering the burnt area. He could feel their frustration strongly now, and it was clear what was causing it. Even with the strong smell of fire hanging in the air, there was something identifiable underneath it: the scent of humans.

Near the center of the destruction, two Ferals were on all fours, digging frantically at the ground. After a moment, one of the Ferals disappeared.

Firefly turned to Jaden. "What the hell was that?"

"Only one way to find out," Jaden answered. "Ready your weapons."

The vampires drew their swords and followed Jaden into the fray. After a year of killing Ferals, they were experienced fighters, and they made short work of the disoriented creatures. Jaden didn't even bother drawing his sword. He just watched with an appraising eye as the team worked.

When it was over, he said nothing, but gave Firefly an approving nod. It was all Firefly could do not to smile with pride.

Jaden waved Firefly over and the two of them walked to the spot where the Feral had disappeared. Jaden reached it first. "Well, I guess we know where it went."

Firefly stepped up next to him and saw the hole in the ground. He swallowed hard. Was this what Alex and the GMT had been trying to cover up with the explosion? "What could be down—"

Before he finished speaking, the Feral leapt out of the

hole, screaming as it came. Firefly started to raise his sword, but Jaden was already in motion. He drew his blade and removed the Feral's head in one neat stroke.

The creature's momentum carried it forward and it landed next to the hole with a thump, its body three feet from its severed head.

It took Firefly a moment, but then he noticed something odd about the creature: its feet were on fire. "What the hell?"

Jaden's eyes narrowed when he saw the creature's feet. "Let's make this fast. Other Ferals will be headed this way to investigate. Have your soldiers watch our backs." With that, he jumped into the hole.

Firefly silently cursed, then he turned to his troops. "Set up a perimeter and wait for us. Radio me if more Ferals start showing up. We won't be long."

Then he followed Jaden into the hole.

19

WHEN FIREFLY LANDED at the bottom of the shaft, the first thing he noticed was the darkness. Normally, he was aware of darkness, but it didn't inhibit his vampire eyes from seeing clearly. This place was dark in a way he hadn't experienced since his days of being human.

Something wasn't right. It was like someone had turned down the volume on his eyesight.

Then he noticed something else—he was dizzy. And his stomach was clenching in a decidedly unpleasant way. It was another feeling he hadn't experienced in two years: that of being sick.

He put a hand on the wall to steady himself, but quickly pulled it away.

"Ow!" he shouted. It was as if a thousand needles had been sunk into his palm. Thin tendrils of smoke curled off his flesh. "Something isn't right, Jaden. What's happening?"

He looked up and saw Jaden was a bit hunched over. The older vampire took a step and nearly stumbled. Jaden must have been feeling it, too.

"It's silver," Jaden said. "The entire bunker is made of it.

I'm guessing the explosion spread some of the particles into the air.

"We're breathing silver?" Vampires didn't have to breathe for oxygen, but they did take air into their lungs to speak. An image popped into Firefly's head: his lungs exploding in flames, and fire consuming him from the inside out.

"There's not a lot of it, or we'd be dead already. We should be fine, but I suggest not touching anything. Come."

Jaden led the way through the mostly destroyed bunker. Even with his weakened vision, Firefly could see well enough to tell a charge had been placed in every room. Most everything had been destroyed, but there was enough left to tell what the rooms had once been. A storeroom. A living space. A lab.

Jaden was silent as they moved through the bunker. He had no visible reaction, though he did pause in the laboratory longer than in the other rooms.

Then they made it to the final room. It was clear that no charge had been set in this one. Three bunk beds stood unharmed, and there were six corpses.

They stood in silence for a long moment, and then Jaden chuckled.

"Humans. They never cease to amaze me. The GMT went to all this trouble to bury the evidence, and yet they risked it all because they couldn't stomach defiling corpses that have been rotting here for more than a century."

Firefly's mind raced. If Jaden hadn't known the GMT was working behind his back before, he certainly did now. Still, maybe Firefly could defuse the situation. "When the GMT blows something up, it's to take out Ferals. There must have been a battle down here. Maybe they blew up the whole area to take out a nest.

Jaden turned toward him. Even in the darkness, Firefly could make out the serious expression on his face.

"I think the time for subterfuge has passed. There was no battle here. Besides the distinct lack of Feral corpses, the creatures wouldn't last five minutes in this bunker with all this silver. They don't have protective clothing, like we do. We witnessed that ourselves, with our fiery-footed friend." He paused a moment. "Alex was trying to hide this bunker from me. The only question is whether you are in on her little plan."

Firefly couldn't have felt more exposed if he were standing naked in direct sunlight. For a moment, he wasn't sure he could even move. He considered drawing his sword, but that would only escalated things further. He'd seen Jaden fight, and he was humble enough to realize he didn't stand a chance against the ancient vampire. If Jaden wanted him dead, this bunker would be the last place he ever saw.

His only chance was to stick to his story.

"Alex runs her own missions. You know she's not very forthcoming with information. Especially not with vampires."

"That's true. Normally. But she's also fiercely loyal to the GMT. And she still considers you a member of the team. If she's running secret missions, she would want you in on it."

Firefly considered denying it again, but the certainty in Jaden's voice told him there'd be no point.

"That's what I thought." Jaden put a hand on Firefly's shoulder. "I understand. You're in a tough position. You were human far longer than you've been a vampire. I don't begrudge you your decision."

Firefly tensed, still half expecting Jaden to end him then and there. "Jaden, Alex isn't just loyal to the GMT. She's loyal to humanity. Whatever she's doing, she believes it is in Resettlement's best interests."

"I'm sure," Jaden said. "As I told you earlier, the best intensions often lead to the most horrific outcomes." He gave Firefly's shoulder a squeeze and released it. "Don't worry. I understand where she's coming from, and I still believe this situation can be salvaged. I'm not your enemy. I'm not Alex's enemy. My goal is the same as it's ever been: to help humanity reclaim the Earth."

"So what do we do now?" Firefly asked.

Jaden turned and walked out of the room, toward the exit. "We're heading back to the hotel. I think I know how to solve our Alex problem once and for all."

ALEX RAN through the empty streets of *New Haven*, doing her best not to think of anything at all. Sometimes running was a meditative experience. The pounding of her heart and the rhythmic tap-tap of her feet on the deck lulled her into a peaceful, mindful place were her concerns, her work, even time itself, slipped away for a little while.

Those were the good days. Today was not a good day. She'd woken at four-thirty in the morning, suddenly fully alert and completely aware that she wouldn't be getting any more sleep. So she'd thrown on her workout clothes and started running. And try as she might, she couldn't seem to push away the thought that had woken her so abruptly and completely. Today was the day she'd be meeting with the City Council.

CB had made it sound easy, of course. All she needed to do was keep her mouth shut unless she was asked a question, in which case she was to answer as succinctly and professionally as possible.

Easier said than done. At least, for Alex. It was difficult to imagine sitting in front of the people who held every lever of power on *New Haven* and not pointing out the dire situation they were facing.

Still, she knew CB was right. They needed to have all the information before they tried to present their case to the Council again. And that couldn't happen until Brian finished digging through the computers they'd found in the bunker.

Since she didn't have anything better to do, she decided she might as well check in on Brian. There was a good chance he'd be working already. She turned left at the next junction and headed toward the GMT Headquarters.

Though the hour was early, the ship was filled with sunlight, as always. While many might understand the day and night cycle of the Earth on an intellectual level, Alex was one of the few people on the ship who'd experienced it. No one on the Council had ever watched the sun trek across the sky or felt the creeping terror as it approached the horizon, knowing there was no way to stop the darkness from coming. They'd never stood helplessly as a horde of monsters raced toward them. They'd never seen the stars at night.

Maybe that was part of what made Alex's perspective different from theirs. She understood at a fundamental level that their way of life was unnatural. That even though their lives had the illusion of safety, they were in constant danger. She silently promised herself she'd remember that during the Council meeting. Maybe it would help her hold her tongue.

She reached Brian's lab and was pleased to see that the

lights were already on. She opened the door and started to speak, but stopped herself as she saw her two friends sleeping. Brian sat in a chair, leaning back and snoring softly, the bank of computer monitors in front of him glowing. Owl sat at another desk, her head down on the keyboard.

She felt a sudden wave of gratitude. Both Brian and Owl had dedicated themselves fully to the task, giving up everything else in pursuit of the truth. As she turned to go, she noticed something, and it made her smile. Owl's hair was now blue.

As she left the lab and eased the door shut, Alex felt the peace that had eluded her on her run. She had one hell of a team.

A few hours later, CB and Alex sat side by side as the Council meeting was called to order and General Craig asked for new business. Ambassador McCready quickly stood.

"I have great news about the Resettlement efforts. As some of you already know, the transport ship Agartha has been working on is now complete. This means that Jaden's team can handle resupplying and communication between Puerto Rico and my city."

CB and Alex exchanged a worried glance.

"Jaden has decided to lead the mission to clear the island himself," McCready continued, "and he has carefully orchestrated a strategy to do just that. As such, I've been asked to let you know that the GMT will no longer be needed on the island. They're free to resume their primary mission of salvaging supplies for *New Haven*."

Surprised looks appeared on every face around the table.

After a moment, General Craig spoke. "This comes from Jaden?"

McCready nodded. "I spoke to him personally this morning when we passed over Puerto Rico. I'll touch base with him weekly, and I'll keep the Council informed."

The room was silent for a long moment, and it was all Alex could do to stay silent. CB cleared his throat. His face was a light shade of red, but his voice was calm when he spoke.

"Due respect to Jaden, but I feel this requires a little more discussion. The GMT has an important role to play in clearing the island. Jaden can only work at night. If the GMT works during the day, we're doubling our efforts. And the numbers have shown that GMT can be very effective."

Horace crossed his arms over his chest. "CB makes a good point, McCready."

The Ambassador's face darkened. "Jaden was quite clear in his direction. In fact, he insists."

Now, Alex couldn't stay silent. "I'm sorry, he *insists*?"

McCready looked a little uncomfortable when he spoke again. "I didn't want to bring this up, but I suppose I owe you the truth. The GMT's presence has been causing problems on the island. The Ferals are generally spread out and don't pose a major threat to our vampires. But the human scent that the GMT brings with them is causing changes. They are growing more aggressive. They are gathering in hordes. Firefly lost a number of soldiers to such a horde after one of the GMT's recent missions."

"Hang on," Alex said. "That's not—"

"Let him finish, Captain Goddard," General Craig growled.

"Thank you, General," McCready said. "Jaden has made it clear that the only way to effectively and safely clear Puerto Rico is to have no human presence on the island. At least, for the time being."

"This is bullshit," Alex said.

CB gave her a long look. Alex expected to be reprimanded, but CB's response surprised her. "I tend to agree with Captain Goddard's assessment."

"Don't get me wrong," McCready said. "We value your partnership on this project. Jaden indicated that in a few years, once they'd thinned the herd, so to speak, the GMT would have a part to play. But this initial phase needs to be carried out by vampires, and vampires alone."

General Craig scratched at the stubble on his cheek. "I must say, this is a surprise. But we did all agree we would proceed with caution. The last thing we want is a repeat of Fleming's disastrous attempt. And it would be nice to have the GMT back to their regular duties full time. CB, what's your take?"

CB leaned forward and looked McCready dead in the eyes. "Is it possible that there's another reason why Jaden doesn't want us on that island?"

"Ah," the Ambassador said. "I was afraid this might come up." He glanced at General Craig. "This is a bit of a sensitive topic. Perhaps we should handle it privately?"

Craig grimaced. "Goddard and CB are adults. They can handle whatever it is you have to say."

"Very well. Jaden mentioned that the vampires who've been working with the GMT have grown a bit concerned. Apparently, Alex has become obsessed with her conspiracy theory that Jaden is hiding some secret weapon on the island. Jaden explained that he's looking for nuclear codes, but she doesn't seem to have believed him."

CB and Alex looked at each other for a long moment. Then Alex gave CB and nod. It was time to come clean.

"It's more than a conspiracy theory," CB said. "On their last mission, the GMT discovered a hidden bunker. It was filled with lab equipment and computers. They brought the hard drives back, and Brian McElroy is going through them as we speak. We'll be able to present his findings to the Council very soon."

"Yes," McCready said, his voice as dry as fire. "That was the other sensitive topic we needed to discuss. Jaden believes those hard drives may contain information on the very nuclear codes he's looking for."

"That's not accurate," Alex said, her voice rising. "It's a weapon, yes, but—"

"Let him finish, Captain," General Craig snapped. "I won't warn you again."

McCready looked at Craig, his eyes heavy with concern. "General, I've enjoyed working with you, and I fully believe our cities can build a brighter future for humanity together. But if your military is running secret missions to find these nuclear codes under the guise of looking for some mysterious weapon that doesn't exist, I have to ask myself why. And the answers are very troubling."

Horace's eyes widened. "Are you accusing us of something?"

"No. I'm simply conveying the questions Jaden is asking. We have vampires. You do not. I have to consider the possibility that you learned about these nuclear weapons, and you decided acquiring them might be a good way to even the playing field."

"That's ridiculous," Craig scoffed.

"I'm not saying the Council knew. Sometimes the military oversteps their bounds."

"Ambassador, that's a serious accusation."

"Then set our minds at ease."

Alex squeezed her hands so hard that her nails dug into her palms. "Are you kidding me, right now? You think we'd actually try to get these nuclear weapons? We're not interested in an arms race."

Craig's eyes were cold. "And yet, you did find computers with possible military information and you did not inform the Council. I trust you, Alex. But I can also see how this would cause some concern for Agartha." He turned to Ambassador McCready. "How can we ease Jaden's mind?"

"It's simple. We have just two requests. One, followed Jaden's directive to keep the GMT off the island. Let the vampires do their jobs."

"Directive?" Alex asked. "I thought Resettlement was a joint effort. Since when do we take orders from Agartha?"

"CB," Craig said, "keep her under control, or you're both gone."

CB gave Craig a long look, then nodded. "Alex, not another word."

"What's the second request?" Craig asked.

"Turn those hard drives over to us," McCready said. "You've had time to go through them. We deserve to have the same information. Unless you have something to hide."

CB leaned forward. "Jaden will be on the island, and we won't. That means he'll be the only one who's able to follow up on the information on those hard drives."

"Jaden's already made it clear what he's looking for. He's been transparent that he wants the weapons destroyed. If you want to win back our trust, this is how you do it."

A long silence filled the room.

Finally, General Craig said, "Council, any concerns with this plan?" He waited a moment, but no one spoke. "Done. The GMT will stay off the island until further notice, Ambassador. And you'll have the hard drives by the end of the day."

McCready smiled. "You've made the right call. Our two

great cities are going to make the world a better place. Together."

The rest of the meeting was mercifully brief. It appeared the Council didn't have the stomach to discuss other issues after that bombshell. CB and Alex walked out of the Hub five minutes later.

"What the hell was that?" Alex asked, her voice hollow.

"Jaden screwed us," CB said. "He's thousands of miles away and he still managed to get the upper hand."

Alex's heart was racing. After everything, this couldn't be the end. Their chances of finding Project White Horse were fading fast. "Maybe we can talk to General Craig. If we explain everything we've found on Project White Horse, maybe—"

"No," CB said. "I hate to say it, but it doesn't matter what we show him. I can't see the Council going against Jaden. They're gun shy after everything that happened with Fleming. They won't risk making Agartha an enemy."

"So, what do we do?"

"Get the team together," CB said. "We have some tough decisions to make."

20

BRIAN AND OWL were eating their lunches when Alex and CB walked in. Brian choked down the bit of food he'd been chewing. "Hey guys. How was the meeting?"

"Not great," Alex said. "Tell me you've found something on those drives."

Brian took a sip of water. "We've found a lot. It's mostly raised more questions, though. We're working on the answers."

Owl pointed at her monitor. "These videos logs are amazing. I feel like I'm really getting to know the scientists in the bunker. I'm only a few weeks into the timeline, but I think Carol and Jack are going to fall for each other."

"What?" CB asked. "Who are Carol and Jack?"

"Carol's one of the senior scientists, second only to Dr. Webber. Jack's just a technician. He's like ten years younger than her, and he's pretty hot. But the way he talked about having lunch with her in the last log, I could practically feel the sparks."

"Okay, forget I asked." He turned to Brian. "What about the weapon? Any leads?"

"Unfortunately, no. There's another level of encryption. The password got me into the computer, but I'm going to have to do some hacking to get to the important stuff. Unless you can find a key in the bunker."

Alex raised an eyebrow. "The bunker we blew up? How long's it going to take to break the encryption?"

Brian shook his head. "Hard to say. Days. Possibly weeks."

"Damn," CB said. "We don't have that kind of time."

Owl stopped eating and set down her fork. "That sounds...dire. When you say the Council meeting went not great—"

"They grounded us," Alex said flatly. "Well, from the island, at least. Jaden wants to handle things on his own. And we have to give Agartha the hard drives."

The room fell silent.

"So, that's it?" Brian asked. "Jaden beat us?"

Alex shot him a sideways glance. "Have you met me? We're not giving up. Not by a longshot. Have you backed up the data from the hard drives?"

"Of course. That was the first thing I did."

"Good. How long will it take Agartha to get into those hard drives without the password?"

"A while," Brian said. "Ambassador McCready doesn't strike me as much of a hacker. So he'll have to send the drives back to his city. That'll buy us a day or two before they even start working on it."

"Good." She looked at Owl. "CB and I are going to be busy for a bit. I want you to contact the team. Have them meet us in the hangar in one hour."

Owl suddenly looked a little more alert. "Roger that."

Alex turned to Brian. "I know this isn't your area, but

how would you feel about coming to the surface with the GMT?"

Brian's eyes widened. "On a mission? Terrified. And honored. I'm in."

Alex smiled. He hadn't even asked where they were going. "Excellent. Load the backup data onto the away ship. You'll have to work on it there."

"What are you and CB going to do?" Owl asked.

"We've got a delivery to make."

AN HOUR LATER, CB and Alex left the Hub, the cart that had carried the hard drives now empty. They'd presented them to Ambassador McCready, just as he'd asked. Alex had delivered something else, too. And she was none too happy about it.

"I can't believe I apologized to that bastard."

"Just think of it as a mission," CB said.

"An apology is not a mission."

"It could be. A mission calls for complete focus, right? Your body wants to run from the danger, but you have to force it to do the opposite. This is no different."

"Ambassador McCready is an asshole."

"You bought us a few hours. He thinks he's cowed you, and he might back off. Or at least slow down a little."

"I get it," Alex said. "I followed orders, Colonel. But you owe me one."

CB raised an eyebrow. "That's not how orders work."

They drove in silence toward GMT Headquarters, the tension of what they were about to do hanging over them.

"What did Jessica say?" Alex asked.

CB sighed. "She didn't love it. But she agreed that it's our best move."

"There could be trouble for her."

"She knows. And she's fully prepared to deal with it."

"You don't have to do this," Alex said.

"Yes, I do. I'm sick of pushing papers and sitting through meetings and dealing with asshole ambassadors. It's time to do something real."

They found the team gathered in the hangar, waiting next to the away ship. Brian looked awkward in his ill-fitting GMT uniform, and he shifted from foot to foot uncomfortably. Ed and Patrick were oblivious, playing tic-tac-toe on a dry erase board next to the ship. Chuck looked nervous. He clearly knew that something was up.

The cart pulled up just as Owl was stepping off the away ship.

Alex hopped off the cart. "We ready, Owl?"

The pilot nodded. "The ship is. Not sure I am."

The tension was thick as Alex stood there in silence. Ed and Patrick even put down their markers and got to their feet.

"I'm going to lay this out plainly," Alex started. "The Council is shutting us down. No more missions to the island. Jaden gets to find whatever it is he is looking for, and there's nothing we can do about it."

"The hell there isn't," Patrick growled.

Alex held up a hand, silencing him. "I think you all know where I stand. Somewhere on the island, there is research pertaining to a virus capable of wiping out all the Ferals, maybe in a matter of days. I would like us to go find this research before Jaden does."

Chuck's eyes widened. "You want us to go against orders."

"Yes," Alex said. "If we do this and I'm wrong about the

virus, we'll lose our positions on the GMT. Probably even do some jail time. We won't see the surface again until Resettlement. But if I'm right? We won't just take back one island. We'll take back the world."

"And CB?" Ed asked. "He's going to cover for us here?"

CB smiled. "Hell, no. I'm coming with you."

"I guess I am, too," Brian said. He looked like he might be sick.

"Listen," Alex said. "You each have to make your own call on this. I'm not ordering anyone to come. It's illegal, it's far from a sure thing, and it's dangerous as hell. But we'll be in position to leave in thirty minutes, so decide quickly."

There was a long silence. Then Chuck spoke. "I don't see the point of this, Alex. It's already early afternoon. What are the chances we find this research before nightfall? And if not, what, we come back here and get thrown in jail? That's a big risk on a long shot."

Alex met his eye. "You're right. The chances of finding Project White Horse in one day are very slim. But we're not coming back here tonight. We're not coming back to *New Haven* until this is over." She paused, taking in the shocked expressions on her teams' faces. "Now, who's with me?"

FIVE MINUTES after they took off from *New Haven*, Owl spoke through their headsets.

"Uh, guys, we've got a call, and I think we might want to take it."

"Who's hailing us?" Alex asked.

"General Craig."

CB sighed. "Can you put it through to me, Owl?"

"Gladly."

"Patch me in, too," Alex said

A moment later, there was a click in their headsets.

"This is General Craig. Who's in control of that ship?"

"General, it's CB."

There was a long pause. Then the general continued in a softer voice. "What the hell are you doing, Arnold?"

Alex swallowed hard. She hadn't heard anyone call CB by his first name in years.

"You're not going to like it, General, but the GMT and I are on our way to the island. I need you trust me that what we're doing is in the best interest of *New Haven*."

"What you're doing is disobeying an order," Craig growled.

"General, you've known me for a long time. You know I wouldn't take this step lightly. Check the Council's secure drive. I had Brian upload the data we got from the bunker on the island. Check it yourself and you'll see why this is so important."

Another long pause. "If you have information that proves your case, you could have brought it to me. Turn around, CB. We can still fix this, but we have to play by the rules."

CB's voice was hollow when he answered. "I'm sorry, General. We don't have time to go through all the hoops we'd need to in order make that happen. Besides, we're disobeying Jaden, here. If we fail, I'd rather have this be the action of a rogue group, rather than the official orders of *New Haven*'s Council. If things go badly, you can honestly say we were disobeying orders."

"Arnold, please. If you don't come back now, I won't be able to protect you from the fallout."

"I know. I'll take responsibility for my actions. Owl, please disconnect the call."

The line clicked off before the General could respond.

The ship was quiet for a long moment.

Finally, Chuck said, "I guess we shouldn't plan on getting raises this year."

Alex smiled as she looked around the ship. They were all risking their careers, their very lives, and not one of them had hesitated in agreeing to the mission. She'd never been prouder of them.

CB looked a little shell-shocked. Alex understood. General Craig had been his mentor. After CB's original team had been wiped out, it was Craig who'd helped him rebuild the GMT. In many ways, Craig was as much a father figure to CB as CB was to Alex. Betraying him like that couldn't have been easy.

"Hey," Alex whispered to him. "I'm sorry you got dragged into this."

CB shook his head. "You have nothing to be sorry for. This is the job. Protecting *New Haven*, even when it's hard. Especially when it's hard." He paused a moment. "Listen, Alex. I might be your commanding officer, but I haven't been to the surface in years. I want to make this clear. We'll discuss strategies together beforehand, but once we get in the field, you're in command. I want us to have the greatest odds possible, and you're the best field commander on this ship. I'll want you to lead us into battle."

Alex blinked hard. "Are...you sure?"

"I'm sure." He smiled. "Besides, I need to repay you for all those times you were a pain in the ass under my command."

"So, what's the plan?" Ed asked. "If we're throwing away our careers, I hope we have a good strategy."

Alex and CB exchanged glances. "It's sort of a work in progress," Alex said. "Brian's working on decrypting the hard drives. Once that's done, we hope to have the location of the other Project White Horse labs."

Brian was madly typing away on his tablet. "Actually, I'm working on something else, right now."

Chuck raised an eyebrow. "Something more important than the encrypted White Horse files?"

"Yes," Brian said without looking up.

Chuck shifted in his seat uncomfortably. "Alex, don't you think maybe he should—"

"No," Alex said. "I have no idea what he's up to, but he's a genius. We're going to let him do his thing. In the meantime, let's put our heads together and think. What info do we have that could narrow down our search?"

Brian spoke again, still typing madly. "The one thing I know is that the powers that be were incredibly secretive during the infestation. They didn't want anyone to have any information that wasn't crucial to their role."

"Makes sense," Chuck said. "When any one of your people could be turned into a vampire slave and forced to reveal everything they know, it's better to keep things on lockdown."

"Lockdown," Owl said. "That reminds me of something Carol said in her video log."

Alex rolled her eyes. "As much as we'd all love to be regaled with the saga of Carol and Jack, now's not the—"

"No, this might help," Owl insisted. "Listen, Carol said that before they were taken to the bunker, they were on lockdown for two weeks in a bigger Project White Horse facility. She didn't give its location, but she did say they were blindfolded, and that the trip to their new bunker took about forty minutes. She also said she was glad Jack could finally stop being such a baby about all the bugs at their previous location."

Brian looked up for a moment. "Hmm. Dr. Webber mentioned his ears were popping in his first entry. Maybe there was an elevation change?"

Alex nodded slowly. "This is good. Owl, how far do you think the old surface cars could travel in forty minutes?"

Owl thought a moment. "It depends. But on the roads around that little village? There's some rough terrain. I can't imagine it was more than twenty-five miles."

CB smiled. "So we're looking for a location within twenty-five miles of the bunker you found. Probably at a higher elevation."

"And lots of bugs," Patrick pointed out. "I'll bet it's in the jungle."

"Excellent," Alex said. "It's still a lot of ground to cover, but that helps narrow—"

"Done!" Brian shouted. He looked up and saw everyone staring at him. "Sorry. I probably shouldn't shout into my headset mic."

"No, probably not," Ed said, with a scowl.

"What did you do?" Alex asked.

"Simple," Brian beamed. "I reprogrammed the ship's radio to broadcast a high frequency signal and detect the bounce back." He paused. When no one responded, he continued. "I made the ship a giant metal detector."

Now the team responded.

"Awesome, Brian!" Alex said.

"My man!" Patrick said.

Brian looked a little uncomfortable with the accolades. "It won't specifically detect silver like you wanted, Alex, but I figure this area is so remote that any quantity of metal large enough for us to register from the sky is worth investigating."

Owl flew the ship low over the mountains twenty-five

miles from the village, traveling slowly. They got their first ping on their second pass. Owl landed, but it didn't take long to discover it was just an old water tank covered in mud and vines. They didn't get their second hit until over an hour later. This time it turned out to be a relay dish and power unit.

"Your junk detector works great, Brian," Patrick said dryly, as they got back on the ship.

Brian's face was drawn in concern. "Could be there's too much metal out here. This might be a longer process than we'd hoped."

It was late afternoon by the time they got their third ping.

"Two hours until dark," Owl said. "Should we mark this spot and check it out in the morning?"

Alex looked at CB.

"Your call," he said.

"Let's take a quick look now so we can rule it out," Alex said.

Owl set the ship down near the spot, and the team exited the away ship. Brian and Owl stayed back, Brian, to continue his decryption efforts, and Owl, to set up the solar panels to charge the ship.

"You know, CB, I've never actually been on a mission with you," Patrick said as they stepped off the ship. "I'm excited to show you what I can do."

CB hoisted his rifle into position and chuckled. "Worry less about showing off and more about keeping up. I'll show you how we used to do things in the good old days."

Alex tried not to smile. "How about both of you chill and stay in formation? This is a quick recon mission. There will be plenty of opportunities for pissing contests before this is over."

They walked a few minutes through the thick jungle before reaching the spot marked on Alex's tablet.

"This is it." Alex nodded toward the mouth of a cave. She saw that it wasn't a natural formation—a man-made wall was built over the entrance, and a door-shaped hole stood in the middle. Her heart was suddenly racing. This wasn't just some old tank or dish. There was a pretty good chance they'd found a bunker.

"Check it out," Ed said. He kicked away some dirt with his foot and revealed a piece of metal that had to be two feet thick. "I think this was the door."

Alex took a closer look and saw he was right. The massive metal door must have once protected the entrance. "Well, let's see what's inside."

The team switched on their headlamps and stepped into the cave, Alex leading the way. It looked to Alex like a man-made tunnel carved into the mountain. The lines were too clean for a natural cave formation. It was also clear that this place had seen some action. The walls and ceiling were scored with bullet marks and there were chunks missing here and there.

They made it through the tunnel quickly and reached a second set of doors. These were much smaller than the one at the mouth of the tunnel, and they'd only been bent and twisted rather than completely pulled off. Alex hesitated for only a moment outside the doorway, then she led the team through.

On the other side, they found a medium-sized room dominated by a large desk. Some sort of security check point, maybe? There was also something else. Three something elses.

"Ed, you got the one of the left. Patrick, take the center. I'll hit the one on the right."

"Roger that," Ed said.

"Ready," Patrick announced.

Alex raised her pistol and took aim. "Fire."

The three of them fired simultaneously, each taking out one of three sleeping Ferals in the room. When she was sure all three were dead, Alex held up a hand. The team waited silently.

It only took three seconds before they heard the first howl. It was quickly echoed by three more. The pounding of dozens of feet rumbling across the floor quickly followed.

"Fall back," Alex said. "Don't stop until you feel sunlight."

The team moved quickly, staying in formation as they retreated down the tunnel. By the time they reached the end, dozens of Ferals were pouring into the tunnel.

The GMT fell back until they were safely in the sunlight, ten feet beyond the mouth of the tunnel. Then they raised their weapons.

"Let's clear them out," Alex said.

The team went to work, eliminating three dozen Ferals before the creatures stopped coming. A few leapt toward the team from safety of the tunnel, but the sunlight took care of those. It was over in less than two minutes.

"You think that was all of them?" Chuck asked.

"Doubt it. My guess is there are some deep sleepers still in there. We'll find out tomorrow." She glanced at CB. "I guess you do remember how to use that gun."

CB grinned. "I gotta admit, it feels pretty good. Sure we can't clear out the rest of the command center?"

Alex glanced at the horizon. There was only an hour of sunlight left. "We'd better get to safety, if Owl's succeeded in finding such a thing. We'll come back and take out the rest in the morning. Assuming we live through the night."

21

"THAT'S IT?" Alex asked as she peered out the cockpit window.

"That's it," Owl said.

They were looking at a metal structure ten miles from the north shore of the island. Alex noticed a flat platform on the left-hand side. "They even left us a place to land."

"Apparently, helicopters were the primary transportation to and from these oil rigs," Owl said.

Alex shifted her gaze toward the western horizon. "We've got, what, twenty minutes until sundown? We'll have to clear it fast."

"I doubt there's many Ferals on this thing. I would think any that were here would have jumped ship and headed for shore looking for food a long time ago."

"Maybe. But we're not going to risk it. The team's freaked out enough already."

Owl reached up and flipped a switch on the control panel, and the ship hovered in place just above the oil rig. Then she pressed the yoke and the ship gently began to descend. "Can you blame them? We're about to do the one thing we've been taught since day one of GMT training would mean certain death. We're spending the night on the surface."

Once the ship touched down, Alex headed to main cabin to check on the rest of the team.

The cabin was oddly quiet. Even Patrick and Ed weren't making their usual jokes. A sense of dread hung over the fuselage. CB had a particularly dark expression on his face. Alex walked over and put a hand on his arm.

"You okay, CB?"

He nodded. "It's just, not counting the couple nights I've spent in Agartha, the last night I was on the surface after sunset, I lost team members."

An image flashed in Alex's mind: Drew being pulled into a snowbank and torn to shreds. She shuddered. She turned to the rest of the team. "We don't have a lot of time, so let's make this fast. Owl's uploaded a copy of the oil rig's schematic to your tablets. We're going to spilt into two teams and search this place. It'll be Patrick, CB and Chuck. Ed, you're with me. Owl's going to prepare the ship for the night."

"What about me?" Brian asked. A bit of sweat stood on his brow, and he looked even paler than usual. Spending the night on the surface was scary enough for experienced GMT soldiers. For someone who'd never set foot on the ground until a few hours ago, it had to be terrifying.

"You keep working on decrypting those hard drives. Let's go, team."

It only took ten minutes to give the rig a thorough search. They checked every room, every storage area, every closet, every deck. There wasn't a corner where they didn't shine a light. In the end, Owl's suspicion proved correct. If vampires had ever been here, they'd abandoned the rig at some point. Still, Alex would sleep better knowing they'd checked. Not well, but better.

They reconvened at the ship and found Owl and Brian in the main cabin.

"We good?" Owl asked.

"Clear as my brother's social calendar," Patrick said. "This place is pretty sweet. I'm starting to think we could stay here long term. Make it our base of operations."

"Not a good idea," Alex said. "Our scent is eventually going to draw Ferals."

Patrick scoffed. "We're ten miles from the island. You're telling me they can smell something ten miles away?"

"Bears can," Brian said, without looking up.

Patrick turned toward him, surprised. "What's that have to do with anything?"

Brian continued typing on his tablet as he spoke. "We don't have any good data on how far vampires can smell. I studied the issue a few years back, trying to see if there was a way we could mask our scent from them. Prior to the vampires, bears were the mammal with the best sense of smell, so I used that as my baseline for what's physically possible. To be safe, I assumed the Ferals can smell at least as far as a bear."

"And how far is that?" CB asked.

"Black bears have been known to head on a direct line for food up to twenty miles away. Grizzlies could smell an elk carcass submerged at the bottom of a lake."

Ed raised an eyebrow. "Twenty miles? I suddenly feel less comfortable."

"If you think that's impressive, wait until you hear about polar bears," Brian said. "They've been observed heading straight for food up to forty miles away. And they can smell food through three feet of solid ice."

Owl clapped Brian on the shoulder. "Man, those are some good facts. I'm impressed."

Patrick looked at Alex. "You're sure we can't just go back to *New Haven*?"

"Not unless you want to spend the next few years locked up," Alex said. "We've done our best to keep ourselves safe, but this is a good reminder that we can't get too comfortable. We'll take turns sleeping, half of us awake at all times. We'll watch the monitors for any movement outside."

"Staying awake isn't going to be a problem," Chuck said. "I don't think I could sleep down here if you paid me to."

"I hear you, but do your best," CB said. "I have a feeling opportunities to rest are going to be few and far between in the coming days."

As CHUCK HAD PREDICTED, none of the GMT got much sleep that night. While they didn't end up seeing any Ferals, there were enough noises and splashes in the water to keep anyone from resting easy. Add to that the fact that the cargo hold wasn't exactly designed for sleeping, and it made for a stressful, uncomfortable night for everyone.

At least they had food. While Alex had been swallowing her pride and apologizing to Ambassador McCready, Owl had loaded the ship with two weeks' worth of rations and supplies. The food was a small comfort, but at least it would keep their energy up a little.

Alex didn't think she'd ever been so happy to see the sunrise.

"Can we get the hell off of this metal piece of shit now?" Patrick asked.

"Yes, please," Alex said. "It's time to go to work."

Owl wasted no time in prepping the ship and getting them off the oil rig.

"We'll have to use a different rig tonight," CB said. "We can't risk our scent attracting Ferals. For all we know, there's a horde walking along the bottom of the ocean headed for the rig right now."

"Agreed," Alex said. "But if we find what we're looking for in that command center, maybe we won't have to worry about it."

They landed outside the command center less than an hour after sunrise. Alex decided to play it safe and wait on the ship for another half hour, wanting to make sure the sun was high enough in the sky to provide them safety even with the thick vegetation. She also used the time to plan with her team.

"Let me guess," Owl said. "Brian and I are stuck back on the ship."

Alex gave her a smile. "Sorry, Owl. We need to make sure the ship is fully charged and ready to go. If anything happens to it or if it runs out of power, we're dead. That means we need you back here manning solar panels and monitoring the power levels. Same goes for you, Brian. I need you working decrypting the drives."

"You don't have to convince me," he said. "I'll take encrypted drives over creepy tunnels any day."

"The rest of you, let's get ready to move out."

When the team reached the tunnel, Alex let out a quiet curse. It was clear from the tracks through the inky-black Feral blood on the ground that a large number of the creatures had traipsed through it during the night.

"Damn it all to hell," Alex muttered. "Our scent attracted them. If I'd been patient instead of racing in here last night, we'd have a much easier job ahead of us today."

"Ha," Chuck said, raising his rifle. "You think any of us joined the GMT for easy?"

"Nothing we can do about it now," Ed said. "Like the bard says, 'What's past is prologue.'"

"The bard?" Patrick said.

"Point is, we need to get this done today," CB said. "Each time we come back here, we're leaving a stronger scent. There will be even more Ferals tomorrow."

The team made their way through the tunnel, moving quickly onto the next room. When they entered, Alex saw a huddled form in the corner.

"I got this," she said softly to the team. Then she drew her sword. She approached carefully, making sure the floor was clear of any debris that might make a noise under her feet. As she stepped into range, she drew a deep breath and the stench of decay filled her mouth. She pushed back the urge to be sick and raised her sword. It came down in a flash, and the Feral's head slowly slid off its body, falling to the floor.

To Alex's surprise, there were no other Ferals in that room. Or the next one. As they quickly discovered, this complex was much bigger than the last bunker they'd encountered. It seemed that every time they stepped out of a room, they discovered another hall with more rooms branching off of it. The team moved slowly, marking each wall as they passed, so that they could easily find their way out.

Alex felt a twinge of regret at some of the items they passed. Filing cabinets. Power supplies. Work stations. They could probably spend a week digging through all the stuff down here. But they didn't have a week. They had today. And Brian had made it clear what they needed to look for: a server room. The hard drives should be in a central location.

They needed to find it, get the hard drives, and get out. The rest was distraction.

As they passed a workstation, Chuck stopped and squinted down at something. "Guys, check this out. Someone else has been here."

Alex turned and saw what he meant. The hard drive had been ripped out of the computer.

"Damn it," CB said.

"Think it was the recon team?" Ed asked.

"Impossible to say," Alex answered. "For all we know they might have been here weeks ago."

"Or last night," Chuck said.

"Yeah." Alex didn't want to think about that now. They had a job to do. They wouldn't know if they'd missed their window until they found the server room.

Twenty minutes later, they finally found it. The room was at the end of a long tunnel in the deepest part of the facility. Rows of cabinets filled the room, each cabinet containing drives and servers.

Alex held her breath as she checked the first one they came to. Much to her relief, it appeared to be intact. "All right, let's work fast and get out of here. We want every drive in this room. And stay frosty. Just because we haven't seen many Ferals yet doesn't mean they aren't here. Let's see if we can get through this without any more trouble."

The team worked quickly and silently, loading their packs with the drives. Alex could tell from the uneasy expressions on their faces that they were feeling as nervous about this place as she was. All those tracks in the tunnel, and they'd only encountered one Feral. They hadn't come close to checking all the rooms, but it still felt like something wasn't right.

A thin layer of sweat covered her brow by the time they

were finished. She took a final walk through the room and then hoisted her pack onto her shoulders. "Okay, we've got what we need. Let's get out of here."

She turned to go, but a light from outside the room shined in her eyes, momentarily blinding her. A dark figure held the flashlight in his hand.

"Thanks for getting those drives, Alex," Jaden said. "We'll take them from here."

22

ALEX BLINKED HARD, clearing her vision. Jaden and four other vampires stood twenty feet down the hallway. In the glow of her headlamp, she recognized the other four vampires: Janet, Stanley, Griffin, and Daniel, all members of the recon team.

She drew both her pistols, keeping them ready but at her sides for the moment. "Isn't it past your bedtime? Why don't you get some sleep, and we'll talk about this later?"

Jaden smiled, though it looked a little strained. Whether that was because of daysickness or the discomfort of the situation, Alex did not know. "It's over, Alex. I knew you were suspicious of me, but I didn't think you'd go rogue. Going against the Council's orders? Not smart."

"I never claimed to be."

"Look, this doesn't need to be difficult. Leave the drives with me and go. Turn yourself in to the City Council. Leave Resettlement to my vampires, and maybe you'll actually get to live down here someday."

Alex raised her pistols. As she did, she felt something change. She'd pointed her guns at Jaden; there was no going back. Her course was set. "The drives stay with us. I suggest you step out of our way."

Jaden sighed. "I appreciate your iron will, but please see the reality of your situation. We have you cornered. I don't want to hurt you, Alex, but we will subdue you if necessary.

"I take it you followed us here?" Alex dropped her left hand and made a quick double swiping motion as she talked. She silently prayed Chuck had seen the hand signal.

Jaden's face was unreadable. "We followed your scent last night. I was worried you'd cleared out the drives, but once I saw you hadn't, I knew you'd be back. Kudos on finding this place, by the way. You beat us here, and we've been looking for some time."

"We humans can surprise you every once in a while."

A shadow passed over Jaden's face. "I would have loved to work with you on this, Alex, but I think we no longer share the trust such a project would require."

"You think right." Both her guns were trained on Jaden now. "Last chance, old man. You really don't want to test us."

Behind Jaden, two of the vampires chuckled.

Jaden sighed again. He turned and spoke over his shoulder. "Try not to hurt them. We just need them subdued so we can take the drives."

And suddenly, the four other vampires were in motion. They raced past Jaden, moving almost too quickly for the human eye to follow.

Ed and Patrick fired simultaneously, but the vampires they were aiming for leaped out of the way, each reaching an opposite side of the tunnel's ceiling and diving toward one of the two brothers. The gunfire echoed loudly down the hall.

Somewhere in the back of Alex's mind, she realized that

any Ferals hiding in the facility would be awake and probably headed toward them.

"Now, Chuck!" she shouted.

There was a loud click as Chuck activated his daylight.

A<small>LEX</small> <small>SAW</small> the absolute terror in the vampires' eyes as the artificial daylight hit them. All four of them dropped to the ground, frantically covering their faces with their jackets. Thin tendrils of smoke rose off of Griffin and Daniel.

"No kill shots," Alex shouted as she took aim at Stanley. She fired four shots, putting two rounds through each of his kneecaps. Vampire healing was damn impressive, but she was sure that would slow him down for at least the duration of the fight.

CB fired, hitting Janet just above the knee. Before he could fire again, a throwing knife spun through the air past him, embedding itself in Chuck's daylight and knocking it out of his hands.

Alex looked up just in time to see Jaden charging, following the path of the knife he'd just thrown.

With the daylight destroyed, Griffin was the first to leap to his feet. He lunged at Ed, grabbing the barrel of his gun. Ed fired, but Griffin pushed the barrel as he did, and the shot went wide to the left, missing Chuck's head by inches.

Griffin hissed, drawing back his fist and aiming it at Ed's face. But CB fired again. This time his aim was true, and his bullet found Griffin's elbow. The vampire screamed and his arm feel limp at his side.

Daniel had found his feet as well, and he dove at Patrick, knocking the gun from his hand and driving his shoulder into Patrick's stomach. Patrick crumbled to the ground, gasping for air. Apparently satisfied that Patrick was subdued, Daniel tuned to Ed and CB.

But Alex had him in her sights. She squeezed the trigger and—

Before she fired, the gun was knocked from her hand. Jaden stood in front of her, his dark eyes alive with resolve.

Alex almost smiled at the poor position he'd put himself in. She pointed her other pistol at his right knee and squeezed the trigger.

His leg moved so fast that it seemed to flicker, and Alex's mouth dropped open. Somehow, impossibly, Jaden had dodged the point-blank shot.

Daniel turned toward CB, his face a mask of rage. But before he could attack, Ed reached out and grabbed him, gripping him by the shirt and shoving him into Stanley. As Daniel stumbled backward over his fallen teammate, Ed helped his brother to his feet.

A series of howls came from a distant part of the facility.

Jaden grabbed Alex's wrist and pulled her close, wrapping an arm around her body. As he did, Alex grabbed his forearm, pressed her pistol up against it, and fired, putting a bullet through his wrist.

Jaden grunted in pain, but he didn't fall back.

Alex took aim again, this time at his shoulder.

Before she could fire, Jaden's leg shot out, catching her in the chest with a solid kick, lifting her off her feet. She flew backward and hit the wall hard. Her head slammed against the concrete, and her jaw clamped shut, causing her to bite the inside of her cheek. She cried out in pain as blood began to fill her mouth.

She drew in a deep breath through her nose, centering herself, and she pushed off the wall and back toward Jaden.

Out of the corner of her eye, she saw Chuck reach into

Patrick's pack and pull something out. Then he sprinted down the hall, dodging the fallen and the fighting. When he was past the vampires, he activated Patrick's daylight

The vampires reeled, stumbling away from the light, covering themselves as quickly was possible.

"Let's move!" Alex shouted. "Head for the exit."

The team grabbed their fallen weapons. Patrick, still gasping for air, threw one arm over CB's shoulder and another over Ed's. Together, the two men helped him down the tunnel.

The GMT raced down the winding hallways of the facility, their hard-drive-filled packs hanging from their shoulders. Chuck was in the rear, the daylight aimed behind them. Alex thanked her lucky stars that they'd taken the time to mark the walls along their route. It would have been far too easy to get lost down here, especially during their panicked retreat.

From somewhere in the distance, they heard more howls. And from behind them, the sound of padding feet as the vampires gave chase.

"Jaden," one of the vampires called. "Can we use deadly force now?"

There was a long pause before he answered.

"That's not necessary. Just don't let them get outside with those drives."

Blood was still filling Alex's mouth, but this time she didn't swallow it. She just held it as she kept running.

"Alex," Chuck said. "They're right behind us."

"Up ahead!" Ed shouted.

Alex looked and saw two Ferals racing down the hall toward them. She raised her pistol and fired, putting a bullet through one creature's head even as Ed shot the other. Ed's aim must have been thrown off from the way his was supporting his brother though, because the round went through the creature's shoulder. It was enough to slow it down, but not enough to stop it.

It had almost reached them before CB fired, dropping it with a shot to the head.

Alex stepped over the Feral's body and cursed at what she saw ahead. They were approaching a large room with six doors, each leading to another hall. Even from where she was, she could see dozens of Ferals pouring into the room from every direction.

"We're not going to make it!" Patrick said with a gasp.

Alex disagreed, but it was tough to relay the sentiment with a mouthful of blood. She reached back into her pack and pulled out her daylight.

As they entered the room, she raised her light and switched it on. The smell of burnt flesh filled the air, and the Ferals in front of them scattered, giving the GMT enough space to sprint through the room.

"They're almost on us!" Chuck shouted.

Alex fell back, letting her team move past her out of the room and into the hallway beyond. She turned the daylight, shining it toward the center of the room.

And suddenly, Jaden was standing in front of her. He kicked the daylight from her hand, sending it skidding across the floor.

It was all Alex could do not to smile. Instead, she spit, splattering Jaden's chest with blood and saliva. Then she turned and sprinted, knowing her life depended on it.

Behind her, she heard the Ferals screaming and howling, worked into a frenzy by the smell of fresh blood. They swarmed Jaden. The last thing Alex saw before she ran out of the room was the flash of his sword as he defended himself from the sudden onslaught.

As they reached the exit, Alex glanced back. She heard the sounds of battle in the distance, and neither Feral nor vampire appeared to be pursuing them anymore. They were too busy fighting each other.

"What just happened?" Ed asked as they stepped into the sunlight.

"I bit my cheek during the fight," Alex said. "Then I spit a mouthful of blood at Jaden."

"Gross," Chuck said.

"Not if you're a Feral. They seemed very interested in the blood on Jaden's chest."

Patrick took his arms off of CB and Ed, finally able to walk on his own. "I can't believe it. We survived a fight with Jaden."

"Barely," Alex said. "Let's just hope these drives are worth it."

"So what now?" CB asked. "Find another oil rig?"

Alex thought a moment. "Not yet. We know where Jaden is, so we need to take advantage of where he's not. This could be our last opportunity to talk to Firefly."

"Are you sure this is a good idea?" CB asked quietly, leaning close to Alex as the away ship touched down outside Firefly's location. "Are we sure where Firefly's loyalties lie? If he's with Jaden on this, walking into a building full of his vampires might not be a good idea."

Alex unstrapped her harness. "I know Firefly's let us down in the past, but he's changed. We're alone down here, CB. We need help, and I think he'll give it to us." She stood up and addressed the team. "Owl, stay ready for takeoff.

Brian, keep working on those drives. The rest of you, hang back. I won't be long."

"Hold up," Chuck said. "You're going in alone?"

"No way," Ed growled. "That ain't happening."

"I appreciate the concern, but I didn't ask for a vote." Alex started toward the back of the ship. "Look, there's over a hundred vampires in that building. I trust Firefly, but there's no use risking more than one of us."

"Can't you send Chuck?" Patrick asked.

"I should be back in fifteen minutes. If I'm not, get the hell out of here."

Owl stepped into the cabin. "Alex, are you sure—"

"This one's not open for discussion," she snapped. Her voice softened. "We don't have a lot of time. I'll see you in a few minutes." With that, she opened the cargo doors.

The building where they'd picked up Firefly's tracker was some kind of old office building. Based on the tracker location on her tablet, it looked like Firefly was on the lower level. She walked into the building and immediately felt a chill, though she didn't know if it was from nerves or it the air was actually cooler in there.

She made her way to Firefly's approximate location based on the tracker and found an empty hall with dozens of rooms off it. "Firefly! It's Alex. Are you here?"

For a few moments, there was no reply. Alex stood, waiting, trying to decide her next move. As much as she trusted Firefly, she wasn't about to go room to room waking vampires until she found him. It would only take one vamp waking up cranky to get her throat ripped out.

"Firefly!"

"I'm here." The voice came from a dark figure standing in a doorway halfway down the hall. "Come, we're back here."

Alex walked toward him, every step echoing loudly in the hallway. She resisted the urge to put her hand on her sword. If this went badly, it would do so very quickly. There would be no use fighting. She stepped into the shadows of an old office and saw Firefly and about twenty other vampires, all still shaking off the grip of sleep. And among them was Helen.

Alex stopped when she saw the female vampire.

"Where's the rest of your team?" Helen asked. Her voice was hard as stone.

Alex ignored the question. "Firefly, I'm not sure what Jaden has told you, but—"

"Just the usual," Firefly said with a smile. "The GMT's gone rogue. Acting recklessly. Putting the mission at risk. You know, the stuff Fleming used to say basically every meeting." He paused. "He was also clear on what we should do if you showed up. We're not supposed to hurt you unless we have to. We're to hold you here until he gets back. He wants to talk to you."

"He and I already talked this morning." Alex glanced at Helen and saw she had her hand on her sword. "So, what happens now?"

Helen drew her sword. "I think you know."

Firefly's eyes were fixed on Alex. "Get her."

Alex tensed as five of Firefly's vampires sprang into motion. But they didn't attack Alex. Instead, they went for Helen.

Hector grabbed one of Helen's arms while Mario grabbed the other, wrestling her sword from her hand. Another vampire wrapped up Helen's legs in his arms, tackling her to the ground. Two other vampires holding chains fell on Helen, pinning her arms behind her back and securing them.

"Traitors!" Helen shouted. "You've betrayed your kind for this... this human!" She spat the words out as if they were bile.

Hector wrapped another chain around Helen's feet, locking her in place. "One thing you gotta understand, lady. We were *New Haven* folk long before we were vampires."

"You're fools!" Helen shouted. "Jaden will make you pay! You haven't seen what he does to his enemies. He doesn't forget!"

Firefly gave her a long, pitying look. "Get her out of here."

It took four vampires to subdue her chained, wriggling form, but they eventually managed to carry her out of the office.

When she was gone, Firefly finally smiled. "That felt good. How's the rest of the team?"

"They're fine," Alex said. "We ran into Jaden this morning and things... They didn't go well. You know how I tend to escalate situations."

"Yes, I do."

"My streak is alive and well. I'm pretty sure he's not going want to have a friendly chat, next time he sees me."

Firefly stared toward the empty hallway. "No. I imagine not."

Alex leaned against an old desk and looked Firefly in the eyes. "We could really use your help here. If we want to find the weapon before he does, we need someone to run interference."

"What are you thinking?"

Alex hesitated a moment. "Firefly, you need to really think about this before you agree to help. Jaden held back this morning, but I don't think that'll be the case next time around."

"We've got him outnumbered about two hundred to five."

"Maybe so, but there are other factors to consider. If you do this, you'll seriously piss off both *New Haven* and Agartha. The people who supply you with blood. If they cut you off—"

"Yeah," Firefly said flatly. "That had crossed my mind." He paused a moment. "When I first got to Agartha, after Mark and Aaron died, Jaden told me some things about the past. He said that he and his vampires worked closely with the humans during the first and second waves, but by the third wave there were some in the human government who stopped trusting him. They hid information. Even though he was involved in the initial design of *New* Haven, they hid the last stages of the program from him and launched the ship without his knowledge."

Alex tiled her head. "What's that have to do with this?"

"This weapon, I think it was one of the things they hid from him. He took it very personally. He believes that if the humans would have shared information with him, he could have ended the war before humanity fell." He paused a moment. "Look, Jaden's a good man. A great man, even. He has the best interests of humanity at heart. I really believe that. But he's been a vampire for so long that part of him thinks he's above us. Not in a Helen kind of way. More like, he underestimates us and thinks we need him to decide what's best for us."

"Yeah, I kinda got that idea," Alex said dryly.

"He's been working behind the scenes for centuries, pulling strings, manipulating events for the good of humanity. But here's the thing. He shouldn't get to decide what's best for humanity. Humanity's future is its own." He looked Alex square in the eye. "If you find that weapon, you're the one who has to decide whether to finish it. You and the other humans. Jaden doesn't get a say in that. Neither do I. We're just dead things, who've forgotten how to die."

"Firefly, you're not—"

He held up a hand. "I'm not feeling sorry for myself here. I'm just saying, I have your back. I believe the GMT is going to pull this off. But if you don't, I won't go Feral. I'll find a quiet place and watch one last sunrise."

Alex swallowed hard, feeling the full weight of what was at stake here, not just for her and the GMT, but for every human and every vampire.

Firefly gave her a little smile. "So, what do you need us to do?"

23

OWL SET the ship down gently on the oil rig an hour before sunset. As they landed, Alex surveyed her team.

Chuck was nodding off. His head drooped as his eyes slowly closed. Then, as his chin touched his chest, he snapped awake and raised his head, and the cycle began again.

Patrick stared into the distance, holding one hand over his stomach where the vampire had hit him. Owl had checked him out and said there wasn't any internal damage —though a massive bruise was already starting to form— but it was clear that his confidence was shaken.

Brian frantically typed on his tablet, as he'd been doing for most of the last thirty-six hours. Every once in a while he glanced up and Alex saw the fear in his eyes. The poor guy was clearly terrified at the thought of another night on the surface.

In all, they looked about how Alex felt: tired and discouraged. Yes, they had beaten Jaden earlier, but that brief encounter had illustrated how daunting their task was.

If Jaden and his team stopped holding back, the GMT was in trouble.

"All right, we've got one more job before we can rest," Alex told them. "Same as last night. Let's clear this rig. I know you're tired, but focus up. If we miss one Feral, none of us makes it through to morning."

As they stepped off the ship, Alex looked around the rig. It looked decidedly less stable than the one they'd stayed on the previous night. Up ahead, she spotted the crane laying on deck, broken and covered in rust.

"We're sure this thing won't fall into the sea tonight?" Ed asked.

CB grinned. "It's stood this long. That would be bad luck, indeed, if it crapped out now."

They split into two teams. Alex, Chuck, and Owl took the main level while CB, Patrick and Ed cleared level two.

They moved from room to room, the rig creaking and groaning with the rise and fall of the ocean around it. Because she was so tired, Alex went extra slowly, making sure her drooping eyes didn't miss a single locker or dark corner. To their surprise, they found one hunched form huddled in a room in the interior of the rig. Owl was the first to respond, shooting the creature in the head before it knew they were there.

Alex nodded at Owl, impressed. "I forgot how quick you were with that thing. I should send you into the field more often."

"Agreed," Owl said with a smile.

They waited two minutes to see if the gunfire would draw any Ferals out of hiding. When none came, they resumed their search.

When they'd finished, they reconvened with the rest of the team on the deck. To the west, the sun hung low, it's edge just kissing the horizon. The team watched in silence, and for a moment, the world seemed still.

Chuck nodded at something on the horizon. Another oil rig. "Let's hope we're not close enough for any Ferals on that one to smell us."

Patrick glowered at him. "Thanks for ruining the moment. There goes any hope I had of sleeping tonight."

When they climbed back onto the ship, they saw Brian sitting cross legged on the floor of the hold, three tablets in front of him, his eyes and fingers furiously jumping between them.

Alex cleared her throat, and Brian's head jerked up, his eyes wide.

"Don't do that," he said. "I'm freaked out enough already."

"Sorry, I'll try not to be so stealthy next time." She nodded toward the tablets. "What have you found?"

His lips curled upward in a wide smile. "A lot, actually. One of the drives you brought back today has the encryption keys for the other bunkers."

Alex's eyebrows shot up. "So, we're in?"

"We're in." His smile faded a bit. "The problem is sifting through all the data. Now I have the drives from the first bunker *and* the new drives to dig through. For all I know, we've got the location of the other bunkers, maybe the formula for the virus itself. Who knows? The problem is that it's going to take forever to find it."

CB stepped up next to Alex and crossed his arms. "Owl, how many tablets do we have?"

"Five total," she answered.

"Okay, that means two people can sleep at a time. The rest should be helping Brian. We'll switch out every two hours, that way everyone can get at least a little rest before morning."

"Sounds like a plan," Alex said.

Chuck sat down next to Brian and picked up a tablet. Then he looked at Alex. "Say we do find the next bunker. Then what?"

Her brow furrowed. "What do you mean? We search it. We get the next piece of the puzzle."

"And if Jaden's there with his vampires?"

Patrick and Ed had joined them now. The whole team was crowded into the hold.

"Look, I'm not trying to be the naysayer guy," Chuck continued, "but, if it comes down to it, how the hell are we going to make a stand against centuries old, superhuman warriors? They'll be ready for the daylights next time."

A heavy silence fell over the ship. Alex scanned the others' faces, and she knew that even though they weren't saying it, at least some of them felt the same way.

"You're right," Alex said. "They have superhuman powers. You know what else they have? Knees. Shoot them in the knees and they can't stand."

"Come on, Alex," Chuck said. "How lucky are we gonna have to be to—"

"I'm not finished," Alex said flatly. "They have shoulders. Shoot them in the shoulders, they can't lift their arms."

"Again, you're counting on super accurate shots. The way they move, that's a long bet."

"That's not our biggest advantage." An image flashed in Alex's mind: Stanley and Griffin's panicked faces when they saw the daylights. "Our biggest advantage is that they're scared to die."

"Aren't we all?" Ed asked.

"We're GMT. We basically signed up for short lifespans.

And if we somehow survive our tour of duty, we've got, what, eighty years total? Not them. If they don't die in battle, they have forever. They know this. You can see it in their eyes. Most of them have spent centuries avoiding death. We're going to show them what they've been missing." She grabbed a tablet off the seat. "But first, we need to find those other bunkers."

———

WHEN NIGHT FELL, Firefly awoke with a start and headed straight for the office where they were holding Helen. His sleep had been brief and fitful, but he'd forced himself to take it. He knew he'd need his energy for the night ahead.

Helen sat on the floor of the office, chains around her arms and legs. Four vampires stood around her, watching her every move.

She glared at Firefly as he entered. "Release me, and I'll ask that your life be spared."

Firefly ignored the comment and addressed her guards. "Thank you for staying up with her. I know it was painful for you."

"Her comments didn't make it any more pleasant," the vampire named Lee said.

"I can imagine." Firefly turned to Helen. "If I released you, you'd have a sword in my back in seconds."

Helen pressed her lips together and stared at him for a moment. "Perhaps. But it's nothing compared with what Jaden will do. He doesn't like traitors. Not at all."

"Traitors, huh? Some might say Jaden betrayed all of us. Alex told me about the virus. Jaden lied when he sent us on this mission, and he had you and your little recon team lie to us about what you were doing here. Maybe if he'd been straight with us from the start, it wouldn't have come to this."

Helen let out a bitter laugh. "You think he owes you anything? Please. Jaden told you what you need to know." She paused a moment. "It's always been a tradeoff. How do you think we lived in the days before blood banks and IV lines? We drank straight from the source, and their blood pumped onto our mouths, feeding us, sustaining us. We killed hundreds of humans to live. But in return, we were humanity's protectors, defending them from the things they were too weak or short-sighted to handle on their own."

Firefly took a step close, his eyes burning with anger. "Quit trying to sell me this *protector* shit. Jaden told me about the wars after the infestation. Don't pretend to be the hero. Vampires destroyed humanity. They turned them into the mindless things wandering the Earth now."

Helen shook her head. "You think you know so much. The so-called vampire who caused the infestation was a newborn. Days after her transformation, she began her twisted plan. We have rules, a system to make sure the price humanity pays for our protection isn't too high. But she didn't follow the rules. She thought she knew better than the rest of us." She looked Firefly up and down. "Reminds me of someone else I know."

"We're done here." Firefly looked at her guards. "Don't let her get in your heads. Get ready to move her."

Helen tilted her head in surprise. "Where are you taking me?"

"We're going to hunt down your boss. I can't leave you unattended, so it looks like you're coming with us."

Firefly gathered his commanders and told them to prepare their teams for travel. When they were ready to leave, Mario picked up Helen, carrying her over his shoulder, her arms and legs still bound with chains. The team moved out of urban area where they'd spent the day, and toward the more mountainous region to the west. The further they traveled, the more Ferals they encountered. Strangely, the Ferals paid Firefly and his troops almost no mind. They traveled in the same direction as Firefly's troops, occasionally sniffing the air as they made their way to the command center, the scent of humans who visited the spot two days in a row drawing them.

By the time Firefly and his soldiers arrived at the command center, there were hundreds of Ferals gathered around the entrance.

"Well, we did say we wanted to find more Ferals," Hector said.

"Yeah, I guess we found them," Firefly replied.

He gathered his squad of twenty and told the rest to wait outside, doing their best not to cause any conflicts with the Ferals. Then he and his team made their way into the command center.

They paused at the entrance to the tunnel. Hector glanced nervously at Firefly. "Are you sure about this, Captain? If one Feral gets jumpy, we're dead."

"I'm sure," Firefly said. Then he stepped forward, leading his team into the mouth of the tunnel.

The Ferals were packed so tightly, it was almost as if they were a single, wriggling mass. Waves of revulsion washed over Firefly as he pressed his way through them. Their stink filled his nose, and he felt the corrupt odor crawling down his throat. He felt their collective mental connection thrumming in his core, more powerfully than he'd ever felt it before. Hector was right; these Ferals were agitated, and it wouldn't take much to push one over the edge. And a single attack would be like a match in a powder keg. Firefly and his squad wouldn't stand a chance.

Still, he pressed forward. As sickening as their powerful scent was, their physical touch was even worse. Their leathery skin brushed against him with every step, and it never failed to make his skin crawl.

As revolting and terrifying as the experience was, it passed quickly. The Ferals were so enthralled with the strong human scents that they paid no mind to their fellow dead things.

Firefly and his squad made their way out of the tunnel and into the first large room. While there were a dozen or so Ferals milling about, the room was much less densely packed than the tunnel had been. Firefly wondered if he'd find Jaden's body here. From the way Alex had described it, the vampires had been woefully outnumbered. If he did find the body he wondered how he'd feel about it.

But the only corpses he found were those of Ferals. It was clear there'd been a battle here. Severed heads, limbs, and fallen bodies with horrific sword wounds were littered across the floor.

Firefly pressed on, moving past the Ferals sniffing the air, searching futilely for the humans Firefly knew were no longer there. He searched for another twenty minutes, though he was already certain Jaden's team was gone. Then, much to his team's relief, he told them it was time to go.

He and his team cautiously emerged from the bunker, working their way through the ever-growing horde of Ferals. The creatures were still ignoring them, enraptured by the lingering human scent. But Firefly knew that wouldn't last forever. They would eventually grow frustrated with their ability to smell their prey and their inability to find them.

He found Mario waiting at the head of his army of vampires outside.

"She escaped," he said with no preamble.

Firefly's face was blank. He looked at the chains on the ground, slick with black vampire blood. "Did she kill anyone?"

Mario shook his head. "No one's died, at least not yet. But she messed up Lee and Peter pretty badly. I think they will recover, but I'm still new to vampire healing."

"She's not in the greatest shape herself," another vampire added. "She broke her own arm and ripped half the flesh off her hand getting out of the chains."

Firefly grimaced. "Make sure Lee and Peter are tended to. When did she escape?"

"About fifteen minutes ago," Mario said.

"Let's hope this works," Firefly said, pulling a tablet out of his pack. "I put my tracker on her when she was chained. Let's give her another five minutes. I don't want her to hear us following her. Hopefully, she'll lead us right to Jaden."

Mario stared at him blankly, his mouth open. "You wanted her to escape? Why didn't you tell us?"

"I couldn't risk it. She had to believe that the escape was real. If she suspected something she would have checked for a tracker or she may not have gone to Jaden."

Mario looked at him for a long moment before speaking again. "I had to pull a sword out of Pete's neck. I think he might have liked to know the plan ahead of time."

"I took a risk," Firefly said. His eyes were hard. "I didn't think Helen would kill a vampire. She practically thinks we're holy creatures. But make no mistake, what we're doing now is dangerous, and it'll be even more dangerous if we find Jaden. We have to play like we mean it if we want to have a chance of surviving this."

Five minutes later, Firefly checked Helen's location on his tablet. She was moving quickly through the jungle and seemed to be heading toward the coast. As he watched, she doubled back, crossing a stream. Firefly smiled. She was clearly trying to cover her tracks, a good sign that she didn't suspect they were tracking her electronically.

The vampire army moved out, traveling much slower than their top speed in order to keep a safe distance between them and their prey.

A FEW HOURS into the research, Brian was still working in a frenzy, but some of the others were slowing down. Alex couldn't much blame them. There was so much information to go through, and they had so little idea what exactly they were looking for. Something might seem promising at first, but after spending ten minutes looking into it and asking Brian what he thought, it would turn out to be worthless.

Still, they'd made some very interesting discoveries. CB had found coordinates for all four Project White Horse bunkers, which had at first seemed like the discovery they'd been waiting for. But then they'd noticed the coordinates didn't match the locations of the two bunkers they'd already found, and they'd realized it must be written in some kind of code. CB had been trying to crack the code ever since.

Alex glanced at Ed and saw he had a wide, childish smile on his face. She was about to ask him why when she noticed Patrick softly snoring, his tablet still on his lap and his head down on his chest. Ed gleefully pulled back his hand and let it fly, smacking his brother square in the face.

Patrick's eyes shot open and he leapt to his feet, his hand going for his side arm as he scanned the area for danger.

Then his gaze landed on his brother who was now laughing hysterically.

"What the hell!" Patrick shouted as he touched the red mark on his cheek.

Ed held up his hands and feigned a look of innocence. "Hey, I'm just trying to help you stay awake. You should be thanking me."

"I'm mighty happy to repay you." He drew his fist back.

"That's enough, boys," Alex said. "Patrick, try to stay awake. Ed, don't hit your brother."

"And you said you weren't motherhood material," CB said, with a grin.

Alex turned to Brian. "How are things coming on your end?"

He answered without looking up. "You know, I think I'm actually getting somewhere with this information on the virus."

"Yeah?"

"Look." Brian shifted his tablet around so she could see it. Not that the scientific equations meant much to her. "The first bunker we found was so close to completing the virus. It's a brilliant design. It's a hybrid virus, an airborne pathogen that spreads a CRISPR gene editor. In theory, the virus is harmless to humans, but it tricks the vampire's anatomy into attacking itself. Between the information from the two bunkers, I'm well on my way to understanding this thing."

"Can you finish their work?"

Brian hesitated a moment before answering. "Given enough time, sure. Well, time, materials and equipment. But, if I can see the work from the other bunkers, it might help me get there faster."

"If we don't get there fast, we probably won't get there at all."

Brian smiled weakly. "Then I guess I'd better get back to work."

Alex took one more look around at her team, struggling to stay awake. In about forty minutes, it would be time to wake up Chuck and Owl, and Patrick and Alex would take their turns sleeping. Until then, she vowed to herself that she'd set a good example for the team.

She turned back to her tablet and clicked on the next file.

The work was a strange combination of exhilarating and frustrating. There was something inarguably fascinating about digging through files and firsthand accounts from the time before *New Haven*. The information she'd looked through painted a picture of a shell-shocked group of people, struggling desperately to hold onto the world they'd always known, and slowly realizing they were failing. They meticulously documented everything, which made it difficult to separate the valuable from the routine.

Looking at the files in front of her, she saw one called 'The Starling Incident'. Though it wasn't the next one on her list, she couldn't resist clicking on it.

A video file opened and began play. It showed a wide exterior night shot of what appeared to be a military base. Large spotlights illuminated the walls of the compound, and guard towers stood at various points along the wall. Even though the footage quality wasn't the best, Alex spotted snipers in the towers.

A group of soldiers marched into the frame and took up a defensive position. The odd part was, they were facing a wall.

Suddenly an explosion rocked the grounds and pieces of

the wall flew through the air. Two dark figures charged through the newly created hole in the wall.

Alex sat up a bit straighter at the sight of the two figures. Though she couldn't make out enough details to tell if they were male or female, they were definitely moving too fast to be human. These two were vampires.

The two blurred figures attacked, moving from solider to solider. While the creatures were moving too fast to be seen clearly, the carnage they left in their wake was all too visible. Some of the soldiers were stabbed. Some were dismembered. The first man they attacked was still wriggling on the ground, holding a hand over the wound in his chest even as the final one of the thirty soldiers was decapitated. It was over in seconds. The soldiers were dead and the two vampires headed into the base. Nothing moved in the frame except the slowly growing pool of blood under the dead soldiers.

The camera cut to another scene, this one in a barracks. An alarm blared as soldiers scrambled to get dressed, pulling on shirts and pants and stepping into boots. Then the vampires arrived. This time, three blurs shot across the screen, hardly pausing as they slaughtered their prey. The unarmed solders fell to the ground, one by one, as the shapes moved past. One confused, terrified solider tried unsuccessfully to hold his intestines in after one of the blurs sliced him open.

The camera cut again, this time to some sort of medical bay. Four occupied beds filled the majority of the space. Two doctors stood between the beds and a closed steel door. As the doctors looked on in horror, something began pounding on the steel door.

One of the doctors ran to the door and shouted into the intercom. "This is a medical area. We pose no threat to you.

We are civilian doctors. Please leave us to tend to our patients."

The other doctor took a step back. Tears ran down her cheeks as she spoke. "Please, I'm a mother. We're only here to help the sick and wounded. We're not part of this war."

Suddenly, the door was blown off its hinges. A single blurred figure ran inside, making short work of the room's occupants.

Alex could see from the play bar on the video that there were only twenty seconds of footage left as it cut to one last scene.

Two men and one woman stood near a conference table. Alex could just make out a screen on the far wall with names displayed in different colors: "Project White Horse, Project Black Horse, Project Red Horse, and Project Pale Horse."

The man standing near the head of the table held up a file folder, a contented expression on his face. "Listen, there will be plenty of kudos in the coming days and weeks, but I want to make sure you hear it from me first. Thank you. On behalf of the world, thank you."

The woman grinned. "You had a little something to do with it yourself."

An alarm began to blare and all three looked up in surprise.

"What the hell?" the second man said.

The door burst open and two blurs charged into the room. All three humans were dead in mere seconds.

The vampires stopped, and one of their faces was clearly visible as he raised a radio to his mouth. The breath caught in Alex's throat. It was Robert, Jaden's right-hand man.

"Teams, report in," Robert said.

Alex could hear the answers through the radio

"Bravo team, clear."

"Charley team, clear."

"Delta team, clear."

"Echo team, clear."

Then the other vampire took the radio from Robert and turned, exposing his face to the camera.

"Alpha team, clear," Jaden said. "Nice work, everyone. Let's rig the charges quickly. I don't want a trace of this base left standing."

He handed the radio back to Robert and walked over to one of the fallen men, picking up a folder off the floor next to him. He opened it, glanced at the contents, and shook his head. Then he set it down on the table, took a charge of C4 from his pack and set it on top of the folder.

"We're done," Jaden said. "Let's go."

The video stopped, and Alex stared at the black screen, a hand over her mouth.

24

HECTOR GLANCED down at his tablet and then turned to Firefly. "That's it. She's stopped in there."

They'd been trailing Helen for a few hours and had followed her to a town near the coast. For the first time, she'd entered a building, and she didn't appear to be coming out. Firefly knew Jaden and his recon team had to be inside.

He gathered his squad commanders. "Here's the plan. Mario, your team needs to act as snipers. Set them up on the rooftops. I want every exit covered. The rest of us will form a perimeter around the building."

"And what if they come out fighting?" Mario said. "Do we shoot to kill?"

Firefly hesitated a moment before answering. "Only if we have to. There's one hundred sixty of us and six of them. We should be able to do this non-lethally. Avoid killing, especially Jaden. If he dies, there's a good chance *New Haven* and Agartha go to war."

Even as he said it, Firefly knew he'd cross that line if it became necessary. To protect Alex and the GMT, he'd kill every last vampire in that building without thinking twice, consequences be damned.

Within a few minutes, everyone was in place. Firefly stepped to the front of his team and yelled up at the building.

"Good evening, Jaden. I want you to know that the building is completely surrounded."

For a moment, there was silence. Then Jaden spoke from a dark window. "Firefly, I admire your initiative and your loyalty to the GMT, but I suggest you stand down. I still have much to teach you, my brother. There's no reason for you or your troops to die tonight."

Firefly felt an unspoken shift in his soldiers at those words. It was tough to believe that Jaden would try to intimidate him when he was so outnumbered. It was even more unbelievable that it was working.

"I'm in favor of any plan that keeps us all alive," Firefly replied. "How about this? You go back to Agartha. We'll carry on with Resettlement, just as if all this never happened."

"If you can convince Alex and the GMT to head back to *New Haven* first, we have a deal."

Firefly frowned. Jaden was just playing with him, now. "You know Alex won't stop until she finds the information on that weapon. Maybe you should just let her have it."

"I went to great lengths to dispose of it a long time ago. I had hoped that it was gone forever, but here we are." He paused a moment. "I'm afraid this conversation isn't getting us anywhere. I'd like to talk this through with you, but I'm guessing that we lack the necessary trust to make any real progress."

"Yes, trust is a must," Firefly said. "I don't see how you

could expect me to believe anything that you say at this point."

"I think you have potential, Firefly. I will try not to kill you and your soldiers."

"Good. We'll try not to die." Firefly looked at his troops and saw the fear in their eyes. He grabbed his radio and spoke to them.

"Remember, we don't need to beat Jaden. We just need to contain him. As long as we keep him in that building, he can't stop the GMT. I want every inch of that place covered. If anyone or anything tries to leave, shoot it."

The next two hours passed slowly. No one tried to leave the building, and Jaden didn't address them again. Morning approached, and soft light began to glow on the horizon.

Some of Firefly's soldiers were getting antsy, shifting from foot to foot. He felt it to, the nagging urge to move, to get away. The first hints of daysickness hummed through his body like a dull ache, an ache he knew would soon grow much worse.

He picked up his radio and addressed his squad leaders. "Hold your positions as long as you can. Based on where the shadows fall, some of you will be able to hold out longer than others. We'll sleep here for the day. Find cover in the surrounding buildings when you have to. It's looks like we're not going anywhere for a while."

They waited another ten minutes, and the first beams of sunlight began to peek over the horizon. On the buildings around him, Firefly could see the snipers calling it a day and moving into the buildings. Most of the other teams were heading inside too. He decided it was probably time to find cover for himself and his squad.

Just then, the windows above his head shattered, and

pieces of glass rained down on him. Six vampires leapt from a fourth story window high above. They landed spryly, already in motion, and took off running north.

Firefly stared for a moment in disbelief. Then he shouted. "Go! Stop them!" He started running, hoping his soldiers would follow.

Jaden and the vampires led them north through the town, sprinting at full speed, dodging between buildings. Every moment, the sun grew higher.

Firefly's head pounded with mounting daysickness and fear as he ran. Beams of sunlight were peeking between some of the buildings now, leaving the soldiers' path a minefield of deadly shafts of light. Even looking at them made Firefly's eyes burn.

He heard a grunt from behind him and turned to see Caleb stumble and fall toward a shaft of light, only to catch himself at the last moment.

It seemed Jaden's team was having no such trouble. Not only were they faster than Firefly's team, but they seemed to have an uncanny ability to avoid the beams of light. They jumped, ducked, and made hairpin turns, somehow always avoiding the ever-spreading sunlight.

Firefly pressed on, vowing to himself that he wouldn't stop until they did. Or until he'd burned to death, whichever came first. With every step, he became more and more convinced that this was a suicide run. Still, though he didn't trust Jaden's honesty, he did trust the older vampire's wisdom. Jaden had a plan, and it didn't include burning in the sunlight. As long as Firefly followed suite, he and his team would live through this.

Firefly rounded a corner and saw a warehouse up ahead. A large, open lot stood in front of the warehouse. The lot provided no cover; Jaden and his team would need to either to turn left or right.

To Firefly's surprise, they did neither. Impossibly, they began sprinting even faster than before, charging straight into the lot. Smoke rose from their heads and hands as they ran. One of the vampires—it looked like maybe Stanley—let out a scream as his hair caught fire in the sunlight, but still, he kept running.

A moment later, Jaden's team reached the shadow of the warehouse and raced into the building.

"Damn it!" Firefly shouted. His team couldn't make it through that lot, and he knew it. He pointed at the building closest to the lot. "There! We need to get inside."

His squad of twenty made it into the building. From the window, they had a clear view of the warehouse. Not that they'd be watching. Firefly and his team needed sleep, and soon.

He sat down a safe distance from the window, and Hector joined him.

"What we just saw..." Hector said. "What they did... it's impossible. I don't care if there are five of us and twenty of them. I don't think we can beat them."

Firefly felt the heaviness, the sense of failure, behind Hector's words. Yet, they hadn't failed, had they? "Remember what I said earlier? We don't have to beat them. We just have to keep them contained. Let's get some rest. We need to be ready at sundown. Jaden sure as hell will be."

Firefly closed his eyes, hoping he'd done enough to protect the GMT for one more day. Yet, somewhere deep inside, he knew there was a reason why Jaden had headed for that particular building. Even though Firefly had succeeded in keeping Jaden's team contained, he couldn't help feeling like he'd somehow lost a crucial battle.

As FIREFLY and his team hid from the morning sun, Alex and the GMT welcomed its appearance over the ocean. It had been a long, stressful night, filled with terror about both the potential threats outside the ship and the very real danger they'd discovered within. Alex had shown each person the footage of Jaden's massacre. It hadn't been easy to see the mounting horror on their faces as they watched the video, but it had been necessary. Now they all understood the stakes. They'd seen proof that when it came down to it, Jaden would kill without hesitation or remorse. If they wanted to have a chance the next time they faced him, they needed to stop holding back. It was time to go to work.

Thankfully, they now had a pretty good place to start. Working through the night, CB and Owl had managed to crack the code to the bunkers' locations by using the two locations they'd already found. Brian had spent the last few hours figuring out what gaps still existed in the virus research and what information he'd need to have a chance of actually creating it.

They'd also found more information on the footage Alex had watched. Apparently, the military base had been Fort Buchanan, right there on Puerto Rico, the headquarters of the entire Four Horsemen program. After Jaden had destroyed the base, White Horse had gone into hiding, setting up four secret bunkers to attempt to recreate the work Jaden had destroyed.

Alex sat on the floor next to Brian. "So what do you think? Is there a chance the info you need still exists?"

Brian looked his tablet for a long time before answering. "Honestly, this is all a long shot. The one thing we have going for us is that the labs were isolated from each other, to keep the information as safe as possible. The first bunker made great progress on the CRISPR gene editor. The second one was further along in making it airborne, but there are still gaps. Once I have all the puzzle pieces, I'll cobble them together and see what's missing. We might have enough...or it could take me years to fill in the gaps. It's so complex. Every piece of information we pull from a bunker could save me months of research. I'll also need lab equipment we don't have back on *New* Haven. I'm hoping we can grab that today." He paused. "This is all assuming Jaden doesn't get to the bunkers first. We've seen how he deals with people who have information he doesn't like." He suddenly shivered.

"Look," Alex said. "Jaden's an incredible warrior. I can't take him, toe-to-toe. But I've got something he doesn't."

"What's that?" Brian asked.

"You. I'm counting on you, today. We need to get the information from the labs and get the hell out of there. We need to get you safely back to *New Haven*."

CB stepped up beside them. "Remember, today's all we have. We can't go back to the bunkers tomorrow. Not with our scents all over the place. Best case scenario, the labs will be crawling with Ferals. Worst case, Jaden is waiting there to destroy your work and kill every one of us."

"Damn, CB," Patrick said. "That's a little dark."

"Hey, I said it was the worst-case scenario."

"The point is, this needs to happen today," Alex said.

Owl sighed and got to her feet. "Well, it wouldn't be the GMT if the pressure wasn't on. So, which lab do we hit first?"

Alex thought about that a moment. It was a monumental decision that could determine their success or failure. For all they knew, one lab had everything they needed to complete the virus, and the other one had nothing. And yet, they had nothing to go on. It was a blind guess.

CB looked at Alex. "I think we should split up."

Chuck raised an eyebrow. "Is that a good idea? There are only seven of us already. Strength in numbers, right?"

"We might not have that luxury. We've got thirteen hours of daylight. My suggestion is we get Brian set up in the first lab and start pulling out the equipment he needs. One group stays with him, and the other makes a run at the second bunker. What do you think, Alex?"

Alex thought a moment, then nodded. "I don't like splitting up, but it's our best option, here. CB, Chuck and I will stay with Brian."

"That leaves me, Patrick, and Owl," Ed noted.

"Yep. You'll drop us off at the first lab and then head to the second one. Owl, you're the senior officer, so you have field command."

Owl's eyes widened in surprise. Ed and Patrick exchanged a surprised look, too, but no one argued.

"Everyone understand the plan?" Alex asked.

"Got it," Patrick said. "You do some science stuff, and we clear out the other bunker and grab the last set of hard drives."

Alex smiled. "Exactly."

Fifteen minutes later, the away ship landed at the location of the first of the two unexplored labs.

Alex sat in the cockpit with Owl. She took one look at the location and said, "Huh. This is different."

Instead of a small unmarked hatch or a residential home, a large hospital stood at this location. Compared with most of what they'd seen on the island, the exterior of the building looked relatively unmarred by battle scars.

"Let's check it out." Alex started to unbuckle her harness.

"Alex, wait a second." Owl hesitated and looked at Alex, the trepidation clear in her eyes. "I understand why you're sending the Barton brothers to the other location. We need muscle there. And I get that you need me to fly them to the location. But, field commander? Maybe you should send CB along to lead our squad."

"No," Alex said firmly.

"I'm not... I mean, that's never been my—"

"Listen to me, Owl. I know you've been struggling with your identity. Your place on the team. How people see you." She put a hand on her friend's arm. "But this is who you are. You're a warrior. You're a leader. Me and you? We're the last members of the GMT who discovered Agartha. You've been on the team longer than I have. I believe in you. This mission is essential. Our entire future may depend on it. And you know what? There's no one I'd rather have in charge of the mission than you."

Owl looked like she was about to say something else, then she stopped and nodded. "Thanks, Alex. I won't let you down."

"You'd better not," Alex said with a grin. "You're my ride off this island. Now, let's check out this base."

The team moved out and entered the facility, weapons raised and ready. Unlike the other bunkers they'd entered, they knew that there was a good chance this place would be crawling with Ferals. Brian stood in the middle of the group, protected on all sides. Alex had made it clear to the team that keeping him safe was their top priority. If something happened to Brian, this was all over.

They stepped into a large entryway with thirty-foot ceilings and walls made of clear plexiglass. A set of locked metal double doors led from the entryway to a large lobby.

"Silver doors," CB noted. "A very good sign."

Brian consulted his tablet. "According to the records, we're looking for the morgue. It should be on the lowest level."

"Well, no need to be sneaky," Alex said. "If there are Ferals in here, we want to flush them out fast. Chuck, why don't you use your key?"

Chuck grinned. "I love my job."

The team backed out of the entryway as Chuck attached a small charge to the locked doors. He fired the charge, and the doors swung open, crashing loudly against the walls on either side of them.

They waited a moment, expecting to hear enraged howls from the woken Ferals inside. But the howls never came. After two minutes, Alex led them into the lobby.

"Not the most subtle décor," Owl said, looking around the room.

Every surface was covered in tarnished silver, from the chairs along the walls to the desk at the front of the room to the very floor under their feet.

"Well, I think it's fair to assume we won't find a lot of Ferals hanging out in here," Patrick said. "If the rest of the building is like this, we'll be able to smell them cooking before we see them."

"Let's not make any assumptions," Alex cautioned. "Let's find the bunker. Then we'll sweep the building. We don't want any surprises while Brian works."

They quickly found a stairwell off the lobby and started down toward the morgue. The stairs, the handrail, and even the walls were all covered in tarnished silver. Still, it was difficult not to expect an attack at any moment. They'd had bad experiences in stairwells in the past. Every echoing footstep had Alex listening for any noise behind it, for the telltale pounding of Ferals charging toward them.

They soon reached the bottom and made their way through the lower level. It didn't take them long to find another tarnished silver door marked "Morgue." Alex pushed the door open and stepped inside, entering a tomb within a tomb.

Brian looked at his table. "The entrance should be through 26B."

The team looked around for a moment, their headlamps illuminating the dark room.

"Okay, anybody know what 26B means?" Patrick asked. "I don't even know what we're looking for."

"Uh, I think I found it," Owl said. "But you're not going to like it."

Alex followed the light of Owl's headlamp to a set of metal storage units against the wall. The doors were small, maybe two feet by two feet, and they all had letters and numbers on their doors. The one on the bottom right was marked "26B".

"What the hell are those things?" Ed asked.

"This is a morgue," Chuck said. "I'm guessing that's where they kept the bodies."

CB chuckled. "Which poor sap has to go in first?"

Alex gave him a look. "You, since you spoke up."

His smile faded. "Remind me again why I put you in charge?" He walked over and opened the door. Reaching inside, he slid out a metal table, pulled it off its tracks, and tossed it to the side. "It's another hatch. We're going to need the cutter."

Chuck frowned as he climbed in and went to work, removing the silver hatch from its hinges. Within a few minutes, he had it. "CB's still going down there first, right?"

"Absolutely," Alex said.

CB only grumbled a little before squeezing his broad frame into the locker and down the exposed hole. The team followed, and they found a bunker similar to the others they'd discovered. But, instead of coming down into a hall, this ladder led to a large room with silver floors and walls. Several couches were set up under the monitors lining the walls.

"Cool, we found the break room," Ed said.

Several hallways led off the main room and the team explored each of them. Based on the size of the bunkroom and the kitchen they discovered, there must have been fifty people working down here. And based on the condition, their resolve for stopping the end of the world had been overcome by other concerns. The kitchen was barricaded from another set of sleeping quarters. It appeared that things between the lab workers had deteriorated into some kind of civil war.

The good news was that the lab equipment appeared to have been untouched by the conflict. Brian was positively delighted at its condition. "This is perfect. But we're going to need to see what's still functional. Can we get some power down here?"

Alex nodded. "You start pulling the hard drives and digging through the information. Chuck, set up the generator. CB and I will sweep the hospital for Ferals."

Brian opened a glass door and pulled out a metal cannister the size of his forearm.

"What's that?" Owl asked.

Brian frowned. "Biological samples. We'll need something similar, to finish the virus. Too bad this stuff wasn't preserved, but with no power to this freezer unit, they'll be unusable now."

Patrick took out a metal cannister and twisted it open. He frowned at the contents. "I don't know what was in here, but it sure smells gross."

Alex turned to Owl. "You've got another bunker to ransack. Let's get to work."

25

"This is pretty and all," Patrick said. "But where's the bunker?"

Owl glanced at her tablet. "According to these coordinates, it's right under our feet." The three of them stood on the edge of a cliff looking out over the Caribbean waters a hundred feet below. Though the vista was beautiful, the location had Owl worried. "Let's head to that outcropping and see what we can find."

They carefully made their way down a sloped portion of the rocks, and, after a few minutes of confusion, discovered the mouth of a cave.

Ed gave the cave a nervous glance. "In there, huh?"

Owl nodded. "Seems that way. Let's take our time and be careful. I'm guessing this cave isn't lined with silver like the other bunkers."

Patrick chuckled. "Don't worry your pretty little head. I'll protect you. You just take care of Ed. He's scared of the dark."

Owl thought about telling him where he could shove his comments about her pretty little head, but thought better of it for the time being. They had a job to do, and they couldn't waste time squabbling. She turned on her headlamp, readied her rifle, and led her team into the cool, dark cave.

As they made their way into the tunnel, the salty tang of seawater hung thick in the air. Owl wondered if this system of caves led all the way down to the ocean. Under the seawater, there was another odor, a far less pleasant one.

Apparently, Ed noticed it, too. "Look alive, guys. I smell Ferals in this cave."

The team continued slowly down the sloped cave floor. Soon, they could hear the crashing of waves through the cave, adding credence to Owl's theory that the cave led to the water. There was still no sign that this place had ever been occupied by a secret military project. Owl trained her headlamp on the ground as they walked, sweeping it side to side, looking for a silver hatch like the ones they'd found before, but so far there was nothing but rock.

Three hundred yards into the cave, Owl rounded a bend and suddenly froze. Six Ferals hunched close together against the wall up ahead. In the yellow glow of her headlamp, she couldn't tell if they were awake or asleep. She silently debated how to proceed. Take them out quietly or attempt to sneak past? She felt like this was her first major decision as team leader.

Out of the corner of her eye, she saw Patrick raising his shotgun.

"No," she whispered. "Not yet."

But he was already squeezing the trigger. He fired and the sound of the shotgun echoed off the cave walls, making it seem even louder than usual. His aim was true, and the closest Feral's head exploded in a mist of brain matter, bone, and black blood.

"Shit!" Owl shouted, as she raised her assault rifle. "Let's go, Ed. Take them out."

They needed to finish this quickly, Owl knew. The other five Ferals had jolted awake at the sound of the gun shot. Ed was already firing, putting a tight group of rounds through one Feral's chest. Patrick fired again, too, and another head disintegrated.

Owl took careful aim before firing her first shot, a bullseye right through the center of the farthest creature's forehead.

Ed shot his second Feral and Patrick took out the final creature before Owl had a chance to fire again.

Owl turned, scowling at Patrick. "That was reckless. I told you not to fire."

"Sorry, I was already in motion."

"Alex put me in charge. That means you wait for my plan before you go 'in motion' next time, understand?"

His face screwed up in disbelief. "Plan? The plan is we take out all the Ferals and find the bunker, right? What's there to talk about? I thought we were racing the clock, here."

She gave him a hard look. "There are three of us against we-don't-know-how-many of them. That means we need to stay sharp and proceed with caution. If you disobey an order again, I'm sending you back to the ship. Do you understand me, Patrick?

Patrick looked like he wanted to say something else, but then he turned away. "Yeah, fine. I understand. We're wasting time. Let's get going."

He turned and headed deeper into the cave. He'd only made it three steps when something whizzed through the air and collided with his leg. Whatever the object was, it hit him so hard it knocked him off his feet and spun him one hundred-eighty degrees before he collapsed. The loud crack Owl heard could only be Patrick's leg bone snapping.

For a split second, Owl thought Patrick had been shot. Then she saw the large rock lying next to him.

Time seemed to slow for Owl, and adrenaline surged through her body. She saw Ed rush to his brother's side and help him onto his back, the shotgun still clutched in Patrick's hand. Then she turned and shined her headlamp down the cave ahead. The light reflected off the yellow eyes of dozens of Ferals in the distance, all of them rushing at them.

"He's bleeding!" Ed shouted.

Owl raised her rifle. "Ed, focus on the Ferals." She sighted her rifle quickly, picking a spot between two eyes and squeezing off a round. As the Feral fell, she risked a glance a Patrick, and instantly wished she hadn't. A bone in his upper leg was protruding through a hole in his pants just above the knee. His pant leg was already soaked with blood.

She took a few steps forward, moving in front of Patrick, getting between him and the Ferals. Then she fired again.

From the sound of gunfire to her left, she could tell Ed was back in the fight, but she didn't dare glance at him. The Ferals were coming faster now, and they required every ounce of her attention.

Four Ferals were ahead of the rest of the horde, and they raced for Patrick. Owl fired once, twice, three times, not thinking, just trusting her muscle memory to send the bullets where they needed to go. Two Ferals fell, but her third shot went wide.

Ed fired, dropping another Feral, but one remained. Before Owl could fire again, she heard a shotgun blast and the creature went down hard. She turned and saw Patrick, his teeth gritted, clutching his shotgun.

"We need to fall back!" Owl shouted. "If we don't get Patrick into the sunlight, we're dead."

Ed rattled off a burst of fire before answering. "I can't move him and fight at the same time.

Owl glanced at Patrick and saw the blood spreading quickly. He was paler now than the last time she'd looked. She knew Ed was right. There was no way they'd be able to drag Patrick out of the cave before the blood-frenzied Ferals caught up to them. The only way they were getting out of this alive was if every damn Feral in this cave was dead.

She turned, raised her rifle, and went to work. She fired, dropping a Feral. Then another. Then another. She was firing faster than she ever had before, and somehow, almost every shot was true. Ed was working just as quickly, firing deadly round after deadly round. Even Patrick managed to continue fighting, working his shotgun from the ground.

Still, the Ferals kept coming.

Behind her, she heard something metal hit the rocks. She turned and saw Patrick had collapsed. He was flat on his back now, his shotgun lying next to him.

"Patrick," Ed shouted. He was clearly close to panic. He held down the trigger, firing wildly into the oncoming horde. Plenty of his shots hit, but they were no longer the controlled head and chest shots he'd been trained to deliver.

Owl knew it was up to her to keep the Ferals off of them. She fired faster and faster, her rifle sounding almost like an automatic now. She moved the barrel from target to target as quickly as she could squeeze the trigger, all the while praying her training and countless hours on the range paid off now when she needed them most. Conscious thought seemed to slip away completely, and her hands and eyes took over. She felt a blister forming on her trigger finger, but the discomfort was far off, like something from a dream. In the relative darkness of the cave she could see the barrel of her rifle glowing red. She heard Ed screaming and firing at the Ferals somewhere in the distance.

She paused, dropping an empty clip and sliding a new one into place in one smooth motion. From her detached perspective, she was able to marvel at the efficiency of her movements. The only person she'd ever seen reload that fast was Alex.

She fired once, twice, three more times, and then something unexpected happened: the wave of enemies stopped coming. Reality slowly came back, and she noticed the loud ringing in her ears and the pain in her shoulder where the butt of the rifle had rested. Up ahead, the floor of the cave was covered with dead Ferals, some stacked on top of others.

Somehow, they'd done it. They'd killed every Feral in the cave.

She glanced back at Patrick and didn't like what she saw. "We have to move. Now." She looked at Ed. "Grab Patrick. I'll cover you."

Ed was breathing hard, and there was a wild panic in his eyes as he bent down next to his unconscious brother. He put his arms under Patrick and gently lifted him over his shoulder. There was soft grinding sound as Patrick's leg shifted, and he let out a groan. But he didn't wake.

Owl was glad at the groan; it meant Patrick was still alive.

Ed moved backward through the cave, his rifle held in one hand, balancing his brother on his shoulder with the other. Owl followed, her eyes constantly scanning the cave for enemies as they made their retreat.

It might have been one minute. It might have been ten.

But soon, the sunlight kissed their backs and they stepped out of the cave.

Once they were on the ship, Ed set Patrick down in the cargo hold and Owl grabbed the medical kit.

"Get blankets and water," Owl said, as she went to work.

The bleeding had slowed, but the jagged bone was sticking out two inches now. Owl did what she could, which wasn't a lot, as Ed held his brother's limp hand. His breathing was shallow.

When she finished, Owl grabbed the cutter out of Patrick's pack and put it in her own.

"What are you doing?" Ed asked, his eyes filled with tears.

"I'm finishing the mission." She slung the pack over her shoulder. "I won't be long. Then we'll get Patrick back to the team. Maybe Brian can do more. They are in a hospital, after all."

Ed shook his head slowly. "There's no way you're going back in there alone. If you're going, I am, too."

"No, you're not. Look, every Feral in that cave would have been drawn by Patrick's blood. They're all dead. I can handle this. You take care of your brother." She turned and headed out of the ship without waiting for a reply.

OWL CREPT DOWN THE TUNNEL, doing her best to keep her breathing even, her gun held at the ready. "You got this, Fowler," she muttered to herself. "Stay focused."

She rounded the first corner and froze as the light from her headlamp reflected off something on the ground. After a moment, she realized it was a pool of Patrick's blood. The fact that there were no Ferals drinking from it was a very good sign indeed. Up ahead, she saw the piles of Feral bodies, but no movement.

She moved onward, pressing up against the wall to squeeze past her fallen foes. She made the mistake of breathing through her noise while passing the largest pile, and her stomach turned at the stench, threatening to heave up the contents of her breakfast.

She followed the winding tunnel downward for twenty minutes, all the while looking for the silver hatch. Finally, once she'd reached a place where the crashing of the waves was so loud that a whole horde of Ferals could have been rushing up behind her and she wouldn't have heard, she found the hatch.

It took her another ten minutes with the cutter to open the hatch. Just like the other bunkers, a ladder was attached to the edge of the hole.

When she was halfway down, light suddenly filled the room. Owl stifled a scream and grabbed her rifle with one hand, holding onto the ladder with the other. She looked around and saw plenty of silver, but no people. After a moment, she realized the light was coming from fixtures in the ceiling. It seemed impossible, but somehow, this place had electricity.

She reached the bottom of the ladder and looked around again. "Who's there?"

But there was no answer.

After calming her nerves for a moment, she pressed onward. As she entered the next room, it happened again. The lights came on. Her frayed nerves had just about had it, but then she noticed the sensor on the ceiling. The lights were motion activated. It still didn't explain how the place had power. She intended to keep her eyes open. If she could find a passive power source that lasted one hundred fifty years, Jessica would love her. It would make a huge difference to *New Haven*. Assuming she ever made it back there.

She found the control panel a few minutes later. The graphical inference made it clear what was happening—this place was hydro powered. It was using the tide for power. Damn impressive, and it was technology that they could probably put to good use, if Resettlement ever really happened.

It only took her thirty minutes to locate the hard drives. Everything about this bunker was neat and tidy. If the bodies of the scientists were down there somewhere, she didn't see them, and she didn't have time to make a thorough search. She had what she needed, and Alex was counting on her to get back as quickly as possible.

Owl was about to leave when she found something else: a freezer unit, just like the one Brian had lamented in the other bunker. Only, this one had power. She pulled the freezer door open and saw the interior was just like the one in the other bunker too. The metal cannisters inside were cold to the touch as she loaded them into her pack.

The walk back through the cave went much faster than the walk down had. The knowledge that there were no Ferals left in the cave put a spring in her step and made the steep climb feel easy.

When she got back to the ship, she headed straight for the cargo hold to check on Patrick, but she paused at the door when she saw Ed hunched over his brother, speaking in a low voice.

"'And like the baseless fabric of this vision,
The cloud-capp'd tow'rs, the gorgeous palaces,
The solemn temples, the great globe itself,
Yea, all which it inherit, shall dissolve,
And, like this insubstantial pageant faded,

278 P.T. HYLTON & JONATHAN BENECKE

Leave not a rack behind. We are such stuff
As dreams are made on; and our little life
Is rounded with a sleep.'"

Owl's eyes filled with tears as she listened to Ed's rough voice speaking these beautiful, ancient words. When he was finished, he leaned forward and pulled the blanket over his brother's head.

Owl felt a tear run down her cheek as she stepped into the hold.

Ed turned at the sound of her footsteps. His face was wet with tears. "Did you get what you needed?"

Owl's voice came out in a choked tone. "Yes. Patrick... Is he—?"

"Then we should go," Ed said. "There's nothing more to do here. Patrick is dead."

26

Brian hadn't spoken in nearly an hour, but his fingers had been in motion nearly that entire time. He had five tablets in front of him, all synced together. He typed on one screen, threw the data to another and began to tap on that one. He was moving so fast that he might have been playing pretend. But Alex knew he wasn't. He was trying his damnedest to figure this thing out as quickly as possible.

CB and Alex had swept through the hospital quickly, but thoroughly. As expected, they hadn't found any Ferals. The silver had kept them out, apparently, but Alex was glad they'd checked. The only issue they'd encountered was getting the generator hooked to the lab equipment. It was too large to fit through the hatch and down to the bunker. Chuck has eventually managed to rig some cables from the generator down through the hatch and restored power to the generator.

Now, it was a waiting game. Waiting for Brian to have a breakthrough. Waiting for Owl and her team to return with the drives. The only thing keeping Alex sane was the pleasure she got from watching CB glower. He was even worse at waiting than she was.

Suddenly, Brian paused and stared at a tablet for a long moment. Then, a complex-looking chemical equation appeared on the screen of one of the tablets. Brian looked at the screen for a moment, his brow furrowed in fierce concentration. Then he looked at another tablet. Then back at the first.

A slow smile crept across his face. "Oh, yeah... Oh, yeah!" He jumped from his chair and threw his arms into the air.

Alex and CB exchanged a glance and both started laughing.

"Is this what a breakthrough looks like?" Alex asked.

Brian spun around to face them. "Well, yeah. I mean, I figured it out. I've got the formula."

Alex grabbed him and pulled him close in a quick hug. "I knew you could do it."

Brian's face reddened, and CB very conspicuously rolled his eyes.

"So, is that it?" Chuck asked. "Did we just win? Do we have the virus?"

Brian's smile faded a little. "Not exactly. We have formula, not the virus itself. I figured out how to stabilize the virus while it carries the gene editor." He paused a moment. "Everything checks out on the computer models. I'm confident that once we gather the biological materials, I can actually make this thing."

CB crossed his arms. "These biological materials we need... Do they still exist?"

Brian was quiet for a moment. "I'm still working on figuring that out. It's going to take time to determine exactly what we need, let alone where to get it."

The room fell silent.

Alex turned back to Brian. "What happens if the virus is released? What will it do to the Ferals?"

Brian leaned back again a chair. "Well, it should trick their bodies into thinking that their own biology is a hostile substance. Their cells will attack each other, and they'll die. Rather quickly, if the modeling software is to be believed. It seems the Project White Horse folks had the gene editing component completed. They were just struggling with the delivery system. I was able to crack that by using the info from the first bunker."

"So, it'll spread if it's released?" Chuck asked. "What, like across the whole planet?"

Brian nodded. "It's an airborne virus, and it'll quickly multiply and spread. It should happen fast. Any vampire who comes in to contact with the virus will eventually melt down on an internal level."

Chuck grinned. "Holy shit. That's amazing!" He turned to Alex. "We can wipe every Feral off the face of the Earth with this thing."

Alex wasn't smiling, though. Not yet. "What about the vampires?"

Brian tilted his head "What do you mean?"

"Firefly and his troops. The Agartha vampires. Frank. Will it affect them the same way it affects Ferals?"

Brian looks down at the floor. "Genetically speaking, there's no real difference between the Ferals and intelligent vampires. It will affect them the same way."

Silence fell across the room once again.

"Maybe there's a vaccine. Someway to make the intelligent vampires immune."

Brian shook his head. "It doesn't work like that. This is an all-or-nothing kind of deal. It's designed to bond with vampire cells. There's no way to prevent it or stop it, once a vampire comes into contact with the virus."

CB held up a hand. "Let's not get ahead of ourselves. We don't have to make any decisions. This is bigger than us. Once Owl, Patrick, and Ed get back, we'll head back to *New Haven*. With the evidence we have, the Council will have to listen to us. Then they can decide what to do with the virus."

Just then, Alex's radio chirped.

"Alex, this is Owl. We're landing in two minutes."

"Speak of the devil," Chuck said.

Alex touched her radio and spoke into her headset. "Glad you're back. We're in the bunker."

The room filled with chatter as Brian worked on testing the lab equipment to figure out what was still functional and everyone else discussed the possible implications of their discovery.

Owl was the first one down the ladder. As soon as Brian spotted her, he ran over. "Did you get the drives?"

She nodded. Even from across the room, Alex could tell there was something wrong. Her friend's eyes looked hollow. "I got them. And something else, too." She pulled a cannister out of her pack. "The bunker actually had power."

Brian's eyebrows shot up in surprise. "The bunker had refrigeration? Were the cannisters cold?"

Owl just nodded.

Brian's hand went to his mouth. "Oh, my God. This is incredible. If we have preserved biological samples, I can actually do this thing. We might not have to take the equipment back to *New Haven*. I can create the actual virus today."

Alex wanted to respond to the good news, but her eyes were fixed on Owl. "What's wrong? Did something happen on the mission?"

Owl looked at Alex, and tears sprang into her eyes. "It's Patrick."

———

ALEX PUT a hand on Ed's shoulder. "You don't have to do this. I'm his commanding officer. It's my responsibility."

Ed turned toward Alex. His eyes were filled with tears, but they also shone with fierce determination. "You might be his captain, but I'm his brother. I'm doing this."

"Of course." Alex couldn't help but feel a twinge of pride through the sadness. She should have known Ed wouldn't take the easy way out. "Just let me say a few words first."

It had taken almost an hour to gather enough wood for the funeral pyre. Though Alex hated to do it, both protocol and common sense dictated that any GMT member killed on the surface needed to burned. Patrick's body lay on a large pile of wood in front of the hospital. For once, his large body looked small.

The team was gathered around, and time was against them. They needed to do this thing. Alex took a deep breath and addressed her team.

"Patrick was a member of the GMT. No, sorry. He *is* a member of the GMT. Now and forever. He lived a life that few people will ever know. His rough wit made us a family, and his fierce skills helped us survive. He faced monsters. He betrayed his city to fight for what he believed. Twice." She paused, forcing down the lump in her throat. "Look, I'm not an eloquent speaker. My words can't do him justice. But he lived every day to keep others safe, and he died saving the world. I can think of no better legacy."

With that, Alex nodded to Ed.

Ed walked slowly to the pyre. After a moment's hesitation, he lit a flare and touched it to the brush on which his brother's body rested. As the flames spread, he leaned forward and touched his lips to his brother's forehead. Fire singed his hair before he finally leaned back, moving his head just before the flames engulfed his brother.

"Do you think you can finish before nightfall?" Alex asked. Owl and Chuck were double-checking the generator, while everyone else was back in the bunker.

"I think so," Brian said. "We've got what, five hours? The computer models have already finished. I just need to run the formula through the processors. In theory, it shouldn't take long at all."

"Good," Alex said. "Let's make it happen and go home. I'd like to sleep in my own bed tonight."

Brian smiled. "Come on. You know you'll sleep in a cell when we get back to *New Haven*."

"One night, maybe. But not two. Not with the evidence and the virus."

CB shook his head, a look of awe on his face. "I can't believe this could be it. A real solution." He turned to Alex. "You know, my whole career, the GMT has been in maintenance mode. Keep *New Haven* running. Maintain the status quo. But you pushed us forward. Without you, this wouldn't have been possible."

Alex smiled weakly. "The solution was here all along. It just needed someone to find it."

CB chuckled. "So what do you think Firefly would say about the virus?"

"He wants us to decide, and he's good with our decision." She paused. "Jaden, on the other hand, is going to be tougher to convince."

CB raised an eyebrow. "You honestly think he can be convinced?"

"No. He'll fight it to the end."

Just as she finished speaking, a loud crash came from above, shaking the bunker.

"What the hell?" Brian said.

Alex steadied herself and touched her radio. "Owl, what the hell's going on up there?"

It was a long moment before Owl answered. "It's Jaden's ship. It just crashed through the lobby. Jaden's in the building."

27

ALEX GRABBED Brian by the shoulders. It was clear from the look in his wide eyes that he was starting to panic. "Listen to me. There's only one way into this bunker. We are going to protect you. Just finish this thing as fast as you can, and let me know the moment you do. CB, Ed, come with me."

The three of them hustled to the ladder and quickly climbed up to the morgue. When she was through, Alex spoke into her radio. "Owl, you and Chuck get down to the morgue. We need to protect the entrance to the bunker."

Owl's voice was low through the radio, as if she was whispering. "I can't talk, Alex. They're coming for us." The radio clicked off and CB and Ed looked at Alex.

Alex ran a hand over her face. "We have to save them. Ed, I need you at one hundred percent. Are you in this?"

Ed raised his gun. "Shooting vampires sounds pretty damn good right now. I'm in this."

"Good man. First, fill this room with explosives. Then gather as much silver as you can. We want maximum silver shrapnel. If anyone other than a member of the GMT walks through that door, blow it to hell. Got me?"

Ed just nodded. He looked a little rough—and no wonder—but there was a spark in his eyes now that hadn't been there just a few minutes ago.

"Okay, CB, let's go." She started to walk, but quickly noticed CB wasn't following.

"Hang on, let's think about this," he said. "This room is the last line of defense. We have the chance to end all vampires. We have to protect it with everything we have."

Alex shook her head. "We're not losing any more team members today. And I'm not sitting in here and letting Jaden plan his attack at his leisure. He won't be expecting us to straight-up go after him. So that's what we're going to do. You gave me field command. Are you going to let me use it?"

CB paused for only a moment. "Yes, ma'am."

The two of them did a quick weapons check, then headed out.

"No more holding back," CB said, his voice dead serious as they walked down the hall. "We saw on that video how Jaden's going to approach this thing."

Alex knew he was right. Only one team was going to leave this hospital alive.

They made their way through the basement quickly, sacrificing stealth for speed. Even if they'd been completely silent, Alex knew Jaden and his vamps would be able to smell them coming. The fact that the vampires weren't in the basement already meant that Jaden was playing some angle. Alex carefully checked each doorway and blind spot as they moved past it.

They'd discussed their strategy for another vampire encounter back on the ship the previous night. CB had his hand on his daylight, ready to use it to force the vampires into an advantageous position, at which point Alex and her guns would do the rest.

They turned a corner and Alex saw motion. She raised her gun, ready to fire, but it was only a wire hanging from a broken light. The wire was swaying, as if something had just brushed by it.

Alex motioned toward the wire, and CB nodded. They slowly crept forward, on full alert now. Suddenly, they heard gunfire from up above.

Without saying a word, they both headed for the stairs at the end of the hall, moving double time. They were twenty feet from the stairs when the door to Alex's right burst open and Stanley rushed into the hall, moving quickly between Alex and CB.

The vampire swung his sword at a blinding speed, slashing at CB. Somehow, CB managed to deflect the blow with his assault rifle. Alex trained her pistol on Stanley, but he was moving so fast she couldn't risk firing for fear of hitting CB.

Stanley grabbed the barrel of CB's rifle with one hand and swung his sword with the other, this time arcing it behind him, straight at Alex's neck.

CB tugged hard on his rifle, slowing the vampire just enough that Alex was able to lean back out of the way. The steel blade whooshed through the air an inch from her neck. She popped back up, drawing her own sword in one quick motion.

The vampire spun after missing Alex, using his momentum bring the sword around. CB let go of his rifle and gave it a shove, putting Stanley slightly off balance. At the same moment, Alex swung her sword hard, aiming for the vampire's neck. Her blade sang as it cut through the air.

Just as it was about to strike, something above Alex seemed to explode, and Janet was suddenly standing in front of her, deflecting Alex's sword with her own. She'd crashed down through the ceiling tiles.

Alex pushed away the despair that threatened to creep in at suddenly having to fight two vampires instead of one. There was no time for that. Absolute focus was the only way she even had a chance of surviving this encounter.

Janet swung at Alex, and Alex deflected the attack. She was knocked backward by the force of the blow.

Suddenly, the hall filled with light, and Janet screamed. The half of her face exposed to CB's daylight burst into flames. Alex raised her pistol and fired, putting a bullet through Janet's left eye.

Without pausing, she spun toward Stanley, who was stumbling away from CB, desperately trying to protect his face from daylight. Alex rushed forward and drove her sword into the center of Stanley's chest.

Alex and CB stood over the fallen vampires for a moment. The only sound was the creatures' dark blood sizzling on the silver floor.

"Well, I guess talking things out is off the table," CB said. "We're in it now."

"Two down. Five to go. Turn off your daylight. We'll need every moment of power in that thing."

Up above, the fight was still going on. Gunfire and shouts echoed down to them. Alex and CB raced up the stairs and through the hallway. As they stepped into the lobby, they froze.

Jaden, Helen, Daniel, and Griffin stood in the room, weapons raised. Half the lobby was filled with a bright light, but the vampires stood in the shadows.

"Now, CB!" Alex shouted.

CB activated his daylight and shined it toward them, driving them to the left as Alex began firing. The four creatures moved in a blur, ducking into a hallway for cover. They were out of sight in two seconds.

"I think I clipped one," Alex said.

"Didn't seem to slow him down much," CB said, keeping his daylight trained on the doorway where they'd disappeared.

"Over here, Alex!" Owl shouted.

The voice seemed to be coming from a doorway on the far side of the room. Alex and CB hurried toward it, CB keeping his light on the vampires' hallway.

They found Owl and Chuck in a small room off the lobby, and it was immediately clear where the light was coming from. There was a twelve-foot hole in the wall, and sunlight streamed into the room.

Owl stood in the center of the light, her rifle raised. Chuck lay on the ground in front of her, a pistol held in one shaking hand. He held the other arm close to his chest. It was soaked with blood, and Alex saw a massive cut across his forearm.

Alex dropped down next to him. She used her sword to cut one of the sleeves off her own shirt and tied it around his bloody arm.

"Maybe blocking Helen's sword with my arm wasn't the best idea," Chuck said through gritted teeth. "They had us. But then, Owl blew a hole in this wall. Saved our asses."

"Nice thinking, Owl." Alex said as she finished tying the makeshift bandage.

"So much for Firefly keeping them contained," Owl said. "Wherever they had their ship stashed, it looks like they made their way to it."

Alex couldn't argue with that. "We need to get out of here. They're close."

"We are close," Jaden said from somewhere outside the room. "I want you to know, this isn't necessary."

"I'm really starting to dislike that guy," CB muttered.

"The virus isn't what you think," Jaden continued.

"Yeah?" Alex shouted. "Maybe you should be straightforward for once in your very long life and just tell us what it is."

"That's the problem. I don't know."

"Yeah, well, we do. Brian checked it out. It's a quick end to our vampire problem."

"I doubt it will be that simple," Jaden said. "The vampire who caused all this, the one who started the infestation, she infiltrated Project White Horse. I don't know what she did, exactly, but it's safe to say the virus could have unintended consequences. I can't allow you to use it."

"Just like last time?" Alex shouted. "We saw the video of what you did at Fort Buchanan. If not for your actions, the world wouldn't be the hell it is today. I saw the real you, Jaden. You're a monster."

There was a long pause before Jaden replied. "I'm sorry you saw that. But you have to understand, I thought I could stop the third wave. I thought there was another way."

"Yeah?" Alex called. "How'd that work out?"

"I didn't make that decision lightly. The vampire who did this? She's the real monster. If the virus was any part of her plan, it had to be destroyed."

"It wasn't your decision to make."

When Jaden spoke again, his voice trembled with anger. "I gave everything for humanity. I protected you for centuries. Even before the infestation, I protected you."

"Yeah, well, we never asked for your protection. *New Haven*'s done okay without your help for the past century and a half. Maybe it's time you stop using your so-called wisdom as an excuse for murder."

The radio chirped and Brian's voice came from her headset. "Alex, it's almost ready."

Suddenly, they heard the sound of feet pounding the floor. Jaden and his team were in motion.

"Damn it. They heard." She touched her radio. "Ed, they're headed your way. Get ready." She turned to Chuck. "Can you walk?"

He nodded weakly and got to his feet. He didn't look very steady.

Alex shook her head. "Stay here in the light. We'll be back as soon as we can."

With that, Alex, Owl, and CB raced through the lobby and down the stairs.

"Alex, the way Jaden fights... I've never seen anything like it," Owl said, as they ran.

"I don't know if we can beat him."

Alex ignored the comment. She didn't need any more reminders of what they were up against.

They made it to the hall leading to the morgue, and, to their surprise, it was empty.

"Ed, are you all right?" Alex said.

"No one's come in here yet," Ed shouted. "But I heard movement out there."

CB had his hand on his daylight, ready to activate it at a moment's notice. "It's gotta be a trap."

The team moved slowly through the hallway, stepping carefully over the two fallen vampires. They looked the same as they had when they were alive, except one had a hole in her face. They covered each doorway, ready for the attack that was sure to come at any moment.

When they reached the door to the morgue, CB and

Alex exchanged a worried glance, both wondering what Jaden was planning.

"Ed, we're coming in," Alex said.

They stepped into the morgue and saw Ed at the far wall, crouched behind a desk flipped onto its side.

As soon as they stepped into the room, Jaden's voice came from the hall. "Ed, have you been studying?"

Ed shouted his reply. "'You taught me language, and my profit on't is I know how to curse.'" He paused a moment, then added, "And I'm keeping that damn book, you son of a bitch!"

"There may be some potential in that thick head of yours after all," Jaden replied.

As soon as he finished speaking, chaos erupted. Three vampires dropped from the ceiling tiles, landing near Ed. His rifle was ready, and he fired at the first vampire, Griffin. The bullet went right through the vampire's shoulder and hit the wall near Owl.

Helen was the second to hit the ground, and she immediately charged. She was on Alex in a moment, grabbing Alex's sword hand. Alex aimed her pistol at the vampire's face and fired. Helen managed to get her other arm up just in time and took the round in her forearm.

CB activated his daylight, but the third vampire, Daniel, was ready. No sooner had CB turned it on than Daniel hit it with edge of his blade, knocking it out of his hands and onto the floor. Another strike from Daniel's sword smashed the daylight.

Helen released Alex's arm and reached for her sword. With one arm injured and the other grabbing the sword, that left her vulnerable. Alex aimed for her heart. Before Alex could fire, Daniel's foot slammed into her ribs. She saw the kick coming out of the corner of her eye a moment before impact, and she shifted her momentum to absorb some of the force. Even so, the kick sent her flying through the air and into the wall six feet away.

As she landed, her hand went to her torso, checking for damage. Good, no broken bones. Scanning the room, she saw her team was still all on their feet. But Jaden hadn't shown himself yet. A very bad sign.

Daniel still had his eyes fixed on Alex. He smiled at her fallen form and started toward her. Off to his right, CB raised his sidearm and fired. Daniel pulled his head back, and the round flew by, burying itself in the shoulder of Helen's uninjured arm.

But Daniel's dodge had put him right in Owl's line of sight. She fired her rifle and put a round through his hand. His sword clattered to the floor. Owl sighted her rifle again, aiming for Daniel's head.

Before she could fire, Jaden's voice filled the room. "Enough!"

Then Alex saw a blur as Jaden rushed into the room and grabbed Owl around the chest, pinning her arms to her side. Her rifle crashed to the floor. A look of horror appeared in Owl's wide eyes. Then Jaden sank his teeth into her neck.

"No!" Alex shouted. She jumped to her feet and raised her pistol.

Jaden threw Owl's body aside and ducked behind the doorframe before Alex could fire.

For a moment, all eyes were on Owl's fallen body and the doorway where Jaden had disappeared.

Ed raise his rifle, tears standing in his eyes, but Griffin tore it from his hands. In response, Ed drew his pistol. As he brought it up, the vampire slammed a fist into his forearm. There was a loud snap, and the pistol fell from Ed's hand. Griffin drew back his fist, clearly about to punch Ed in the face, but Alex fired before he could. Griffin collapsed, a bullet hole in the back of his head.

Now CB fired, putting a round through Helen's knee. She fell to the ground with a scream, her three injured limbs a twisted mess.

That left only Daniel standing. And Jaden. Wherever he was.

CB and Alex approached Daniel cautiously. CB fired twice at his chest. The rounds hit, but Daniel managed to dodge enough that the bullets missed his heart. He turned, the twin bullet holes in his chest seeping black blood. Alex dropped low, swinging her sword and striking him in the side of the knee. Daniel crumbled to the ground with a shout.

Alex raised her sword to finish him, but paused as she saw Jaden step back into the room, a sword in each hand and fire in his eyes.

CB didn't hesitate; he just fired. Jaden trained his eyes on the barrel and dodged, moving out of the way before the round left the barrel. Alex had her gun up a moment later, but Jaden was ready. He placed the tip of his sword underneath the sword of one of his fallen comrades. Then he flicked his wrist, and the loose sword flew through the air.

Alex dove left, just avoiding the flying blade.

CB fired, but once again Jaden managed to avoid the bullet, this time by stepping closer. In an instant, he was within striking distance. The tip of his sword lashed out and sank into CB's arm. CB grunted in pain and dropped his gun. Jaden extended his other arm and used the tip of his sword to catch the sights of Alex's pistol, pulling it out of her hands with the flick of the wrist.

Alex let it fall and moved both hands to the hilt of her

sword. She only had one shot to make this happen. She needed to make it count.

With all her strength, she drove the sword forward, aiming for the heart. But Jaden pressed a foot into CB's chest, pushing him off his blade. Then he brought the sword around, deflecting Alex's thrust. He swung his other blade toward Alex's throat.

Alex just managed to get her sword up in time to stop the strike from removing her head. Then she attacked again, putting everything she had into a slash at Jaden's neck.

Jaden easily blocked with one sword, then brought up his other sword, locking her blade between both of his.

With both his hands occupied, Alex knew this was her moment. She grabbed the silver cannister off her belt with her free hand. Jaden twisted the sword out of her hand, and she let it drop. She brought the cannister close to Jaden's face and hit the button.

A silver mist sprayed into Jaden's face, his nose, and his slightly open mouth.

He staggered back, his eyes wide. Then he collapsed to his knees. He let go of his swords and his hands went to his throat.

A strange, strangled sound came from his mouth. Thin tendrils of smoke rose out of his throat and dark blood dripped from his eyes. The skin on his face was already blistering and smoking as the tiny particles of silver invaded its pores.

He looked so pathetic on his knees like that. Far from the invincible warrior he'd seemed only a few moments before.

Alex steeled herself. She bent down and picked up her sword.

Jaden raised a shaky hand and hissed out two words. "Save me."

"Sorry," Alex said. "It's a little late for that." She drew back her sword.

A blur shot across the room, and Alex looked up and saw Owl sprinting toward her. Owl's eyes were filled with terrified confusion, and she moved with the speed only a vampire could possess. She slammed into Alex, tackling her to the floor.

As Alex hit the ground, she caught a glimpse of the room in front of her. Helen and Daniel were back on their feet now, rushing toward their fallen leader. CB was on the other side of the room, close to the wall. She and Owl lay on the ground beside the desk where Ed was crouched. The positioning was the best they were going to get.

"Blow it, Ed!" she shouted.

The charges went off. Explosions came from both side of the room, and the silver shrapnel flew.

There was a brief moment of silence. Then the moans and shouts of pain began.

Alex slowly got to her feet. She noticed a small piece of metal sticking out of her calf. Others had it much worse.

Daniel lay wriggling on the floor, a large piece of silver impaled in his chest. Smoke rose from a dozen other cuts on his face and body. Helen lay close to him, a piece of silver protruding from her cheek. Jaden looked the most messed up, but how much of that had been from the silver mist and how much from the shrapnel, Alex did not know. He was already moving, pulling a large piece of silver out of his side and sitting up.

Thankfully, it looked like CB and Ed had only taken minor cuts from the blast.

Then there was Owl. Her body had protected Alex from

the majority of the shrapnel, and the many smoking wounds in her back told the tale of just how many hits she'd taken. Still, she crawled toward Alex, her weakened body still trying to follow its master's orders.

A voice came from the open hatch. "Alex! It's ready."

Brian climbed through the locker, a cannister in each hand. "This is it. It's done." He handed Alex one of the cannisters.

Alex felt the cold weight of it in her hands. It seemed like such a simple item. A little tube made of glass and steel. And look at all the damage that had been caused in its pursuit.

Then she saw Jaden climbing to his feet. Despite his injuries, his voice was calm and strong. "Alex, you have to believe me. We don't know what that thing does. It must be destroyed."

His hand shot out, moving as quick as ever, snatching his sword off the ground.

With a sinking feeling, Alex realized this wasn't over. Jaden was hurting, but he wasn't done. He was already beginning to heal. There was no way she could take him. She'd played her best hand, and he was still standing. He'd keep fighting until every one of them was dead. Then he'd destroy the virus, and no one outside that building would even know it had existed.

"Do it, Alex," Owl said, her voice weak. "I can't live as Jaden's slave."

There were only two choices left to her: die at Jaden's hands and let the savage truth die with her, or release the virus immediately. It was possible that Jaden was telling the truth, but even if he was, he'd admitted he didn't know what the virus would do.

If she didn't release the virus, Jaden would make the

choice for her. If she used it, at least humanity was deciding its own fate. Didn't they deserve that?

Jaden held up a hand. "Alex, please. Just listen." With his other hand, he raised his sword, drawing it back with perfect form, preparing to bring it forward in a killing blow.

The time to consider her decision was over. She had to act.

Alex pressed the button on the cannister and twisted hard.

There was an audible hiss, and a thick cloud of mist filled the room.

AUTHOR'S NOTE

What? That's the end?

Yes, but only briefly. As much as we hate to cut you off at such a moment, this really is the culmination of Alex's journey to find the savage truth. To go any further would be to get into her next journey...probably the most important one she will take in her life.

But, we have good news for you. We knew we owed it to you to minimize the wait between book four and five, so we waited until book five was finished before publishing this one.

As Ed might say, "The past is prologue." What's next?

Book five, The Savage War, will be released on May 15th. You can pre-order it here. http://mybook.to/theSavageWar

Thanks for reading The Savage Truth. This one really put us through our paces, but we're very proud of the result. We hope you enjoyed it.

Jonathan and P.T.

Made in United States
North Haven, CT
16 November 2023

44084933R10189